MW00910631

2016

2016

Rob Andwood ✳ Stephen G. Bloom
Samantha Canales ✳ Cory Carlton
Chelsey Clammer ✳ Douglas Cole ✳ Sarah Evans
Malinda Fillingim ✳ Briana Forney ✳ Kylie Grant
Barbara Hacha ✳ Debbie Jones ✳ Mark Jones
Christine Lind ✳ Caroline Mansour ✳ Cameron Martin
Alex Clark-McGlenn ✳ Meg Pokrass ✳ Robin Rozanski
T.L. Sherwood ✳ Bob Thurber ✳ John Wells
Melora Wolff

Hopewell Publications

Managing Editor
Brittany K. Fonte

Senior Editors
Matt Ryan   Christopher Helvey   Danielle Evennou
Tim Waldron   Jamey Temple   Joe Peacock
Michele Ruby

Proofreader
Emily Vander Ark

Best New Writing 2016 Copyright © 2016 by Hopewell Publications. All rights reserved. No part of this book may be reproduced or transmitted in any form or by any means, electronic or mechanical, including photocopying, recording, or by any information storage or retrieval system, without permission in writing from the publisher, with exception of reviews.

Published by Hopewell
Publications, LLC
PO Box 11
Titusville, NJ 08560
(609) 818-1049

info@HopePubs.com
www.HopePubs.com

International Standard Book Number: 9781933435503
Library of Congress Control Number: 2015946415

First Edition
Printed in the United States of America

For submission and nomination guidelines, visit:
www.BestNewWriting.com

In memory of
philosopher Eric Hoffer

"Creativity is the ability to introduce order
into the randomness of nature."
– Eric Hoffer

Table of Contents

Introduction
From the Editors

Each year, *Best New Writing* features the finalists for the Eric Hoffer Award for Prose, the top entries for the Gover Prize, and unique cover art. The Eric Hoffer Award is open to any fiction or creative nonfiction of less than 10,000 words. The Gover Prize is given to short works of 500 words or less. All works must be unpublished or published with a circulation of 500 or less. Authors and artists from around the world are invited to submit.

During the judging process, a small subset was isolated for the Eric Hoffer Award "short list" and publicly announced. Each editor was afforded the opportunity to champion one story. These were dubbed, Editor's Choice.

The cover art is the result of an open competition for international artists to feature their work in a space with limited text.

Please enjoy our selections for 2016.

The Eric Hoffer Award for Prose

26 Junctures of How I am a Part of You
by Chelsey Clammer

Accept

Taking sips of waking up. Warmth cupped in my hands. The maroon mug my mother gave me on a day when I didn't want to be me. It was any day. Any year. How I looked at my body, and I said no. How she said yes. Here, have a mug with a woman on it. You need this. This something warm to soothe the worries. Trust me, it's a beautiful body. Those memories of her are right here, my hands pressing into them, soaking back into the shifting sense of no, of yes, of no, of yes, of no really, I can do this. Self-acceptance. Now, months later, years later, it is this morning, it is any day and every day and daily that both hands hold onto something that holds meaning. A woman given to me by my mother. As in, I accepted the present, which is to say myself. As in, to be with the world, not just in it. As in, here is the woman I have become. But also the women who not only brought me here, but also showed me reasons to stay. Made the earth more inviting than the sky.

Birth

Dr. Payne (yes, that's his name) stands around, yawning, wondering when he will finally get to go home. It's been a slow day, as it tends to be when there is a blizzard in Wyoming. And while this woman has been in labor for only a few hours, his patience is waning. Last job of the day. Come on already. You're taking too long. What are you doing in there? Do I have to count to three? And then I crown and his bored hands birth me. 4:17 a.m., Easter Sunday. Thank god. It's about time.

Chi

The flat iron called the Chi found in a chain drugstore's florescent-lit aisle number three. Purchased by three different women, all related. Taken home to three different houses. Plugged in and sitting on three different bathroom counters. Three Chis heating up, preparing to be put to use. Three generations of fierce women who refuse to be tamed, who, by the three different colors of their vaguely wavy manes, do not look related; but when at home, they take the flat iron and use it to coax their undulating strands into soft streaks and the heat from the Chi accidentally meets skin and *sizzle* it bleeds, bubbles, blisters and forms a scab containing bits of a specific protein sequence that says *yes, I am a part of you.*

Duct tape

A different type of family. One that is created, is made out of the belief in freedom, in yes. Duct-taped *x*'s crossing over nipples. Topless women. Bare-chested queers. Cover the female nipples or risk getting a ticket. But it's hot and this is the dyke march and of course clothes are coming off and thus the duct-tape. *X*'s mark what's perfectly clear: how very queer. Queer as in having names like Pidge and Froi and Trouble and Nern. Queer like the polyamorous transgender man with facial hair and voluptuous breasts. We honor him as a man. His name is West. Queer like a spectrum of gender identities accessorized by glitter and hand-kerchiefs hanging out of back pockets. Codes. Queer like unicorn parties where women wear boy-cut undies and plastic horns and duct-taped nipples. Roof parties. Queer like ecstatic. Like everyone is queering themselves silly. This is family. Take pride. The intersex person nicknamed after a bird some describe as a rat with wings. Or the bisexual Brazilian transgender woman with a koala bear tattoo climbing up her upper thigh. How queer? Righteously queer.

Exhale
There is the sound of her expression. The struggle between encouragement and concern. Seventeen years ago I read to my mother an essay I wrote about how I would kill myself. Caught between wanting to whisk me off to the psych ward and wanting to encourage me to express my feelings no matter how dangerous they were, my mother just sat there, in her chair, staring across the kitchen table at her thirteen-year-old daughter, a suicidal writer. She probably said, "That's really good." She probably said, "You're a great writer." She probably said something about craft instead of content, ignoring my grave words, not quite knowing what to do with them. At some point, she probably exhaled.

Friends
Once, when I had friends. (Sad how that sentence is true.)

Great-granddaughter
The great-granddaughter who has more than just the vague waves like the women in her family, but who gets her overtly curly hair from dead great-grandpa. His history of black kinks now blonde on her. And when she's old enough, the Chi she will wield.

Home
Escaping the feeling of a fractured world. Right now, I am at my mother's house.

I
In the first draft of this essay, I somehow forgot to write a section for "I." I find this significant as I'm writing this to try to remember more of myself. Here, I am writing about the women

who help me to locate the me inside of me. But I cannot let go of the fact that I forgot about the core of this essay: me. Where am I?

Jammies

Night. Visit to my mother. In her house. Nine years after a pronounced-dead father. I forgot to bring my pajamas. "Jammies," as my mother calls them. In the rush away from my loneliness, from my lonesome apartment, from the foreboding feeling of this-isn't-going-to-be-a-good-night, the colorless sunset weeping into my bedroom. Yes, in such a rush I forgot to bring a simple something to sleep in. At my mother's house, getting ready to go to sleep with the relief of her presence in the room above me, I put on the jammie pants she lends me. Hot pink. How funny. A color so unlike her, or me. A variety of cartoon moose with sunglasses arching over their stout snouts. The images compose the fabric's outrageous neon pattern. And there are words written in the spaces between each moose. *Don't moose around with me!* I laugh. *Don't moose around with me!* How I want to say that to the penetrating memories of a dead father brought on by a colorless sunset. I slip my body into these hot pink moose jammies, take a picture of me in the bathroom mirror, a smile unable to contain itself. And, later, when I look at that picture after months of forgetting about it, I will fall in love with the fact of the jammies. How they will remind me of her, my mother, and how at least one ominous night turned out all right.

Knitting

The brown yarn woven together then presented to me as an example. A swatch of knitting. I'm watching her movements, trying to learn. My friend who is more like a mother so I call her my mentor has been knitting for years. I look up to her, this mentor with a knack for crafts. "Stress-reliever," she says. Mentor mentoring me on how to take care of myself. How to be proud of myself. How to *be* myself. How to weave this woman which is to say myself into this world.

Living
I'm trying. The women are helping. (We breathe.)

Mouth
Eighty-eight years old. No one else at the table volunteers to say a prayer. Great-granny knows a blessing from the time before we— husbands, boyfriends, mother, aunt, me—were born. She says it's four lines long. And she says no will understand it but her. In regards to facial structure, I am just like her. In regards to being understood, I, too, am just like her. We are not. As in family members find our thoughts confounding, too eclectic. As in who I am is rooted all the way back to who she has been and more. The specific protein sequence that connects us, that says I am a part of her. She speaks. Four lines in which the word *divine* appears four times. I count them. All four of them. I forget the other words until the amen in which we follow her lead, lips un-close, say A-MEN, heads un-bow, hands un-clasp and break away from positions we only take once a year. The postulations of prayer. And the *amen*'s N is pushed out from being lodged in the space between tongue and roof of mouth and to somewhere it is better received. Such as an ear. How do you know god is listening? Or rather, what are you thankful for? Now pass the turkey down to the men. And we ladies begin to serve each other salad, and Christ this feels like the stereotypical and gag-inducing gender shallowness and socially constructed expectations and a prevalence of the forever dieting female and a stupid, horrible what-the-hell-are-we-doing-just- eat- ing-salad subtext. Into our mouths the tradition of what it means to be a woman goes. The salad has figs in it. And low-calorie dressing. Dig in. But then great-granny grabs a roll and slathers butter onto it and the mashed potatoes quickly makes their way down the table to her as my mother and my aunt and I don't touch them and then she heaps three, calorie-heavy mountains onto her large plate. More butter. And gravy, too. Her stomach that says it's okay to eat. She's been alive for eighty-eight years. She knows better now. Such

as accepting her body for what it is. She sits there smiling at all of the food in front of her, sits there looking enlightened. Divine.

Number

Eating Disorder Not Otherwise Specified. EDNOS. DSM 307.50. A number my mother would be a good fit for. A number I'm a good fit for. So good that the doctor will give it to me. The present of a diagnosis. Though my mother gave it to me first. Tradition passed down. Too many women in this society have been assigned this number. So many of us in this situation. Sitting in the waiting area at the doctor's office, waiting to be weighed, praying for the correct number that proves our capability in this battle against our bodies. The waiting room is stuffed with anticipation. The receptionist tells me the number of women who will be called before me. Please have a seat.

Obese

An obese woman talks to her dog. A rambunctious muscular thing. "I told you you'd do that." She laughs. The conversation continues. The dog runs in circles around the basketball court because for once the court is not littered with small children bouncing flat rubber balls. "You're having fun, aren't you?" An obese woman talks to her dog. And all the fat-phobic judgments society shoves down my throat come spewing out. I can't believe I'm thinking this. How she must be so lonely with such an unlovable body. Yes, an obese woman talks to her dog. And I wonder if this is the only conversation she'll have today. I walk by. I do not wave. We do not say hello.

Potatoes, Part II

Once, when I had friends, we women would get together on the day every American is expected to eat a dead bird. To stuff themselves silly, too (and the fact of women and their salads). We queer female friends forming our own family served ourselves more than just salad. As in, rolls. Mashed potatoes. Tofurky. Pass the butter. Among the six of us we shared six bottles of Three Buck Chuck. We called it Thankstaking.

Quarters

Breaking away for a moment now, it is time to place a man in this essay. Out of the wings. Stage front. Guest appearance. The memories. That one moment.

You. You don't look like him. You don't like him. You the daughter, he the father, and you not knowing how to be his daughter. But there's the fact, again, of more protein sequences that hold meaning. Because you the daughter are a part of him—your father. Blood, yes. But not apparent. Because you do not look like him and you did not like him. He knew this, easily surrendered to the truth of it. Though there were the times he tried to be a parent. Why believe this? Because you hold out hope. Because he used to wash your truck for you. A subtle sign of care. Because when he washed your truck for you, he filled it up with gas and he filled up the console with a stack of eighteen quarters. It's all that would fit. Fifty cents short of something complete. Whole. The holes of your relationship. He bought that truck for you, even though you didn't know how to drive it. Stick shift. He would have to teach you. An intention of quality time? You will never know. Regardless, the necessary lessons at the top of the hill. *Now keep her still.* There was something there, idling. Attempted parenting, perhaps. There was something there that tried to find a greater meaning than the $1.50 in dimes that would be found five years later counted out on his dresser the morning he died. Suicide? The dimes perhaps about to be put to use to purchase a newspaper. His Sunday ritual. Died before he could do so. Fifteen dimes worth of signs. And that unanswerable question of his intention, of his desire consumes you, still. And now nine years later, and still. You try to drive away from the memories. Shift gears. Desperate. Peel out.

Move on.

Red

For my sister.

Immediately after the fifteen dimes, you and I will disagree about everything. His death, mainly: your grief verses my relief. Daughters with different views. Sisters insisting different causes of death. Regardless of our differing reactions, there's the fact of you and me and what we felt with each other after the fact of him being no longer. Such as lost, perhaps. Though we can never really lose each other. We have, in fact, and will always be, in fact, enmeshed by the inner thrust of rushing red, yes, the underlying red. That red. That red that from the outside looks like pipes full of blue. They are not. The red inside filled with similar protein sequences. Linked. How even though we disagree on the meaning of a dead father there is the ratio of how I am a part of you. Of how you are a part of me. Of how we have this we.

Strawberries

My mother's garden in Colorado. Decades ago, when I was only a decade old. How she tried to give me a green thumb, to include me in the joy of gardening, the activity rooted in my matrilineage. Three generations of women who will not be tamed, who like to get their hands dirty. The garden more than a hobby, a lifestyle, a need. A type of creativity. Though there is the problem of deer. Strawberries stolen each year. A blow-up owl on a fence post works for a night. But just one night. The deer quickly realize the owl is unusually patient, how it stays too still for too long, even for an owl. The following dawn, fence hopped over again. More strawberries stolen. Red ingested. Though they never touch the rhubarb. Red stalks remain. A pucker of a taste. The only produce that will be a product of my mother's garden. I will grow up on rhubarb recipes, never able to decide if I like the taste of them. Then, a decade later, when I had a friend named Pidge, she decided she wanted to make rhubarb pie to take to a roof party. But she didn't know what rhubarb looked like. I took her to the market and thought of my mother. Memories planted within me. I tend to them.

Texture

Dusk. The final touches of a sky turning orange, the switch to pink, no, now purple. Watch as everything continues to shape-shift, color-shift, bringing on a sense of an end-of-day hue. No longer colorless. The blurring of bodies, mother and daughter watching the day give way to night. Silence between us. We say everything by saying nothing. We connect with the knowledge that I am a part of her. We are a part of each other. Yes, her support. The woman on my maroon mug. The present she gave me of no really, I can do this. Here, now immersed in a midnight blue, the air between us strokes my skin. The texture of what connects us.

Understanding

The women in my life. Our stories tucked in tight with each other. We create an us. How together we knead nouns into new meanings, let them settle, bask as we consider ourselves, consider each other, and then put them into action, enliven them into verbs. Don't moose around with me. And I ask the women in my life, can I essay you? They encourage me to create, no matter how dangerous my words. How it is we create together. How it is we understand each other. How I understand all of what our language can hold, contain. I cocoon into the fact of family, into you.

Veer

The first time I kissed my father's forehead was when I was twenty-one and he was lying dead on a table before me, the announcement made moments ago that he was too dead to be revived, skin graying, growing cold, no longer slack or wrinkled with worry, but thickening skin settling into the fact of him now gone, succumbed to death, successfully veered away from the direction of living as now he is lying dead on a table, a daughter leaning over him, her affection finally showing. I uncocoon myself to him, but only momentarily.

Written

The stories written on my body. How people try to read them. Though some don't want to know. Some try to avoid staring, but cannot help it. Like looking at cleavage, their eyes linger. Another fact of being female. But more. I know the downward spikes of eyes so well. Then, the look up, the adamant eye contact, the trying not to double-take at what they think they just saw. Lines of scars on her arms. No, it can't be. She seems so happy. Such a confident and optimistic woman. She's so accomplished. What does she have to be anxious about, sad about? Another glance at the lines on my arms to try to understand my story and why I wrote it like that. The lines are from a time when my language went missing, when flesh met razor because I couldn't think of any other way to relate my story. What else is there to say? That was four years ago, today. The scars won't ever fully fade. But now I'm armed with a language that feels right on my skin. Something I want to slip into. I write differently now.

Xenophobia

The take versus the give. We take, you give; if you don't give, we still take; and we take everything, which includes your lives. Please define genocide. Tell me: what are you thankful for? The female friends with whom I celebrated Thankstaking, thankful for each other's company on a day that could be lonely with the reminders of genocide and fractured family and dead fathers and lost friends. The latter of which I hold the feeling of now. Good women gone. And yet, my story moves on.

Youth

Image: a younger version of my uptight aunt let loose at my mother's wedding. The picture of this in my hands is older than I am, and how I hold a portrayal of attitude uncoiling, of how my aunt's teeth are clenched on a rose's stem, up-turned lips not worried about thorns. Bride in the background. The petals of kin. Blood. Red. All held in her mouth. They are so different, though here in this photo their smiles match for just one day. That wedding day. And I wonder, when did she let go of the idea of letting go?

Zippo
The naked woman's torso has a gun for a head. A butane flame sparks out of the revolver when I pull the trigger. The rest of my hand caresses her breasts, the curve of her ass. No legs needed. Just the torso, the ass. The breasts with pointed nipples. The gun where there should be a face. But first, New Year's Eve. 2002. Waco, Texas. The weird vibe of being a drunk surrounded by other drunks I do not know. I'm with my girlfriend wondering if these Wacoans are taking note of the woman with a shaved head following around the other woman, the one they know, their old friend from high school. We walk through the living room and past a coffee table that is more of a collection of splinters than a sturdy piece of home furnishing. A jagged pile of objects strewn on its surface. A broken bong lying on its side. A slew of *Hustler* magazines. A zippo lighter. A woman's torso and a gun instead of a head type of lighter. Too completely terrified to even think about these people, about what type of person would want to own that Zippo, I follow my girlfriend out to the backyard, crowd around the keg of Natty Light with her, and contemplate how I want to steal what scares me. That lighter. Such extreme misogyny. And how I'm in love with how offensive it is. Such creativity. Admirable innovation. So many ways to hate. And how I want proof of this— this unbelievable offense. *No really, check this out!* I imagine saying to my feminist friends later. They *must* see this. Yes, I *must* have it. "I'm going to the bathroom," I declare. Girlfriend shrugs. No Wacoan cares. I cross the backyard, tall weeds crashing into my shins as I walk through them. I enter in through the screen door

that snaps my ass when it sharply closes behind me. There, the lighter still lying amid splintered wood. No one else in the room. Just me and the gun-headed half-woman, now in my pocket. Liberated.

Chelsey Clammer has been published in *The Rumpus, Essay Daily, The Water~Stone Review* and *Black Warrior Review*, among many others. Clammer is the Essays Editor for *The Nervous Breakdown* and Senior Creative Editor of insideoutediting.com. Her first collection of essays is *BodyHome*. Her second collection of essays is *There Is Nothing*.

Editor's Choice Award

Apricot Ridge
by Rob Andwood

The flowerbeds tangled a spell of orange and white and deep maroon on both sides of the narrow dirt pathway that led up to the wooden gates and so were considered a foremost attraction by all who visited Apricot Ridge—pruned daily by a team of six gardeners, they received the kind of attention usually reserved for an only child.

On the nineteenth of July, however, with the mercury bobbing above ninety, the blossoms drooped as if they'd tried to unearth the reason for their existence, had failed, and were now overwhelmed with despair. The gardeners battled the wilting all morning to little purpose, for the two dozen visitors who were dragging their feet along the pathway in approach could not have cared less about the quality of the landscaping. It was the hottest day of summer thus far in eastern New Hampshire, and, red-faced and sweating, they were being thoroughly pummeled by the sun.

A boy wearing a T-shirt striped yellow and blue suddenly fell onto his backside, dust rising around him and mingling with the tears on his cheeks. His mother knelt next to him and whispered hard into his ear. The boy leaned away from her.

"I want to go home," he said, elongating all of the vowels.

Seizing one of his thin wrists, the woman tried to pull him to his feet, and succeeded only in dragging him a few inches along the path, for which she was rewarded with several exaggerated cries of pain and looks of alarm from the rest of the group, all of whom momentarily forgot the heat amidst the expectation that the boy's arm had been yanked from its socket.

"We paid money to be here," she said to him. "Be respectful of that."

But he'd anchored himself in the dirt and was sobbing madly. Weary from the exertion, his mother gave up; sitting down next to him, she dropped her voice to a murmur and rubbed the tapered span of his back.

A few yards in front of the column of visitors, a man in dark pants and a straw hat craned his neck to watch the boy's antics, maintaining his backpedal all the same. His white shirt was heavily starched and rolled to his elbows, and a brown vest was draped over his forearm. Five minutes earlier, he'd met the newcomers at the mouth of the dirt pathway—where they'd gathered, as planned, beneath the shade of a large tree—and introduced himself as Samuel.

"Looks like we've lost a couple already," he said, a grin creasing his face, "which is no surprise to us here in Apricot Ridge. On average, two out of every ten travelers making their way to or from the village fall short of their intended destination."

This bit of pleasantness elicited no sympathy from the remaining twenty-two, many of whom appeared on the verge of trending that statistic upward—in particular, an older gentleman wearing his eternal uniform of slacks and a navy-blue polo shirt, who was so red in the face that Samuel had asked twice already if he wouldn't like to stop for a rest and join up with the group later on.

Then a loud creaking, as of the joints in the old man's knees, ripped through the windless, heat-choked air.

"That'll be Tom with the gates," Samuel said.

The visitors peered beyond him to see that the wooden square in the distance had indeed separated into halves that were slowly coming apart, a sliver of light growing between them until it became a framed image of the village.

Passing through the gates and underneath a carved wooden sign, they found themselves in a gravel clearing, where Samuel halted.

Viewed from above, the layout of the village might have echoed a jagged slice of wagon wheel: four roads arrayed as evenly as spokes shot off from the clearing, and a long incline curved to meet them all at their endpoints. At the moment each was brimming with villagers, scurrying up and down despite the heat as they pursued the day's business. Men in shirtsleeves carried armfuls of wood into thatched houses, while others in black formal jackets and salt-banded top hats dashed around corners, papers tucked beneath their damp underarms. The women, meanwhile, formed two unbalanced subdivisions: most wore white dresses and black bonnets, and stood in backyards hanging laundry over stretches of rope, but a group of three or four walked leisurely under floral-printed umbrellas, fanning themselves and carrying on as if there was no work to be done at all.

None of these people seemed to notice or care that twenty-plus strangers had just marched into their home, with the exception of one: a man in a dark suit, who smiled briefly and lifted his hat toward the newcomers before dashing up the left-center street, from which jutted a white steeple in the middle distance.

"Welcome to Apricot Ridge," Samuel said.

Beckoning the group forward, he continued in reverse down the gravel road furthest to his left and their right—two words painted on a small building of wooden slats called it Molasses Lane.

"This is our stable," Samuel said, gesturing to the building, which showed a wide, empty space intended for three equine heads; the twenty-two raised their own in anticipation, but Samuel only frowned and shook his. "Unfortunately, a band of Iroquois made off with the horses several months ago, cutting off our ability to trade with villages to the south."

This, of course, was a lie: Apricot Ridge had been horseless from the beginning. The alleged stable functioned primarily as a storage space for cleaning products.

Continuing along Molasses Lane, the group approached a two-level house opposite the stable, its gray stone interrupted only by a knobbed rectangle of black—the door. An apparently heat-immune girl near the front desisted from skipping to raise a hand.

"Is that the jail?"

Samuel laughed.

"I'm afraid not. The jail is northwest of here, at the intersection of Rattlesnake Slope and Puddle Street. This is the smithy, where Titus Windaloo, our blacksmith, forges iron products to meet the village's needs, both domestic and military."

There was interest in the last word, and the girl's father spoke up directly.

"Are we going inside?"

"Not today," Samuel said, glancing at the metal door as he passed it. "A day like this makes it impossible for Titus to work—contained by all of that stone, the heat from his furnace would reach a dangerous level. He much prefers the winter, I think."

There was a coo of disappointment, but it was quickly forgotten—on a scorcher like July the nineteenth, it was hard to feel anything beyond one's own suffering.

But as the group continued on toward their first destination within Apricot Ridge—the cooper's lodge, hidden behind a pine grove on the other side of Molasses Lane—a hint of something appeared on the upper half of the stone monolith, though it went unnoticed; indeed, Samuel seemed to deflect attention away from it, changing the subject to the pine tree's origin in the region, "a rather fascinating tale, more of an epic, really… "

A curtain matching the stone's hue had been pulled back to reveal a window, and a dark form which observed the retreating visitors. As they disappeared into the grove, the curtain was dropped back into place, and the smithy took up a façade of lifelessness once more.

Upon curtainfall, the sunlight that had peeked eagerly into Titus Windaloo's living quarters for the first time in over a day was refused further access, and an electric lamp on the nightstand became solely responsible for illuminating the room. As the blacksmith turned to face the hundred square feet that were his own, the weak glow drew his eyes to two things—a small pile of clothes on the carpet next to the twin bed, and, atop the mattress, the heartbeat pulsations of Beatrice Miller's spine, concealed by nothing except a thin layer of skin.

"Are they gone?" Beatrice asked, voice obstructed by the pillow into which she'd buried her face.

"Yeah," Titus said. "I saw Samuel at O'Leary's last night and told him we'd be up here."

"Samuel's the best."

Stepping over a pair of leather work-boots, Titus padded to his side of the bed. Spread-eagled, Beatrice occupied far more than her usual share of the cramped space. Titus squeezed into the last vacant plot of white sheet and, elbows bumping against the headboard, planked his legs over hers. With a groan of annoyance she straightened herself, untangling their limbs, but he was already dancing the fingers of one hand between her shoulder blades as if needing to maintain contact.

Abandoning any designs on further slumber, Beatrice rolled onto her back and opened her eyes. Titus watched her pupils expand within bleary green irises.

"What time is it?" she asked.

"I don't know. My phone's on the nightstand."

She dug her hands into the linens and pushed herself upward until her back ran parallel to the headboard, then fetched the small black rectangle and squinted at its illuminated display.

"Shit."

"What time is it?"

"Just before noon."

The half-burnt stub of a joint materialized between her lips, and from thin air she conjured a yellow lighter. The smoke that rose off the end upon ignition fractured the lamplight into golden shards.

"You on today?" she asked, passing the stub to Titus. "You can finish that."

He took a hard pull and exhaled a fleeting white cloud; somewhere in the middle, he shook his head.

"Paula told me not to bother, on account of the heat."

"She likes to keep you comfortable, doesn't she?"

Beatrice was referring less to the excusal from work, and more to the portable air conditioner that hummed in a corner of the room—Paula had dropped it off midway through a record-breaking heat wave the summer before, leaving everyone else with malfunctioning three-speed fans. Titus let another drag excuse him from answering.

"I should get moving," Beatrice said, though she didn't immediately follow through on the notion. "I'm doing two to eight at the mansion, and Paula's got new lines for me, of course, and I haven't even looked at them."

Paula Goodstone had managed Apricot Ridge for twelve years, nine of them with her husband, Ralph, before he'd dropped from heart failure on an August afternoon not unlike July 19th in its potential to incinerate. Paula's own dietary habits suggested a reunion in the near future, which would undoubtedly please much of her current staff.

"And how will you be serving the Goddard family today?"

"Fuck off," Beatrice said, and in one fluid motion hoisted herself onto the carpet.

She stood, back to him, in skin-tone underwear; through the smoke that had accumulated in the tiny room, she looked artificial, as if at any moment she might disintegrate and join the vapors which crept along the ceiling in search of an outlet. Picking her clothes from the mound next to the bed, she transformed herself piece by piece into an exact replica of a serving girl.

First she hooked together a bra which matched the shade of her underwear, then forced her arms through the sleeves of a white T-shirt. A pair of black athletic shorts on indefinite loan from Titus was folded over once at her hips, and there the process came to a momentary halt, as she looked over her shoulder toward him and smiled.

"I want you to remember me like this, okay?"

He nodded, and was on the verge of saying something when he felt a singing pain against his thumb and index finger; with a muttered curse, he killed the joint against a corner of the nightstand.

From the carpet, Beatrice gathered up a bundle of white fabric, through which she wriggled her arms and head. When she let the bundle drop, cloth unrolled to her ankles, revealing a plain white dress identical to those suffocating the majority of the women outside. She looked down at herself, as even in color and texture as the building that contained them; after a long sigh, she wrapped a black apron around her torso, and tied its gossamer strings behind without having to look.

Throughout the weeks following Beatrice's rise to her current position—she'd started as an usher in the playhouse, known to Titus and everyone else as Eleanor Greenbush—she had needed his help with the apron strings; not quite a year later, she performed the task with ease, her fingers moving as nimbly as a sharpshooter refilling his musket with gunpowder.

She crowned herself with a black bonnet, tucking the folds of her dark hair underneath it. Thus five minutes' labor had produced Beatrice Miller, serving girl in the Goddard mansion on Alchemist's Road, so named for Mr. Thomas Goddard's ability to gild any venture upon which he lay his manicured hands. Lifting the hem of her dress, she curtsied slightly in Titus' direction, and upon straightening bit her lip in a way that never failed to jellify his heart.

"Say it."

She shook her head.

"Come on. Just once."

Snarling at him, she curled her lips upward and folded her hands atop the black apron. When she spoke, her voice abruptly held the residue of a transatlantic accent, one that had been dying off, month by month, but would never—could never—be fully eradicated.

"How do you do? My name is Beatrice Miller. I'm twenty-four years old, and I've been employed in the Goddard mansion since arriving in America last year. My responsibilities include the organization of Mr. Goddard's papers, the preparation of Mrs. Goddard's breakfast, and the warmth of little Emily's bath. And I'm going to bloody kill myself if I have to do this a single day longer—oh, shut up."

She reassumed her off-duty voice for the last three words—Titus had broken into laughter halfway through her speech. She harrumphed, then stepped lightly toward him; bending at the waist, she pressed her lips against his.

They held there for several moments longer than what might be expected of the typical goodbye—like everything impossible beyond the closed door, the gesture was one that they relished. Titus spread the fingers of one hand over the back of her skull, where they could get lost in the dark realm of her hair.

"Careful," she said, breaking away and checking the integrity of her bonnet.

"Will I see you tonight?"

"I don't know. I think Paula might be suspicious. Plus," and she smiled wickedly, "there's always your wife to be concerned about."

Titus groaned.

"Don't call her that."

The smile grew—she took pleasure in torturing him.

"Would Martha Windaloo be upset if she knew I was here?"

"Stop."

She laughed, and kissed him again before walking to the door.

"I think I'll go to O'Leary's tonight," he said as her hand brushed the knob. "Will you be there?"

Her green eyes caught the lamplight, flashing through the smoke as she looked at him. "What does it matter, Titus? We wouldn't even be able to stand next to each other."

And then she was gone—Titus listened as her footsteps descended the stairwell and then paused while she inspected Molasses Lane for observing eyes; after a moment, he heard the front door close heavily.

Already half-stoned, he rolled onto his stomach, and threw an arm across the place where she'd just been.

His problem was not unusual: He did not love his wife, who loved him very much.

His problem was that he loved Beatrice Miller, who was certainly not his wife.

Titus had no qualms over the nights they'd spent together—no lingering guilt over his violation of marriage's sacred bonds, no internal wrestling at breaking the trust of his neighbors—but really, in the end, there was no reason why he should.

After all, his wife was not really his wife, either.

Paula Goodstone enforced a single rule, which had in turn spawned countless offspring.

Performers at Apricot Ridge were never to break character.

As such, a man and woman whose nineteenth-century personas were married were to act married during the village's business hours of ten to eight, and be cordial to one another outside of them; cordial, but never intimate, for the natural yield of intimacy is romance, and love has a way of cutting through illusions that made Paula Goodstone see it as a legitimate threat to her business.

Paula had informed Titus of this stricture on his first day, in the office she kept beneath the welcome center which stood like an outpost fifty yards outside the gates. Titus had slotted it near the back of his mind, behind questions of salary and benefits; at the time, he'd thought he could sidestep his heart as easily as if it were a tree branch obstructing a footpath, especially since he was penniless and the gig was of the hard-to-come-by variety.

And then, two months later, Beatrice Miller had stepped off the express bus with a torn suitcase and those fucking eyes. Of course, she'd been Eleanor Greenbush then; though her name had changed, the eyes hadn't.

Two minutes after the closing hour on the nineteenth of July, as the day's final tour group passed through the gates and separated into its component units to argue dinner plans and shower order, Tom freed the rope that kept the wooden halves separate and, easing it hand over hand, guided them together once more. Their reunion caused a slight boom which echoed up Molasses Lane and woke Titus Windaloo, still drowsing on his unmade bed.

"Shit," he said, without opening his eyes, for he knew she'd be on her way.

Martha had asked if she could come by directly after close to run lines for the next day's exhibition, claiming she had difficulty recalling the various heights to which a blacksmith's wife might build his furnace-fire in order for him to adequately rework certain quantities of iron and steel.

Not a minute later, he heard footsteps in the stairwell, and a quiet knock thrice repeated.

"Come in."

Martha Windaloo appeared at the foot of his bed, wearing street clothes and a fragrance of cigarette smoke. She sneered at him, baring yellowed teeth.

"I see you've accomplished a lot on your day off."

Titus didn't say anything, only reached for the pages on his nightstand, where they'd lain untouched since he'd received them from Paula two days before. He swung his feet over the edge of the bedframe, and handed the script to Martha; while she shuffled through it, he transferred a dirty T-shirt from the carpet to his torso.

"Sit down," he said, eying the twisted sheets next to him; though he wouldn't enjoy such proximity, the room held no other furniture.

She complied, flopping on the mattress and sighing contentedly as she leaned back on her elbows.

"I thought you quit," Titus said.

The noise she made was tellingly noncommittal, landing somewhere between a sigh and a dismissive grunt.

"I went out today to the matinee, then O'Leary's on a whim. It's harder after drinking."

Titus nodded and gestured for the pages.

"Start from the beginning?"

They ran lines for half an hour, until Titus, exhausted by Martha's presence, declared her halting recitation of the proper way to go about forging an iron gatepost to be perfection incarnate, and rose from the bed so that she would follow suit.

"Everyone's going to O'Leary's tonight," she said, as if this was news—the dive bar was the only source of recreation for miles. "Will you be there?"

"I don't know."

"Well. Maybe I'll see you later."

He didn't say anything, and after repeating the possibility she left.

Once he heard the door close, Titus let himself fall backward, cutting a diagonal across the mattress. He would go to the bar that night, of course, if only for the chance of seeing Beatrice, which he figured was pretty good. For the time being, he settled for thoughts of her, pale substitutes for that dark hair, and those green eyes, and the way in which her breasts challenged the upper seams of her apron; the memory-flecks burned hot and steady, like sparks leaping yellow and orange from an anvil.

As he stepped past the night-shift doorman and into O'Leary's, the most prominent of the offspring rules surfaced in Titus Windaloo's head: Performers at Apricot Ridge are forbidden from knowing each other's birth names, lest one slip out midway through an exhibition. Aside from the doorman and the rotation of bartenders, Titus referred to everyone by the characters they'd assumed, the collected fiction of Paula Goodstone.

Jameson Till, a red-cheeked carpenter who would've stank of an all-day whiskey habit if not for the thick aura of sawdust clinging to him, was standing next to the supposedly teenaged Emily Goddard—lingering baby fat allowed her to play a dozen years below the amount she'd compiled. Titus nodded to Theodore and Abigail Richardson, sitting in a corner booth; they owned the hardware store on Miner's Way and, much to Paula's concern, were as inseparable as the Richardson & Son painted on a board above the entrance. Titus leaned against the wooden counter next to Jameson.

The bar ran around O'Leary's in the shape of a squared-off U, and was halved by a two-tiered shelf lined with glistening bottles. Squinting through the dim light to the other side, Titus made out Pastor Worthy, a man of forty-two and ample vices who spent his days white-collared, reciting the cardinal virtues, and his nights sitting backwards on the nearest toilet lid, snorting lines of cocaine off the porcelain tank. Alongside the pastor was Beatrice Miller, mouth open in laughter at something he'd just said, teeth glinting underneath the fluorescents. To ward off the jealousy that clawed at his stomach, Titus ordered a shot and entered a discussion ongoing between Jameson and Emily.

"Did you see the guy with the scar?" she was asking.

"I wasn't on today," Titus said.

"What kind of scar?" Jameson asked.

"It was bad, like half of his face. You'd remember him."

"Then I didn't see him."

"Anyway, he wouldn't stop staring at me. Doesn't he know I'm supposed to be fifteen years old?"

"Maybe he figured out that you aren't," Titus said.

"That's not the point."

Facing the bar, Titus struggled not to glance across toward Beatrice; after five minutes, his neck began to cramp with the effort of holding still. So he was relieved when a finger tapped his shoulder; he rotated to find Martha, leaning in a way that indicated how she'd spent the hours since leaving his room.

"You didn't think to tell your wife you'd be out late?"

Titus forced a smile—Martha told the joke at least five times per week.

And then very suddenly he was sitting across from her in the booth with Theodore and Abigail, distributing the contents of a half-priced pitcher between four glasses.

"How's business?" Theodore asked him, then cut his eyes toward Martha, including her in the question.

Titus felt something rising in his throat and, to combat it, drained his glass in one breathless slug. He set it down and refilled it immediately.

As the alcohol filtered into his bloodstream, a haze descended upon the bar, or at least upon his perception of it. First came the facial arithmetic—turning his head too rapidly caused Martha to quarter and then exist as four clones, a nightmarish prospect; subsequently he noticed that the lights hanging from the ceiling and those stuck into the walls were beginning to spill from their bulbs and shades, bleeding electric into the smear of faces until he was squinting as if through murky water just to see the glass in front of him, his only anchor. Voices separated from their origins to exist as floating entities, little packages of anecdotes and witticisms with no return addresses, and Titus laughed every minute or so at the things they contained, if only to ensure he hadn't faded into nothingness.

And then, unexpectedly, the gloom cleared halfway through an improvised scene.

"Not here," Beatrice was saying, and he was standing next to her, arm wrapped around her, fingers exploring the spaces between her ribs.

"Not here," she said again, but leaned into him all the same.

Titus Windaloo looked up, then, like the God-fearing man he pretended to be every day between ten and eight, and his not-wife's face, slack-jawed and wide-eyed, resolved itself from the darkness across the bar.

Though his memory ran dry after that, Titus woke the next morning to three things, which blended to make chaos of his senses: a mouthful of dark hair; the image of Martha's face—most unamused—filling his aching head; and, lastly, an authoritative rapping against his door.

Tom kept the gates open five minutes later than usual that evening, allowing the blacksmith—wearing his leather boots and work shirt despite being recently off-duty—to slip through on his way to Paula Goodstone's office. Titus nodded to the gatekeeper, who returned the gesture in a mournful sort of way, informing Titus that he had already heard, most likely along with everyone else.

Paula had certainly known what to expect in coming to his room that morning—she'd elbowed around Titus, her thick shoulders rising and falling like unsure mountains as she observed the sleeping form of Beatrice Miller; when she made her exit, it was accompanied by the laser-beam glare usually reserved for everyone in the village but him.

"My office, right after close," she had said, and then vanished, the stairs groaning underneath her weight.

The impending meeting had dwelt in the foreground of his thoughts all day, distracting him from his work—midway through an exhibition, he nearly branded his palms when he left a sheet of metal dissolving in the furnace; alerted to it by one of the visitors, he had tried to snatch it out without first putting on his leather gloves.

"Be careful," Martha had said afterwards, but Titus hadn't responded, part of a daylong vow of silence in which he addressed her only when the script called for it, and then without making eye contact.

A patch of trees on Titus' left gave way to a small clearing filled entirely by the welcome center, a two-story building made of red bricks and a cheery disposition. The latter was taken care of by a series of placards mounted lectern-style along a gravel path branching to the front door, which related facts about the village in a clean-cut humor that gunned ambitiously for every demographic possible.

Everything within Apricot Ridge is made by the villagers themselves, their luck included, one read.

The heat had finally broken with an early afternoon thunderstorm, and so, for the first time in days, Titus felt no perspiration cooling on the back of his neck as he opened the door and entered the air-conditioned lobby, though his palms were slicked with it.

Tina, the woman who worked the front desk, was formerly known to him as Genevieve Harris, a farmer's wife often to be found elbow-deep in a pail of milk, relating to half-interested suburbanites the ins and outs of bovine anatomy. She'd tired of the part six months before, and had been granted a transfer to the business end of Apricot Ridge.

"She's waiting downstairs, Titus."

Thanking her, Titus descended the staircase to the basement, where a long hallway ended in a single door, on which was stenciled, in thin black letters, *Paula Goodstone, General Manager.* He knocked twice—considerably less than Paula had that morning—and heard her voice telling him to enter.

Paula was bent over her desk, face shucked of its prior ill-temperedness such that, on first glance, Titus thought she'd already moved beyond the morning's anger; upon looking up, however, her face made a whiplash-inducing three-point turn back toward it: nostrils flaring, eyes narrowing, mouth flattening. Titus avoided eye contact, shifting his gaze around the office as if he were unfamiliar with the newspaper articles framed on the wall behind her desk and the white plastic chair perpetually set up before it, into which she gestured him.

"Sit down," she said, and he did. "How was it today?"

The question not being one he'd anticipated, Titus took a moment to forge his response.

"It was fine."

"Martha get the new lines down alright?"

"Yeah. Alright."

"She was worried about them this morning, I know."

"Well. She did okay. Better with practice, I'm sure."

Paula nodded, then pressed her fists into her desk, using the leverage to push herself upright. After catching her breath, she set herself in motion, waddling back and forth through the gap between her pushed-out chair and desk; by pausing briefly at each end before reversing direction, she began to resemble a slow-moving pendulum. Titus' eyes jittered back and forth, following her.

"How long?" she asked, turning sharply toward him.

"How long what?"

"Don't play dumb. Martha sees you acting familiar with Beatrice Miller last night, and I find her nude in your bed this morning. That kind of thing doesn't just happen once. I want to know how long it's been."

Thinking it best to mislead her, he sighed as if giving in.

"A couple of months. It's not a serious thing, Paula."

"You have a wife."

"She's not really my wife."

"Exactly the kind of attitude that infects an operation like ours."

Titus rubbed two fingers across his unkempt beard, a requirement of his profession.

"Are you in love with her?"

He gawked, and stammered. This seemed to be the wrong response, for her eyes slitted and a dark color flowered in her cheeks.

"It's been two months," he said.

"You can fall in love in two months. I fell in love with Ralph in two days."

He raised a hand in exasperation. "I didn't know that."

Paula returned to her seat, another lengthy process, and burrowed her elbows into the desktop; leaning toward him, her face unfolded into a rare expression—if it wasn't kindness, it was close enough.

"It's no secret that I like you, Titus, and contrary to popular belief, I understand that all of you are human beings, with needs and attentions that want fulfillment. But this is my business, and I have a rule which I believe helps make it successful."

She reclined in her chair before continuing.

"If you're going to stay on at Apricot Ridge, I can't have you seeing her anymore."

For a moment he hesitated, considering the option implied, but then the moment passed and he nodded, the movement as slight and near-invisible as a heart unraveling.

He left her office, Titus Windaloo still.

After briefly returning to Molasses Lane, where he progressed his outfit by a century in five minutes, Titus shadowed the crowd heading to O'Leary's, finding it broken apart and distributed about the bar when he entered. He saw Theodore Richardson leaning against the counter in front of a quartet of beers, while Abigail and Martha were lodged in the same corner booth as the night before; they'd left a space empty, as if expecting an arrival.

On a barstool further down sat the reversed form of Beatrice Miller, her dark hair spilling over her shoulders, her tank top cut low to reveal thin lines of muscle webbing her back.

A sudden nausea rose within him, a heavy cloud that expanded until his breath came hard and short. Titus backpedaled to the entrance, mumbled gibberish to the doorman in the vein of something forgotten, and then rejoined the night. After a period of stillness on the concrete, he turned and headed toward the liquor store up the road.

The confrontation came two evenings later in a narrow alley behind the playhouse on Alchemist's Road, where once, cloaked in after-midnight darkness, they had shared an illicit embrace, one of countless private displays of affection occurring over a yearlong stretch. As he spoke, her green eyes dulled under a rising tide.

"How did she find out?"

He didn't answer. The silence was partly filled by muffled dialogue from that day's fortieth run-through of a five-minute scene plucked from Oscar Wilde, which spilled through the theater doors.

"All I'm trying to say, dear—"

The predicate was overcome by clanging swords—the militia was running their demonstration a block over.

"I don't think we can do this anymore," Titus said.

Frustration slipped through the few gaps remaining in her gritted teeth.

"She can't tell us what to do."

"We work for her."

Beatrice looked toward the dirt beneath her slippers, baked into clay by yet another hot one.

"We don't have to, you know," she said. "Work here, I mean."

"Do you have a better option?"

She lifted her eyes and shrugged.

"I've been talking to my mother lately. I'm thinking of moving back to New York, taking another shot at it."

"Oh yeah?" She nodded.

"You could come with me. We could get a place in the cheap streets. Hit auditions. Support each other. Do it together, while we still have time."

Imitating her in looking downward—though his eyes glazed into a stare, as if the earth were a crystal ball—Titus remembered his life as Jonathan Bedford: the mattress on the floor of the studio apartment, the three daily meals of microwaved noodles, the false hope giving way to inevitable rejection. These images were distorted with the addition of Beatrice's silhouette, conjuring whispers of pre-audition encouragement, eating together at five-dollar buffets, and barrel-bottom cocktails at Village bars crammed with dozens of their kind.

After a few seconds, it all faded, yielding only the cracked layer of brown upon which he stood.

"I'm sorry," he said. "I just can't right now."

Her face breaking but revealing nothing underneath, she abandoned the playhouse wall, walking up Alchemist's Road toward the Goddard mansion.

The swords stopped clanging as he watched her go.

"I've finally realized for the first time in my life—"

But the shouts of two passing children drowned out the ultimate clause.

She didn't tell him when she left. Her name bounced around his skull for a couple of days before he realized it was inappropriate, as her name wasn't Beatrice Miller anymore.

Titus learned of her departure from Emily Goddard one evening after close, when he just so happened, as he'd convinced himself, to be walking up Alchemist's Road past the mansion. Emily was crouched atop the stone wall out front, a cigarette dangling from her lips.

"Shame about Beatrice," she said.

Titus blinked.

"You heard about that?"

"It's hard not to notice someone's gone when you see her every fucking day of your life."

Not wanting to give away that they'd been on different pages, he didn't ask her to specify.

Instead, he wondered if she had any extras in her pack.

Beatrice had told him she was going, but he hadn't expected her plans to crystallize so quickly, like molted iron cooling in an instant to a flesh-piercing edge. Though he couldn't blame her, the sudden lack of her took him somewhere, numb days that had vacationers staring as he fumbled through exhibitions, had Martha Windaloo asking if he might not let her stand next to the fire, instead, if only for an hour or two.

Within two weeks, he'd nearly come to terms with losing her; without her electricity, however, his life dulled considerably, paved over with the monotony of working-class routine. He rose two hours after dawn every morning and met Martha downstairs, where they'd quickly run lines followed by exhibitions from ten to eight, breaking for an hour somewhere in the middle to eat lunch together outside. Nights he spent in O'Leary's, drinking until his memory fragmented, so that he woke knowing little except that the first group of the day would be coming through in twenty minutes, and he had better take a shower before they did.

Thus the summer passed, the days gradually shortening until the leaves began to turn and the crowds to swell.

Autumn was often said to be the most beautiful season for a visit to Apricot Ridge.

Paula Goodstone stumbled across her husband's path one morning that November, discovered facedown in her office by Tom after failing to emerge for her customary welcome of the day's first guests.

She and Ralph hadn't left an heir, and control of the village remained up for grabs until the cusp of spring, when the lot was purchased by a small team of property developers; soon after, the developers announced plans to knock down the tidy arrangement of outdated buildings to make way for a budget department store.

Though newspapers statewide decried the proposal in opinion pieces and letters to the editor, the locals were quietly pleased—after countless middle-school field trips, they'd grown tired of Apricot Ridge, not to mention that the store's second-nearest location was fifty miles away.

The entire staff was gathered in the clearing just inside the gates for the news to be officially broken by an anonymous man wearing sunglasses. He additionally informed them that Apricot Ridge would remain operational for a final week, after which its five streets would become a restricted area, blocked off by wire fences and caution tape.

That night, the primary topic for discussion in O'Leary's—at the bar and in the booths, through scattered groups of two and four, as well as within everyone's heads—was what, exactly, they were going to do next. The immediate answer, scribbled in every water-damaged margin of the place, seemed to be the widespread destruction of inhibitions.

Theodore and Abigail Richardson were creating friction in their usual booth, wasting no time after the implied lifting of the ban on coworker affection. Samuel, the guide, spun unsteadily on his barstool to mouth "I told you so" to Jameson Till next to him; Jameson, in turn, raised two fingers at the bartender, who smirked and shook his head, long-familiar with the bright-red color of Jameson's cheeks. Pastor Worthy went by them on his way from the bathroom, eyes so unnaturally wide it seemed metal splints had to be forcing the lids apart. He fell into a booth next to Emily Goddard, sitting across from her faux-parents, all of them planning a weeklong bender to honor the end of the whole charade.

Behind them sat Titus and Martha Windaloo. His anger at her had faded with the season, and they'd taken to keeping each other company, though he still refused to acknowledge her come-ons, wouldn't respond to any hints at their relationship's further development.

"Are you going to miss this place?" Martha asked, in the silence following a humorous tangent.

"I think dive bars will exist almost anywhere I might choose to."

"No," Martha said. "I mean Apricot Ridge. Everyone here. You know."

"Oh."

Titus looked around at those assembled, eyes flicking through the darkness.

"Yeah. I guess I will."

His eyes glazed slightly, and he focused on the empty space beside her as if expecting something to appear there by magic; though, having spent the past several years of his life pretending to will shapeless metal into concrete objects by sweat and fire, alone, he really ought to have known better.

As the night wound down, and closing time approached, the soon-to-be-former citizens of Apricot Ridge began to disappear in ones and twos and threes; so that after the bartender had wiped the liquid residue from the empty counter and flipped the stools upside-down on top of it, their legs pointing toward heaven, it was as if no one had been there at all.

One week later, a bearded man stood on the edge of the highway in front of a convenience store, a medium-sized suitcase— just enough to fit the contents of a hundred square feet—propped in between his denim-covered legs. There were two cars parked in the lot behind him, one belonging to the morning-shift cashier, the other to a man on all fours on the pavement, trying to replace a dead tire. Above the store hung a gray morning, one bright spot amongst the clouds revealing the position of the sun. Above the bearded man's head hung the initial-laden awning of a bus stop.

The silence was broken by a noise of fumes exhaled from beyond an incline up the road, followed by the rev of a chugging motor; as the man turned, a dirty-white monstrosity on four wheels appeared and coasted down the hill toward him, seemingly relieved to have made it over. Taking his suitcase by the handle, the man removed a folded ticket from a pocket of his jeans. As the express bus pulled onto the shoulder, he squinted at the electric-yellow letters, located just north of the windshield, which spelled out its destination.

The doors hissed open, and the man climbed aboard. He handed his ticket to the driver.

The name on the ticket read Jonathan Bedford, printed in tiny black letters slightly smudged from the paper being folded over.

Holding the suitcase in front of him, the man made his way down the aisle, gripping the metal beam that ran the length of the bus as the engine roared to new life. There was an empty seat in the back, next to a young woman wearing sunglasses and leaning against the window. As his shadow fell over her, the woman looked toward him.

"Do you mind?" he asked.

"Of course not," she said, and he sat down, shoving his bag beneath the seat in front.

He breathed out loudly, as if he'd been holding it for some time. The woman smiled at him.

"Going somewhere new?"

He seemed to consider the question.

"Sort of."

"Me, too."

They fell quiet, then—the brief exchange might've been all had the woman not shrugged, and produced five more words.

"I'm Emily, by the way."

"Titus," he said, after too long a pause.

Rob Andwood lives in Cambridge, MA. He has previously been published in *Writing Tomorrow* and *Cicada Magazine*.

Editor's Choice Award

The Lost Doll
by Alex Clark-McGlenn

A hush covered the city at night. For André Menge the silence came with fear and something he couldn't understand. The wind would not blow. Like the citizenry and like André, it held its breath; God held his breath, too, and, like God, André was filled with uncertainty.

Bartes always drove. It was an unspoken agreement between partners. An unspoken agreement, like so many others they shared; they never spoke about what they did to survive. In times like these, they told themselves, individual morals were reduced to skin and bone.

"You ready?"

André nodded. It was 1:02 a.m.

Bartes started the engine. The darkness of night swallowed the police car's headlights. As they pulled away from the station silhouettes of police officers climbing from the curb into marked vehicles faded into existence. They all appeared stretched and bone thin in the sudden glare of the headlights. *It's as if only darkness will define them, much like it will define humanity.* André shivered and, despite this, cracked the window. He needed air; there wasn't enough in the car.

Another police cruiser pulled in front of them. It braked at an intersection, turned left. For fifteen minutes they followed the cruiser. Neither of them spoke. It was just a job. There were no questions to ask. But. . .

"Are they French?" asked André.

Bartes exhaled through his nose. "The report said Polish."

André set his jaw and nodded.

As they parked, officers were already packing the small city square. Periodically the hush of the night was broken by hoarse whispers, the sound of dirt sliding into a poorly dug grave.

"We've got 213," Bartes told André, adding to the disturbing voices as they stepped from the vehicle.

They crossed the square. More officers were arriving by the minute. The whispering grew and lights came on in some of the surrounding houses. André flicked his flashlight over the doors, counting the addresses. Many officers were doing the same.

"Here." He pointed. The stoop was a distance from the crowd. No lights were on in the house.

The impact of André's knuckles against the wooden door resulted in a knock that drove the hush from the city square, just as the Luftwaffe, two years prior, had shattered the silence of France.

Everywhere in the square officers began to knock on doors. The hush that had felt pervasive now seemed unlikely ever to return. André knocked again. The door eased open. A woman stood there, her face pale in the dim light of the streetlamp.

Bartes pushed his way into the house. The woman shuffled back, feet rubbing the carpet; her nightgown hung loosely, etched lines covered her face, though André could tell they were not from age. Only fear did that to a woman so young.

"Get them up," Bartes said. "Wake them. You're leaving."

The woman shook visibly. "Where?" she asked. "Where? Where are you taking us?"

André couldn't look away from her. The fear that shook her voice was contagious, and he feared, as well. "It's not our decision."

"You have five minutes," Bartes showed her five raised fingers as though he was counting down. "Follow her," he said to his partner.

André only stared, watching as she climbed the stairs to the bedrooms. *She's young for children, yet so close to death.*

45

"Menge." Bartes shook André by the shoulder. "Go with her. Make sure no one gets out by mistake."

Up five steps the stairs took a right; on the left wall, a mirror hung. A small table stood below it on the landing. Family pictures were arranged. A man and two boys. A woman and a small girl, all smiles. Not so long ago, but *before the world moved on.*

André momentarily caught sight of his reflection in the mirror. Were those his creased pale cheeks? His sagging eyes? *Is that the man I am? Or the one I will grow to be? Who is he?*

"Menge!" came Bartes's voice from below.

"Yeah?"

"Ask her about the husband; he's supposed to be here."

"Okay."

André stepped into the bedroom; there was a crunch. Four faces looked at him. The woman, two young boys, and a little girl, all pale, all frightened. André raised his boot. The broken pieces of an earring. He brushed them aside with his foot. He looked up. The woman stood on the other side of the bed. She spoke as she dumped drawers full of clothing onto it. "Go on," she said. "All the clothes you can carry, right now."

André moved from the door to let the children leave. "Ma'am," he said. "Where is your husband?"

She was wrapping her clothes in a blanket. She didn't look up. "I don't know. He didn't come home after work."

"I'm sorry."

Now she looked at him, shook her head. "You cannot be sorry. Where are you taking us?"

"I don't know."

She let out a breath, and another, and a tear. The children returned, each carrying an armful of clothing. The little girl was wailing. She wanted her doll. She wanted her doll but couldn't find it. It was a sound André had made a long time ago.

"Menge!"

André stepped into the hall. His partner was at the turn of the stairs. André could see the back of Bartes's head in the wall mirror.

"Any word on the husband?"

"He didn't come home today. He's not here."

"Maybe." Bartes disappeared around the corner.

An uprising of voices and inarticulate sound came from the bedroom. André looked in.

"We have to leave because they say so," the woman said as the little girl wailed and one boy yelled at his mother, asking why, while his brother sat in silence on the bed shaking his head, face as pale as a porcelain doll's.

A thump came from ground level. The family didn't notice. A crash and the house shook. The woman looked up.

"What is he doing?" she asked over the noise of her children.

André took a breath, not caring to answer. *He's destroying your house.* "He's looking for your husband." André entered the bedroom again.

"He's not here…"

"Papa!" cried the girl and bolted out the door.

Too late the woman sprang around the bed, reaching for her daughter. In a cascade of stomping the woman hurtled down the stairs after her daughter. The two boys followed, then André. It sounded like Bartes was dismantling the house, looking for any place a person could hide. André stopped on the landing. He checked his face in the wall mirror again. *I know you.* It was a man who wouldn't survive. It was a small boy who had cried nearly half a century ago as he looked down at a starved dog, boney ribs showing through skin and fur. He had wailed over that dog as the girl now wailed for her doll. *Why are things like this?*

He turned away from the mirror. At least one of the bottles that had broken filled the room with the reek of alcohol. It burned the nostrils as it would have burned the throat. *What a waste.* A grandfather clock lay on its side, the face broken, the pendulum hanging limply in its casing.

They were all yelling now, the woman and children near the stairs, Bartes across the room, legs hidden behind a hastily moved couch.

"Enough!" This time Bartes reached for his gun and pulled it smoothly from its holster. He pointed it firmly at the family. And at that moment André knew Bartes would survive this. He would survive because the gun he pointed at the innocent never shook.

The hush had returned to the house. The yells and cries from the city square were silenced. All anyone could look at was the barrel of the gun.

"Don't," quavered the woman, as though her word alone could stop the bullet. She held her arms out and in front of her children and André watched her.

She would die in this, to protect them, but her death would not protect. *For some there is no hope and nothing will save them from this world.* He would have done anything for that dog, but it had been beyond help. *Were they?*

He stepped forward. "Time to go."

"Our clothes..."

"It's too late for that," said Bartes. André had moved away from the stairs. Bartes caught his eye and held it. André looked at the ground. *This is why he will survive and I will not.* It wasn't a lack of mercy that Bartes had; he had made a choice. A choice to survive. André knew this.

"Let's go," said Bartes and motioned toward the door. The family moved, the woman and her sons one way, the little girl the other. Her mother tried to catch hold of her but missed and André watched Bartes, as if in slow motion, track the little girl with his loaded gun. The flash and crack of the bullet leaving the barrel left André deaf and stunned. He didn't move, he didn't do anything, and he didn't hear the glass of the mirror shattering.

"Dammit, Menge. Go get her!" shouted Bartes, training his gun back on the family.

André looked up the stairs. The fragments of glass littered the table and the floor. He had expected to see a body, but there were only these tears made solid. No little girl painted crimson.

She was back before he took a step. Nimbly, she sprang over the broken glass and down the last few steps, so strange an image compared to the one he had recently adopted of her. She carried something. It flopped in her arms.

Her mother grabbed the little girl up and hugged and scolded and cried into her hair.

"But look, Mamma," said the little girl. "I found her."

What a miracle she is, thought André. *Breathing, living, not splayed upon the stairs where she could have so easily been killed, comforted by the discovery of her doll. But this isn't about comfort, is it? Death so seldom is. And now there is only the truth of life, and the spitting of metal, and peace is but a distant memory unlikely to return. There will be no salvation for her, and so none for me.*

He took it. Took the little girl's doll. He yanked it from her hands as she cried out, reaching. The doll had flowing golden hair and glassy dead eyes that peered from a porcelain face. The woman said something to him, but André couldn't hear her. Whatever she said was lost in the hush that had come over him. He understood why the wind wouldn't blow. The hush of the city was one of survival. It was the hush of a city waiting for the end. What end he couldn't say. The hush of the city was now in him, as well. It was a hush that told him he would survive this.

He threw the doll back into the house, nodded at his partner, and herded the Jews out the door.

Alex Clark-McGlenn is taking his MFA in Creative Writing from the Northwest Institute of Literary Arts. He was published in *eFiction Magazine*, *Inkwell* at Evergreen, *Slightly West Literary Magazine*, and *Smokebox Literary Magazine*. He currently lives in the Pacific Northwest.

Editor's Choice Award

Tide
by Briana Forney

"When you realize how perfect everything is, you will tilt your head back and laugh at the sky." -Buddha

Eight celestial bodies dance, heliocentric. Sunspots flare, ultra-violet, ultra-violent, providing warmth and burns and life and cancer. It's a galaxy. It's a universe, it's a single-celled organism, it's a soul in a body and it's seeking Nirvana. Ashtanga Yoga bears eight limbs, as an octopus bears suction cups, as Durga, Goddess of Victory of Good over Evil, bears weapons. These are the structural tenets of yoga, the steps to true peace, as laid out by Patañjali in his Yoga Sutras.

Yoga is an inward journey, a self-contained destiny. We are both infinite and infinitesimal, the ocean and the grain of sand, the labyrinth and the lost. My own expedition began in the mud, like a thousand-petaled white lotus.

Yama | ya·ma | (observances towards others)

I don't remember when I started comparing myself. It's not something that just happens all at once. There was no *Mommy, what does 'fat' mean?* No pointing at a commercial or billboard or magazine and asking, *Am I gonna look like that?*

Inexplicably, I do remember one moment of my youth, around 8-years-old. I was playing with my Barbie dolls in their fire truck–red convertible, and I imagined how I would look at sixteen—a lifetime away. I imagined myself with yellow-blond hair and a glowing white smile as I waved to some fabulous friend. Then, I reimagined the scene, asking myself, but what if I get fat? Same yellow-blond, same happy smile, but this time the waving arm jiggled as it shook. I remember erasing the thought like an Etch-a-Sketch and resuming play. It wasn't that I was peering down at Barbie asking my God, *Why can't I look like her?* It was nothing so dramatic. That was just the first moment I realized that the fate of my body was something to be controlled, something to be feared.

The first limb of ashtanga yoga is *yama*, the code of conduct to live a life of harmony. In yoga, this means being non-violent, humble, and giving up an obsession with material goods. I just tried to live in harmony with the girls to whom I compared myself. They told strangers they were pretty, so I did. They talked about their own flaws as if it meant they were embracing them, so I did. I thought if I did as they did, I would be happy like they seemed. I tried to follow. I tried to fit in. The code became one more thing that other girls were better at than me.

I never found out who said it, and I don't remember who told me, but it was notorious that someone said in reference to me, *She got big boobs and turned into a bitch.* I laughed when I heard it, but it was true. I had filled out from birth control and I began to regard "nice" as a curse. It was probably some "nice" girl who said it about me, and whoever heard it probably argued that I was "nice." "Nice" was what you called someone when you had nothing good to say. "Nice" was redemption for vapidity, compensation for ugly, fat. I hated "nice." I would not be "nice."

I suspected that the comment may have come from my skinny, small-breasted best friend and resented her for it in secret. I would later learn that she was bulimic. She was the first person I told after I first had sex. Afterwards, I saw a page of her journal on which she wrote simply *Bri—whore.* In my vague recollection it only made sense for me to open or look over at the journal, and I take that to mean that, on some level, she wanted me to see it, though I never told her I did. Our mutual friends would joke to her, *It's because you're so fat*, as reason for anything. It was clear they were joking. I resented her for that, too. Why would nobody joke that I was fat? Why was stating my fatness not a clear untruth? It was truth by omission, admission by silence, insinuation by fear. I had observed others. Others were better, happier, skinnier than me, and correlation implied causation.

Niyama | ni·ya·ma | (self-imposed disciplines)

At some point in early high school, the hazy cloud of dislike took root, manifested itself right behind my belly button, right in my third chakra. I hated my stomach. I hated its roundness. I hated the sideways "S" curve down to my pelvis when I looked at it in profile. I hated how I could take it up in my hands, bulging between my fingers like wet clay, but I did it anyway, repeatedly. *If I could just get rid of this.* There was no consequent to the thought, no 'then.' There was only the desire to be rid of it, no concept of what would be left.

Niyama are ritualized spiritual observances. These are similar to the code of conduct, but are more internal. Each limb of Ashtanga Yoga moves inward, reaching closer and closer to one's core. Where yama are actions, niyama are thoughts.

I don't know where I got my specific disciplines. There was no gray-font-on-a-black-background website of helpful tips, no wiry and shivering friend offering me cigarettes to curb my cravings for food. I seemed to come to my niyama on my own. I sucked in my stomach because I felt like it was protruding. I sucked it in because I thought it would strengthen the muscles and eventually it would just look that way all the time. I sucked it in because I didn't want to have to look at it. And I jiggled my legs so they wouldn't just sit there, the fat pouring into the pockets on the side, cottage cheese in a Ziploc bag resting on a rounded sofa arm.

I cut out soda, cut out everything but water. I drank a full glass before a meal, whenever possible. *Our Water, who art in a Plastic Cup, Liquid be Thy name.* Thy Kingdom come, Thy will be done, on

Earth as it is in My Stomach. Give us this day our daily refusal of bread, and forgive us for our carbonation, as we forgive those who drink it carelessly around us, and lead us not into temptation, but deliver us from Fatness. Amen.

Āsana | ah·sa·na | (posture)

In yogic philosophy, āsana are the poses one assumes to create greater self-discipline in meditation. This is what is commonly known as "yoga." This is the active limb, the physical limb.

I played sports my whole life, but it had always been just for something to do. I never thought about fitness. I didn't begin practicing yoga until my freshman year of college, yet until that point I held a strict nightly exercise regimen. Do these before shower. Do this while brushing teeth. Do all this before getting into bed. Do this while in bed. Hundreds of repetitions, performed self-consciously in locked rooms, acutely aware of the resonance of jumping, jogging feet on floor.

I began to perform my own āsana:

Crooked Pretzel Pose: Begin seated, legs bent. Raise one knee in front of torso, leave other down. Hunch shoulders. Best when seated at a desk, to appear defeated while working, creating lowered expectations. Benefits: raised leg hides your hideously protruding stomach, poor posture prevents you from looking like you're trying to look good, so it doesn't matter if you don't.

Unwanted Fetus Pose: Begin seated, both legs bent and forced into chest. Wrap arms tightly about knees, holding everything in. Hunch shoulders. Good for sitting on ground. Benefits: hides all unseemly areas, provides extra warmth, head can be placed on knees, providing privacy for crying or sleep.

Half Surrendered Atlas Pose: With elbow covering as much torso as possible, place hand on same shoulder. Hunch shoulders.

Can be performed seated or standing. Benefits: coverage, warmth, massage shoulder muscles sore from hunching, shrugging, and excessive exercise fatigue.

My parents encouraged my dedication to my health. They figured a life of sports had sparked in me a legitimate interest in being physically fit. I didn't want to be fit. What did it matter how many crunches I could do or miles I could run if I didn't have the body to show for it? I envied the naturally thin, those girls who I thought never did anything and so they never got hungry and so they never got fat. People tell them, *You're so lucky, you don't even have to try to stay thin.* I took that to mean that I wasn't lucky because I had to try. It wasn't that people never said that to me— they did—it was that when they did they were either lying or confused.

Prānāyāma | prah·nah·yah·ma | (control of life-force)

I counted. I limited. I excommunicated. Certain foods were restricted, others forbidden. I developed more ritualized spiritual observances in order to practice prānāyāma. Never finish a plate. Never get a second helping. Never skip breakfast, but all other meals are fair game. I went through phases of writing these things down, lists of rules, lists of foods deemed acceptable, lists of what I had eaten, their caloric content.

8/23/12

I keep feeling like all I do is eat, so here is what I ate today: orange juice, a Lean Cuisine pizza, fruit snacks, some animal crackers, half a salad, some of a piece of baguette, tea, and cheerios. That could be one meal for someone else.

The numbers dropped, prime merchandise to sale item to last-chance clearance, but despite how small the number, how short the list, it always looked too large.

There was one day in particular, back in my senior year of high school. It was the second day in a row I had convinced my mother to let me stay home from school. This was normal for me; my mother called them *mental health days*. They were usually just one day and then I was better. It was my second day home and I hadn't eaten, but my home was filled with junk food as it always was and I broke and I binged and I hated myself and went to the upstairs bathroom and locked the door and knelt before the toilet.

I had never purged before. I thought it would be simple. I remember sitting there, tearstained and shivering, stubby fingers in my gobbling throat thinking, *Why can't I even get this right?*

Prānāyāma refers to breath control, and the connection of this to the mind and emotions. Control of the body and what keeps it alive. To control was to make smaller, and this would continue for years.

Pratyāhāra | pra·tyah·hah·ra | (withdrawal of the senses)

It wasn't that I was convinced what I was doing was fine, normal and healthy. Pratyāhāra is a blocking out of the external world. I blocked out what were clear symptoms because I was focused on the ones that weren't there. I wasn't bulimic, because other than that one incident, I did not engage in those characteristic activities. But I wasn't anorexic, either. I was still eating, daily, what I considered to be too much. I didn't have an eating disorder, wasn't disciplined enough, wasn't good enough for that. I wasn't skinny yet, nobody told me, *You need a hamburger.* My heart rate was normal. My weight was normal. My life was normal. But I wasn't happy.

Dhārana | d·hah·rah·na | (concentration)

I sought therapy on my own near the end of my freshman year of college in what felt like another failure on my part. Where was the shocking moment when a loved one witnessed me changing clothes and saw my ribs and shoulder blades and demanded I get help? Where was my untimely collapse in front of confused and concerned friends? I rationalized that I was *too smart for an eating disorder,* but in moments of lower confidence, *I couldn't even have an eating disorder right.*

I took the entrance test, scoring high for both body image issues and depression, and was assigned a therapist. My therapist encouraged me to use my newfound interest in yoga for positivity and mindfulness, and I began my true practice. I had begun yoga in an ongoing attempt to control my body, not realizing that what I needed was more spiritual. At my therapist's request, I began keeping a journal. While pratyāhāra deals with outside disturbances, dhārāna deals with those inside the mind.

5/4/12

I got into one of those moods where I'm just sad for no reason, and I caught myself trying to attribute it to my stomach. Because I've been aware of it lately, I stopped that, but I was left with this hollow, aching feeling of confusion. My stomach didn't start my low mood, and I suspect that it usually didn't, but was just a quick, easy scapegoat. So while I'm glad my body isn't causing these sad states, I'm left wondering: What is?

My thoughts had trampled dirt paths in my mind, convenient shortcuts through the thorns, but I had begun to forge new ground, more winding but ultimately more scenic. I began to make sense of my mind's internal distractions.

The most important, the thought that was a tide wetting the beach at intervals, *What does it matter what my body looks like?* And, *The beauty of others does not detract from the beauty of the self.* Even still, the moon brings the tide in and out, and each time it's high I'm surprised by its salinity. It always feels like a new wave, a new realization, a new and better understanding.

9/25/13

I described myself as resilient and strong, even when I was in the middle of discussing all the reasons I'm still fucked up enough to want to be in therapy and my therapist agreed. She said I've had a long, positively directed journey, and I would agree with that.

Dhyāna | d·hee·<u>ah</u>·na | (meditative absorption)

Dhyāna and dhārāna are closely related. Dhārāna is focused concentration on meditation, and dhyāna is reaching that same state more easily. Dhārāna is practice and dhyāna is performance. It's writing in pencil and writing in pen. While my dhārāna was changing my mind's associations and thoughts, my dhyāna was yoga.

I shuffle a playlist, light incense, ring a glass like a bell, the purity of sound echoing through the room. My senses begin to heal, and I direct my attention to my breath. I do not judge it. I do not change it. I am lying on my back, my mat supporting as much of my body as possible, and my focus shifts. I imagine a white light examining the darkest notches of my body, from the crown of my head down, like an MRI, searching for tightness, anxiety, knots. I do not judge, I do not change—the change will come. I deepen my breath, and I begin my sun salutations. I feel my muscles release, joints loosen. I choose my focus: balance, strength, flexibility—whichever feels right. I follow the routines I have found for my asana, or I make them up. I listen to my body, its needs, its wants, until I am sated. I return to savasana, feeling the ground beneath me rise to meet my lower back, my knees, my neck. I notice my breath once more, notice how it has changed. I do not judge the change. I shift my attention, imagining my limbs are filling with wet sand, starting from the ends and working in until all of me, limbs, torso, head is filled with sand, and I am heavy. I notice my outline. I do not judge it, but I begin to erase it, allowing the sand to fall, to spread, to shift with the breeze or the lapping tide, until I am unrecognizable, I am the earth, I am everything.

Yoga meant a connection with my body that transcended appearance. Yoga meant a reconnection with the joys of my gymnastic youth, when my body was a toy and not a figure left pristine in its box. I quit gymnastics before anyone ever asked me to change my body, but it may have been that environment that made 8-year-old me ask, *But what if I get fat?* But yoga meant setting goals not based on size or numbers but on ability, and working and attaining, and the pride therein.

I began to tune in with my body, to feed its desires without judgment. When my skin craved the sun and my lungs lusted for grass-scented breath, I indulged. I practiced in the small yard of my apartment complex, on a busy street corner near a busy campus. I became self-conscious of my body in a way I wasn't before. Their eyes were on me, their voices, weighing down my limbs. They saw in me what they wanted to see. I was an ad for yoga apparel, excluding body shapes and colors and abilities, showing off my privilege. Or I was a performer, a contortionist, an exotic dancer, specifically there to please them. They wanted to keep me in the packaging, because, to them, I was there for show, but I was coming to realize that I wasn't only meant to be looked at.

I continued the hilly, winding, inward, seaside path, with crashing waves and erosion and sunny, salty air, onward toward inner peace. I continued to see therapists, I continued to practice yoga, I continued to keep a journal:

1/31/13
I keep having panic attacks... This time I felt really angry and mistrusting of everyone. I was furious, and I couldn't stop thinking about my stomach and the notion that I'm a fucking loser. Even writing those words started to make those feelings come back a little. The bad part was it happened while doing yoga, which is sort of like being extremely tired but not being able to sleep.

Yoga wasn't a pill, wasn't an emotional off-switch. It was a healing garden that I had to constantly tend to. The continu-ing challenges and improvements from the first five limbs of yoga—the physical, the external aids, the bahiranga sadhana—have helped me to love my body for what it can do. The final internal three, antaranga sadhana, remind me that even with that love, I can transcend the physical entirely, and reach samādhi.

Samādhi | sam·ahd·hi | (ecstasy)

It's done. Totally healed, super cured. *Everything is beautiful and nothing hurts.*[1] The tide still goes out. When I've binged on alcohol and I'm puking self-consciously in other people's locked bathrooms sometimes I still think, *This is good, all the fun with none of the calories.* I still sit hidden, shoulders hunched. But now this is the exception, an island rather than a lake, the realizing tide surrounding and not surrounded.

Samādhi is enlightenment. It's interconnectedness of life and oneness with the Universe. Moreover, for me, it's a peaceful quietude of the mind. It's a hushing of doubts, a shushing of demands and expectations.

The depths of my human existence expand ever inward, just as space expands ever outward. *I am large; I contain multitudes.*[2] Patañjali's eight limbs now carry their true yogic meaning for me. I live delicately but surely, watch over my mind, assume postures, breathe, focus my thoughts and let them go, and find my inner peace. The tide comes in. The white lotus blooms. I tilt my head back and laugh at the sky.

Briana Forney is a graduate of the Ohio State University, now pursuing a master's degree in Creative Writing at the University of San Francisco. Her writing has appeared in *Spires Intercollegiate Arts and Literary Magazine, The Found Poetry Review, In Shambles Anthology,* and more.

---

[1] Vonnegut
[2] Whitman

59

Hoffer Award Finalist

The Parameters of Commitment
by Sarah Evans

Day five hundred
Michael Overman has been released. The words cut through my harried morning. My mouth freezes, half-full of half-chewed Cheerios as I turn the radio up.

But I pause only a moment and then I'm back to my usual fly around, swallowing down the remains of breakfast, scooping up the odds and sods needed for my day, searching for wayward keys.

Only once I'm sitting in the lecture hall, heartbeat raised with the hurry, my face flushed from the transition from outside cold to stuffy warmth, do I find time to Google on my phone, gathering further details. The Foreign Office are claiming this as victory in their drip, drip of diplomacy. Several NGOs express delight, alongside concern regarding ongoing human rights abuses. Michael will stay overnight at the British Embassy in Mandia before being flown home. His parents are ecstatic.

"We must never desert the Mandalian people," is Michael's headline quote. "I remain completely committed." A photo shows him smiling broadly and below this is the strap-line: five hundred days.

Five hundred days. It is an impossible measure of time.

Day zero
The questions looped round and round.
Where you from?
Why you here?

Who tell you come here?

Where you from?

The room was stuffed with people, empty of air; it smelt of heat and spicy breath and stale bodies. *Michael Overman? You with him, no? You tell us about Michael, perhaps is not so bad for you.*

"I have nothing to say." My throat was parched from endlessly asserting this. "My name is Caroline Watkins. I'm a British citizen. I've done nothing wrong." It sounded less convincing with each repetition.

Where you from? Why you here? It no help if you no answer.

"I am a British citizen." The words failed to cast their spell of invulnerability. "I demand to see someone from the Embassy and a lawyer and could I have some water please." Words like *lawyer, citizen, Embassy* felt out of place, belonging to a different world. Beads of sweat crawled over my skin like insects while panic was rising up and knowledge crashing down: just how far outside known parameters I was.

Day minus one hundred and fifty

I heard it from a distance, a vibrating, humming background. *Om mani padme hum.* I walked as briskly as the crowds allowed, honing in on my destination, following the rhythmic chant. The vista unfolded, the plane trees and Victorian buildings, the square with its shifting, colourful mass. Above the crowd, monks in orange robes were sitting crosslegged on a makeshift platform, their shaved heads nut-brown and gleaming in the winter sun. Voices swelled out: deep, slow, insistent. *Om mani padme hum.* The beat of drums provided an unadorned accompaniment and the chant was taken up by the throng, undulating backward from the centre, somewhat off-key, out of synch, voices rising to fill the open space. Nelson and his four lions; the banded grey sky; the Greek revivalist columns of the National Gallery: They all seemed out of context amidst the blur of reds, oranges and yellow, the sway of flags and slogan-bearing banners, the helium-buoyed balloons.

I lingered on the edges, still outside the barriers separating the in-crowd from the tourists with their cameras and chatter, momentarily reluctant to commit and immerse myself in this sea of strangers. I thought of spending the day frivolously, browsing Oxford Street sales, or strolling London parks.

But my body was already responding to the rhythm, establishing an almost imperceptible sway, and the sounds were rising up my throat. *Om mani padme hum.*

My feet took me forward to join the queue that was being funnelled through the single entry point between barriers, manned by bored-looking cops.

The crowd ahead shifted, opening up, allowing me to slip in and be subsumed amongst the bobbled hats and rainbow scarves. *Om mani padme hum.* My voice was finding itself, self-awareness dissipating, and I was surrendering individuality and becoming part of the whole.

The chanting slowed and stopped to be replaced by slogans, my own voice one tiny element of the horde that spoke discordantly as one. *Mandalia, Mandalia, free, free, free.*

Speeches followed. From my vantage point at the back, mostly it was lost to the breeze and the hiss of the sound system, but I picked out the words that mattered, words like *rights* and *change.* An orange robed man held up his shackled hands to a rising roar. *Peace, democracy* and *freedom.*

We started to move, forming a great Chinese dragon, an untold number, thousands, tens of thousands, all of us with common purpose. The monks and others from their oppressed country were joined to those from here, those of us who cared.

A cordon of police provided escort. The roads had been closed to traffic and cleared, giving us full sway, allowing us to occupy the inner London space.

A brief hiatus to the forward momentum forced us to a stop, leaving me jamming against those in front. I shivered a little in the February breeze, glancing up at the frosted trees, wondering at the monks in their light robes and sandaled feet. My throat ached. I took out a plastic bottle from my bag and swigged, the water tepid and tasting of chlorine. The man by my side—youngish, wiry—cast his glance my way and I offered him the bottle.

"Thanks," he said, his smile open, his eyes—their dark intensity—the sort that draw you in.

Day one
Day one of fifteen years. *Fuck!*

My cell measured seven paces by four. It contained: a wooden pallet; a rolled up mattress, its blue-white ticking stained and split, diarrhoea-yellow stuffing bulging out; a greasy blanket; a red bucket and a pail of water. The concrete floor was covered in fine grit and occasional scuttling roach. The wooden door was reinforced with steel and locked only from the outside. A wide, glassless window allowed in thin light from the corridor and through the metal bars a female guard stared impassively. At me, or through me? I couldn't tell. The air was heavy; it stank of human effluent and fear.

Fuck, Caro! What the fuck have you done?

I sat cross-legged on the wooden slats, closed my eyes and tried to clear my mind. *Om mani padme hum.* The words echoed . strangely but I kept on going, all the while my heart bumped along way too fast. *Om mani padme hum.* I tried to absorb myself in the present, no past or future, existing in this moment.

Om mani padme hum.

It wasn't working. My eyes opened. The whitewashed walls were smeared in yellow, brown and green and I didn't want to even contemplate where those pigments came from. My bum ached. My prison shift was itchy and drenched in sweat.

I won't be here for long.

A sentence of fifteen years—no trial, no lawyer, no court—was good. I imagined how Michael would argue it. Ludicrous enough to hit the headlines and guarantee international outrage.

I won't be here for long; I whispered the words like a mantra. But my heart beat ever faster and my thoughts were whining like a mosquito with just one thing. *Fifteen fucking years!*

Day minus one hundred and fifty

My legs ached, my throat was sore, but the monks had taken up their chant again and the crowd chanted, too. There was still the buzz, but it had peaked and was winding down towards the bubbles-pricked aftermath. Already the edges of the crowd were dispersing, our purpose fulfilled and confidence ebbing just a little as to what we had achieved.

I was close to the front now and the man—Michael, he'd said—was still at my side, still absorbed. *Om mani padme hum.* His voice was decidedly off-key, but that was part of its appeal.

The drummers laid down their instruments. The chants wound down. It was over.

"D'you want this?" I offered Michael the last mouthful of water.

He blinked and I had a sense of catching him in the moment of returning to himself, distilling back out of the crowd. "Thanks." He was older than me, a bit, his skin tanned and weathered. He seemed impervious to the cold, wearing just a thin, denim jacket, while I was bundled up in padded coat and winding scarf.

"D'you want to go somewhere?" I asked. "A drink perhaps." I didn't normally do this, starting up conversations with unknown men, but the two of us were bound by our shared experience.

His eyes flicked uncertainly towards me, and his thud of bumping down to earth was almost audible. "Sure."

"Coffee or alcohol?"

He shrugged. "Either? Both?"

Together, we laughed, misted breath mingling in the air.

The streets were choked with people, the crowd we had been part of now separating out into component strands; it felt colder. "D'you come to many of these?" I asked, instantly hating the way it sounded.

"Some," he said. "Mandalia is a particular interest. You?"

"A few. How did you get interested in Mandalia?"

It took no more than that to get him talking. Telling me about backpacking across Thailand, hanging out in hostels, the chance encounter when he met a group of Mandalian refugees. Listening to their tales of genocide, rape and repression had spurred him to make his first trip into Mandalia. *To see for himself.*

We found a back-road pub, already throbbing with people and smelling of spilt beer and sweat. He battled his way to the bar and we drank deeply from pints of pale lager, the alcohol and froth lubricating the conversation.

I listened with growing awe. Shame at how little I'd ever done vied with a sense of pride that he judged me worthy of talking to, that I was finally touching the centre of where it's at, no longer a silly schoolgirl with her metal badges and opinions that no one took seriously.

"You wouldn't believe how beautiful it is there," he said, "How alive." Conjuring an exotic picture. The vivid foliage, so very many shades of green, so varied it hardly seemed that anyone could need another colour. The wildlife. The vastness of the Eastern sky. The intensity of heat, the monsoon rain, the humid air, the weather always so very full-on. The press and noise, the smells and colours of the market place. "And the people. You'd not believe how open and welcoming they are."

He'd stayed on to teach English to one of the displaced tribes, the village a day's walk along dirt tracks from any town, people quietly trying to live as best they could. "None of them political, not really. Just wanting to bring their kids up and for them to have a future." Before the military junta moved in, arriving with a clash of metal in the night, forcing them all to scatter and flee.

"I couldn't remain silent after that." So he staged a protest, just a small thing, chaining himself to some railings outside parliament and reciting a pro-democracy poem. "Just stating the obvious. Like that freedom was a good thing." It was enough to have him arrested and sentenced to seven years in prison. "But in the end they found it simpler to just chuck me out," he said, his grin belying the gravity of what he'd just said.

"Must have been quite an experience. I mean, awful. But you must really know what it's all about." My admiration fizzed up, leaving me sounding like some teenage groupie.

He smiled. "I've been going on and on."

"No. It's fascinating. Really."

We chatted more widely then, exchanging the essential parameters of our lives: hometowns, study choices, siblings, accounts of apolitical families and never fitting in at smugly middle-class schools.

My senses drank him in, the way he looked, sounded, smelt, wanting to run my fingers over his stubbled chin, to feel the firmness of his lips, to taste his mouth, his skin. We talked about how to change the world; it felt like we could've talked forever.

And I thought how this was what I'd been searching for all through those bored teenage years. This authenticity. This passion. This commitment.

Day ten

Above, the strip light buzzed and blazed. On and on. The next set of gongs would mark three am. Or four. I'd lost count. Below me, the thin mattress did nothing to soften the wooden pallet; it stank of decades-old urine and damp.

Sleep. If I could just sleep.

But my brain still ticked away.

They don't need to keep the frigging light on all frigging night.

Sleep used to come so easily, gobbling up great chunks of time when I had so many better uses for it. I'd lost the way of drifting off. Too much conspired to keep oblivion at bay. Limbs that ached from hard surfaces and with cold; my stomach clenched with hunger; the fact I would be woken anyway by the quarter hour gongs. The lights that blazed, but provided no illumination. Arms wrapped around my rib cage, I tried to think of Michael, the warmth and give of his body, but the images refused to come, even memories abandoning me.

The lights buzzed. My mind started to waft down, down. I snapped awake to the reverberation of a clanging gong.

Day minus sixty

Winter had drifted into spring and I could feel the fall; falling in love with a man, a cause, the two an intricate part of one another.

Weekdays, he spent at his family home, his parents' four-bedroom detached in leafy Coventry suburbs. His time was occupied by volunteering amongst the homeless, participating in online protest forums, along with listening to his mother nagging him to get a proper job.

He visited me every weekend. My room and bed were narrow, the shower dripped in the miniscule en-suite, the kitchen was permanent disaster zone, but he was more at ease here, he claimed; we had greater freedom to be ourselves. And besides, London was where everything was at.

We joined a campaign group and did what we could. Drafting articles for the website. Distributing leaflets. Fundraising and writing letters to MPs. We attended rallies, read, researched, ached with despair and hope. And if my studies slipped, well, really what use were my essays on Shakespeare to anyone anyway? How could tragedy in literature even hope to compete with the real life heartbreak of a people kept in chains?

We stayed up late into the night, talking. We slept locked in each other's arms. Woke to mutual hunger and the slaking of desire, followed by the pleasures of dozing until one of us rose and returned with an offering of tea. Time slipped, it glided along so smoothly.

And all of it culminated in him saying, "I have to go back."

We were sitting thigh-to-thigh amidst the wreckage of the bed, backs against the wall; midday, and we were only just finishing a first mug of tea, brewed strong and hot. Soon, very soon, we'd grab a shower and then we were heading out to another demo.

"Go back?" I sounded shocked, though I couldn't explain why. I'd known that this would come, that talk-talk-talking would never substitute for *doing* something.

He smiled, somewhat guiltily, his hair boyishly rumpled. "I'm planning a trip over to Mandalia again. I have to see what I can do."

The room was silent and still, blood pushing through my veins like slushy snow, skin tightening to goosebumps, the cave of his body no longer offering warmth.

I took my time, wanting to hit the right note, to properly express both support and concern, enthusiasm tempered by caution. I held back from blurting the thing I wanted to: *But what about me, what about us?*

The political over the personal: it wasn't that I didn't understand. "When?" I said. "How?"

He stirred, breaking the skin on skin contact to turn and look at me more fully, his gaze so tender as he pushed my hair back from my forehead, before his eyes shifted to stare ahead, detaching himself from the warm comfort of now.

"Soon." He started to talk and I realised that he'd been thinking about this for some time. Thinking and planning.

"You didn't tell me."

"I'm telling you now. I wanted to get my head 'round it first. No point talking about it until I had some idea what I wanted to do."

"Isn't it dangerous?"

"I'm not planning to do anything illegal," he said, his mouth turned downwards into a wry smile. "Least not at this stage." He'd travel to Thailand. "You can buy a one day visa to one of the border towns in Mandalia for a few dollars." He wasn't sure it'd work, but the checks were likely to be simpler that way than the whole rigmarole of applying to the Embassy here. "Guess I'm betting on them not being that wired up."

"And if they are?"

He shrugged. Don't know yet."

It felt disloyal, but the uncertainty filled me with a kind of hope and it was on the wave of it that I said, "I'm coming with you."

His look was complex. "I can't let you do that."

"Why?"

"You've got your studies."

"They can wait."

"Your parents won't like it."

"It's my life, not theirs."

He looked at me anew and my stomach flipped as I realised that I'd attained another level in his approval, winning his increased respect, and it was this more than anything that meant there was no going back.

"It isn't safe, Caz," he said, and I loved the way he shortened my name. "I can't predict what they'll do." He expected it would be a rerun of last time, if he got there at all. He'd stage his protest—a poem, a song, perhaps some leaflets handed out, some token gesture, but tokens were all we had. He'd be picked up. "Not much point if I'm not." I already knew what had followed, but he told me again. An uncomfortable ride, jostling in the back of a pitch-black police van. The terror of a night in a cell, the sound of rats and roaches, the light blazing above. Unspeakable toilets and being constantly watched. "Even when using the ensuite bucket." He wrinkled his nose.

No one speaking English, no one bothering to explain the legal process, or even if there was one.

The same police van taking him in cuffs to the airport. Endless waiting in windowless rooms. Being bundled onto a plane. His passport thrown in his face at the very last moment.

I tried to picture it, steeling my courage. If he could face it—not just once, but a second time—why not me?

"But it could be worse," he said, his face turning stern. "Much worse."

We exchanged a look and, of course I knew what he meant, but that didn't stop him carrying on.

"They're unpredictable. Vicious." The words *rape, genocide* and *torture* were there, crowding their way into my mind. "Being a Westerner, it's not foolproof protection."

We sat quietly and I thought of recent examples.

The American grandmother sentenced to death for trafficking drugs and no sign yet of the authorities ceding to Western pressure.

The British journalist awaiting trial because he'd ignored the injunction and taken photos of a policeman beating up a teenage boy.

And of course there were cases too numerous to name, their own people, their peaceful stands for freedom, infractions of unjust rules, incurring harsh and fast retribution.

"If you can face it, so can I." My words sounded brave and I hoped my thoughts would follow suit.

He lay back, his arm curving to cradle his head. He closed his eyes. Opened them to look at me. "I couldn't forgive myself if anything happened to you."

"I'm not more important than you are."

"You're younger."

"Female." I said it for him.

He nodded. "I don't mean you're not tough." He was careful, always, in terms of gender politics. "And in some ways women are treated better than men." He grimaced. "By which I mean, less appallingly badly. I just don't want to be the one who's led you into it."

"No one's leading me."

"Your parents..."

"...don't control or own me."

"You need to think it over carefully."

"I know." Except I knew I wouldn't. Better sometimes not to think, if thinking would preach caution and lack of action. I had this sense of standing on a cliff edge and looking down, about to take to the air and trust to the parachute above, testing out the limits of my resolve.

Day fifteen
Metal clanged distantly against metal. Iron-tipped boots struck the concrete floor. Something squeaked. My stomach rumbled in anticipation; it still hadn't learned to abandon hope.

Doors clanged opened, clattered shut.

I put my face up to the metal grille, eyes wanting to see the evidence of my ears. The sentries outside my cell, fellow prisoners elevated to this dreary watching-duty, shook themselves alert, their gaze skidding away from mine. I could hear the rapid chatter of the approaching guards, the fall then rise of alien tones.

Food. Something to assuage the hunger. To interrupt the boredom.

My stomach growled louder. The noises got closer. I stepped back and sat down, not wanting to be caught in such desperate waiting. The key was in my lock and always the opening of the door stirred up an eagerness. Two dishes were placed before me on the floor, the woman—yet another detainee—swooping down gracefully, not meeting my eyes, before being escorted away by those guards in military uniform who never smiled.

I picked up the larger earthenware bowl and inspected, knowing I shouldn't, my eyes inexorably drawn to what they'd rather not see. My finger prodded the red rice, low grade, the grains broken and accompanied by husks along with the usual additions of ants and weevils. Rice that would normally be used as animal feed. The insect life was thoroughly boiled and, in many parts of the world, insects were a luxury. *Extra protein, Caz,* Michael might have said. *Yeah, right!*

Amidst the sludge of rice nestled three—no four—brown lumps, meat from some animal and it was probably better not to know which one. The lumps were coated in a slick of red oil. I tried

71

not to inhale too deeply, but the smell reached me anyway, an unpleasant whiff of something. Like the scum of long-boiled beans. The pervasive smell of wet dog. Of tinned chicken, or dogfood.

For the first few days I couldn't eat, no matter how hard I tried, the need for calories overridden by the imperative to avoid spoiled food. I gagged and retched and failed to keep anything down.

Hunger won out eventually; I no longer hesitated. My fingers felt their way, not drawing back with revulsion as they scooped up glutinous, weevil-dotted rice, together with one of the chunks, rolling it all into a ball which I lifted to my mouth, my gut balanced between appetite and nausea.

I chewed, trying not to feel the texture, or taste the taste, grateful for the annihilating sting of chili-oil, me who always liked her curries mild. Hopefully the chili purged bacteria, as well.

To the side was a cup of vegetable matter. It looked like boiled grass; it may well have been boiled grass. I took a small amount between my fingers and brought it to my mouth. It was bitter and defied chomping. I needed cow-teeth, a cow-stomach.

You need to eat, Caz. I could hear Michael urging me gently on. *Keep your strength up.* I scooped, rolled, chewed and forced myself to swallow it all down.

Day minus thirty

Mum opened the front door and the smell of roasting lamb, of garlic and rosemary drifted out into the summer air, mingling with the heady scent of roses. I squeezed Michael's hand. "This is Michael," I said.

They smiled widely at one another, Mum's expression forced, Michael's genuine. "Lovely you meet you," Mum said, shaking Michael's hand before greeting me with a fragrant hug and hair-ruffle.

"I told you we're both vegetarian," I said, the savoury smell setting my stomach rumbling.

Mum looked so impeccably sleek, her hair neatly styled, clothes precisely ironed.

"Well, we're not," she said. "I bought a nut roast thing from M&S, too. Lamb always used to be your favourite." Knowing how to tempt me.

It felt stuffy and formal, sitting 'round the polished table, eating hot and heavy food while the sun burnt through the windows. I watched my parents try to be welcoming and accepting, seeing Michael through their eyes, his unkempt hair and washed out shirt, its slogan—*Freedom*—faded and frayed.

"So when are you coming home?" Mum asked, the question I'd been avoiding so far.

We'd worked out what to say, but that didn't make it easy.

"I'm hanging on in London for a little while," I said. "Staying with friends." Not mentioning dossing down on someone's floor, or that the friends were from the campaign, not Uni. "And then we're going travelling," I said. "Heading off in a few weeks' time. Spending some time in Thailand."

Mum looked up and continued chewing thoughtfully. Dad placed his cutlery down. I saw the look the two of them exchanged, the wariness, wanting to treat me as a grown up, wanting to tell me absolutely no way.

"Is Thailand safe?" Mum asked, the crease of anxiety between her eyes deepening.

"Oh yes," I said, my voice labouring its certainty. "Thailand's fine."

Which was true. I thought about the FCO website and its list of advice for Mandalia.

There was a high threat of terrorism.

We should avoid all demonstrations and gatherings and desist from taking photographs of the military, the police or protests.

We should stay in the central area and avoid remote regions. We were advised that there were restrictions on freedom of movement and speech and that several hundred political prisoners were in jail.

As if we didn't know that; as if we didn't know that several hundred was a gross underestimate.

Nonetheless, around five thousand tourist visas were issued each year, and most visits were trouble-free. "Trouble-free for non-trouble-makers," Michael said and smiled, excluding us from such coziness.

We read on through the list of risks and things to steer clear of. Avoid intrusive medical or dental work with the risk of poor hygiene and hepatitis. There can be heavy rains and floods. Occasional earthquakes. Homosexuality is illegal.

We laughed, finally. At least one thing that wouldn't apply.

None of this was I about to mention to my parents. Instead, I prattled on about temples and beaches.

"And you can afford it?" Dad chipped in. "I mean the time off studying? And the cost, of course."

I'd only just finished my exams, was dreading what the results would show. University work, exams, they felt like such trivial things.

"Yes," I insisted. "Not much I can do work-wise over the summer, really. And you can get really cheap flights."

"And I've been working," Michael said. Not mentioning that it was all cash in hand and he was on benefits, too.

"It costs next to nothing when you're there."

"Both of us could do with a summer break."

We were like some double act. Mum's eyes flicked from one of us to the other. I could feel my own wavering, knowing the things Mum would ask if she only knew. Knowing the answers would not be convincing.

Day twenty-one

I tried to maintain my straight-backed pose as my lips pushed out the words. *Om mani padme hum.* The sound was barely audible.

Around me were the sounds of prison life. Clatters, bangs and raised voices, squeaking doors and clanging keys. An endless progression of bongs to mark the passage of time.

Om mani padme hum.

My throat was tight, my lips dry, the background noise too strong, my heart not in it. *I can't do this.*

Surely the next bong is overdue, another quarter hour endured.

Time progressed so slowly it barely seemed to move at all, as if this place occupied a different dimension, obeying alternative laws of physics.

Come on, come on!

Bullying was not a good tactic for meditation.

Useless tears pricked my eyes.

Come on, Caro, come on! Something, anything.

I gave in and laid back on the mat, closing my eyes, knowing how I shouldn't do this, not in daylight, this slippage into apathy. Keeping alert by day was the only hope of sleep at night, the only defence against slip-sliding into despair. *If I slide too far I won't get back out.*

I was there as a consequence of my own freely chosen actions. Reminding myself didn't help. The others here had not had the same choices; they endured much worse than I did. Hard labour. Beatings. Overcrowding, food yet more dire than mine. Those thoughts didn't help, either.

I had no books, no radio, nothing to provide distraction from my thoughts.

Focus, Caro, focus!

I remembered a meditation retreat, being there with Michael. The soft-voiced teacher whose words were so compelling, who soothed our minds into a state of responsiveness, of openness and emptiness.

I thought of the walk we went on through the grounds. *Walking meditation.* The aim was to move as slowly as possible. I was lousy at it; Michael was brilliant. I remembered the way, afterwards, my muscles uncurled from their confinement and how I wanted to run and run.

Even through my inertia I could feel it, the longing to uncurl the knots of tension and stretch and run. To be free.

I'd known this might happen; I had not known how it would feel. *Bloody Michael and his saintliness.*

Blaming him was unfair, but what did fairness have to do with anything anyway? I stood up and my head spun. The humid air seemed determined to push me back down. I had to steady myself, one hand against the smeared wall whose every inch I had studied in detail by now, working out its cave-man art.

My head cleared. *Come on, Caro. Come on!* I started to curl down slowly towards the ground. Slowly, slowly, vertebra by vertebra, as my yoga teacher used to say. My fingers brushed the floor. My hair fell forward to sweep the concrete and I wondered when I would next get to wash it in something other than soap that smelt of lard. The close up of the floor allowed me a clear-eyed view of insect life, the bugs and beetles I always loathed; I lacked the energy even for hating them now. I started to curl back upright, thinking through the press-ups and the crunches and the running on the spot that would help to use up time and keep my muscles from degenerating. My head swam, I was covered in sweat, my vision blurred, my legs weakened as I locked my knees tight. *Just a few more.*

I wasn't even halfway though my second roll-down when hopelessness crashed over me, dragging me under, leaving me helpless in its grip. I thought of Michael. Of his certainty and resolve. Of what he might be going through. Remembering the time we spent together.

None of it felt remotely real.

I can't do this.

Day minus ten

The flight took twenty-four hours with two stops. Time passed slowly with the thrum of the engines. My head nestled into

Michael's neck, feeling the rub of his growing stubble. Our breath grew sour, backs and limbs ached with disuse, moods fractured.

We disembarked into the glare of an alien sun, bleary eyed and irritable, out of kilter with the time of day, the heat, with the complete otherness of the place.

We waited in the noon-day sun for a bus that rattled us along to the teeming centre of the city and the backpackers' hostel we'd booked. The heat, the whining of mosquitoes outside the net, the effect of jetlag, the snores through the thin walls, the cumulative smell of bodies that had occupied the narrow bed, all these conspired to keep me awake, despite my exhaustion.

Days of city sightseeing passed in a haze, my mind registering the exotic surroundings, failing to properly feel awe and wonder. The photos we texted to my parents showed me wide-eyed and smiling. Another bus transported us to the coast, the sea breeze offering respite. The clear blue beauty of the sea and sky, the whiteness of the sands, the tourist crowds who we didn't belong amongst: all providing a pause ahead of what was to come.

It weighed between us, spoken of less now we were so near, and after all what—really—was there to say that had not already been said and planned for? Michael no longer asked me if I was sure, his own certainty not allowing room for others' doubts. Besides, I was only playing an ancillary role, not testing the absurd boundaries of legality, myself.

Now was time for relaxation, for simple pleasures, swimming in calm seas, lying side-by-side, our bodies bronzing, eating fish freshly cooked and barbecued on the beach, biting into mangoes, juice dripping down our chins, reaching for each other in the semi-cool lull of night. Allowing ourselves this temporary indulgence.

Time moved us forward and into another slow, rattling, un-airconditioned bus whose seats had been oversold, leaving people sitting in the aisle. We dozed, the disturbed, half-sleep of the traveller, poised between sleep and wakefulness, between reality and dream and nightmare. The light grew in intensity and we watched the landscape pass by beyond the grimy window and I felt suspended, wishing we could stay like this, the two of us, his hand resting lightly on my thigh, the beauty of the early morning, the moon remaining clear against a slowly lightening sky, being transported, on and ever onwards, never arriving, never getting there, never having to confront what must be faced.

Day twenty-five
Not again. I gut clenched. I could both feel and hear the squidging, smell my own vileness. I rose from my pallet and hurtled towards the bucket, the stench growing as I squatted, foul excrement being added in painful, uncontrollable spurts to the rancid mess below. My anus burned; my stomach squidged and churned. My thighs ached; they threatened to weaken and give way. I felt sick.

It had been like this all day, ever since I woke from fractured sleep. Surely there couldn't be anything left inside.

It stopped. Started. Stopped, finally it stopped. *For now.*

I was nearly out of the rough, brown loo paper that had been granted as a huge concession. I could barely stand. My eyes rose to the window where a female guard stood and watched, her features bored and impassive, and I remembered how at first it was impossible to go with an observer looking on and I thought sourly how that was a problem I would like to have back. The stink was worse than anything I could've imagined.

I staggered back to my pallet to lie down, curl up and hope to die. This was the closest it was possible to get to hell.

Day zero
The bus approached the barbed wire fence of the border. Our destination lay just beyond. Everyone had to disembark; Michael and I clung onto our papers, standing quietly, avoiding drawing attention to ourselves, avoiding looking into eyes screened behind dark glasses. My heart battered stupidly, wondering if the men

were on the alert for Michael, whether the buying of a visa the day before—passing without a hitch—wasn't just a trick, luring him here, making him easier prey.

But eventually we were all waved through. We walked hand-in-hand across the border.

The plan was that I would be as unintrusive as possible. A tourist who just happened to be passing by. I'd snap a few quick photos on my phone then make my get-away, disappearing into the small backstreets, making my way back to the border well ahead of the visa curfew.

We had discussed this plan of action many times. I'd tried to argue that I could do much more. He thought he had dissuaded me, and perhaps he almost had, I don't know.

"Keep well back; don't appear as if we're associated," he reminded me of these last instructions as we made our way through the narrow streets which opened into the midst of a busy market.

We lingered on the edges, the bright bustle lying before us. "OK, this is it," he said quietly, and I reached out for one last moment of contact, a hand-squeeze, a fleeting kiss, a meeting of eyes, a smile, but already he had moved beyond me, intent on what he proposed to do. He walked forward without a backward look.

I stood and watched his wiry figure weaving away from me. I felt the absence of his presence at my side, felt how I had lost him, felt the utter loneliness of being here in this foreign, alien place. I thought of returning later to the resort and of travelling home alone. I longed to be continuing at his side, fingers intertwined, his conviction fueling mine; right then, the point when it was far too late to backtrack, I'd have given more than anything to undo the trip this morning, the journey to Thailand, for neither of us to be here.

But already, he was committed, and I was, too.

I snapped out of my paralysis; I'd lose him if I didn't move. I started shadowing him, keeping a good ten paces behind, pretending to browse the small stalls selling food staples, many of them alien to my Western mind, and small crafted items for tourists like myself, the wooden figures and the woven fans, the brightly coloured fabrics. I breathed in the scent of spices, of exotic vegetables, the boiled-cabbage smell of poverty.

I kept my proper focus, my attention to the market just a sham, keeping half an eye ahead as Michael went about the innocent actions that would lead to his arrest. *Not much point if I'm not.* The thought of him joking failed to provoke a smile.

He had a wodge of leaflets and stickers printed with brightly coloured slogans, the words in English on one side and in Mandalian on the other. Calling for everyday things, the rights that back home we took for granted. The release of political prisoners who had done no more than speak out for justice, for the right to freely express political opinion and stage peaceful demonstrations. A call for free elections, which, after all, were enshrined as a principle in the constitution.

I saw how he followed his own list of precautions. No looking at anyone directly. No eye contact. Acting as randomly as possible, not—*not!*—as if he thought anyone was inviting him to engage. *Don't do anything which might be interpreted as collusive*, which might land someone else in trouble for having the misfortune to be a bystander to this suicide-missioned Westerner who was hoping his white skin and British passport would render him bubble-wrapped against the worst types of harm.

His passport was a get-out-of-jail card. Not necessarily for free, not immediately, but nonetheless *out*. We both believed that.

He looked so slight and vulnerable, a little idiotic, a simple-minded fool of a Westerner thinking he could change the world with words, meeting violence with such a gentle protest. I began to follow him quite shamelessly, amnesia setting in, forgetting all we had said, wanting to cast my protection over him, a shadowed guardian angel, as if my tender gaze might keep him from harm.

I had never loved him so all encompassingly. A love that would last forever. That would transcend the separation and cruelties to come. A love that required me to be as brave as he was, to face the things that he would face, the two of us emerging triumphant against the world.

He didn't once look back. He threw his leaflets into the slight breeze of a hot mid-day and they fluttered and fell. He stuck stickers to the posts, choosing those not belonging to any individual stall. He shouted out the words he'd practised, alternating English and Mandalian.

Democracy. Freedom. Freedom of speech.

Mostly the stallholders kept their heads down, disassociating themselves, and I couldn't blame them. They carried on intently about their business, whether for real or for appearances' sake, it was impossible to say. A small child went running up to him, hand held out, wanting to be given a brightly coloured sticker and Michael laughed, his whole body suddenly relaxing as he crouched down and stuck a sticker on the girl's grubby T-shirt. My breath caught a moment. But surely not even a regime as corrupt as this could place blame on a three-year-old child. A woman came hurrying up to pull the girl away, to remove the sticker, a quick smile, perhaps apologetic, in Michael's direction, as she folded it up and threw it away, setting the child off wailing. Just for a moment he seemed to falter as he watched the small girl being dragged away.

Then he resumed his futile dance, which seemed to go on forever. I began to wonder if perhaps there would be no arrest. Perhaps his actions would be deemed too frivolous to take seriously, perhaps the police, the military would not even notice this crazy foreigner shouting out words that nobody could understand.

And then it all happened so quickly.

Day twenty-nine

I heard footsteps along the corridor, but no accompanying clang of metal. It wasn't the right time for food, anyway.

The door opened and a female guard beckoned for me to come. She was one of the ones who never smiled. I scrambled to my feet. Her touch on my arm was firm, but not rough. My feet slipped a little in the soft footwear that was all I was allowed. I would have liked to ask her *where* and *why*, but I knew she spoke no English. I thought of my meeting a week ago with the British Ambassador, his tired air of thinking me a nuisance, his assurances he would be doing what he could and the fact he could make no promises. Sympathy seemed in short supply; after all, I'd made my choices freely.

I was taken along corridors and through heavily locked doors. The small, windowless room for visitors was ahead and, as we got close, I heard voices and my heart clenched to a tight ball, my body understanding before my brain had properly processed this implausible thing. My legs weakened with hope.

The door opened. I stepped inside and was enveloped by my parents' arms and all three of us stood fused together and I didn't know if the wetness on my cheeks was their tears or mine. My mother's hands pressed against my ribcage. "You're so thin," she said. She smelt of the perfume she'd worn since forever; she smelt of home.

Later we sat, me on the plastic chair, Dad on the table and Mum on the floor. A guard stood in the corner and another would be outside. I was conscious of my grubby smock, my birds-nest hair, my bad breath and unclean smell.

"We're taking you back with us," Dad kept saying. "You're coming home." And Mum kept nodding her agreement to this impossibility. "There's just one small thing you need to do."

Day five hundred and thirty

I am anxiously early. My eyes scan 'round the buzzing space of the cafe chosen as rendezvous, but there is no sign of him, not yet.

I wonder if he will cause a frisson of celebrity when he arrives, though four weeks have passed and the item no longer occupies the news.

My phone rings and my heart jumps to my throat.

It isn't him.

I scald my lips on the coffee I don't even want. I remember back a week ago, my phone ringing and the sight of his name on my screen. My finger hovered over the button that would connect us, but failed to act. I waited, then retrieved his message.

"Caz?" Michael's voice was in my ear, jolting through my heart. He said how he was back and feeling great and he just wanted me to know. "We could meet up sometime?"

And here I am. Waiting.

Time has stopped. The digits on my watch refuse to move on. I do and don't want him to be here.

Then abruptly he is. "Caz!" I hear his version of my name and I see his uneven gait lope towards me. He looks different and unchanged. The same intensity to his gaze. His face and frame much gaunter. The same, all-encompassing grin.

We embrace clumsily. He smells different somehow, clinically clean, and I remember the hours I spent bathing when I returned. I can feel his individual ribs through his T-shirt.

"You're so thin."

"Suits me, no?"

My mouth struggles to echo back his smile. I feel my mask crumple and I find that I am crying.

"It's OK," he says. "It's OK." His hand takes mine.

"I'm so sorry." There seem to be so many things to be sorry for.

His gaze is serious now. "It's OK. I understand. I hope you know that," he says. "You did the right thing." And the softness of his voice is killing me, the fact he is being kind, the sort of kindness he'd extend to any stranger.

I pull myself together and we start to chat, this and that, inconsequential things. He tells me about his flight home in an RAF plane, the welcoming committee of press and friends and family, the things I saw only through the medium of the news. About trying to adjust back to ordinary life. Of the campaign he intends to keep going with.

He does not ask me whether I am still involved; he doesn't need to. How could I be? Neither of us seek to formally end our affair, neither does there seem any hope of resuming it. We are both changed, no longer the people we were. And for all we part with hearty assertions that we'll keep in touch, meet up again, I know we won't. I will never say to him the things I long to say.

Day zero

I saw them before Michael did. A half-dozen burly men, dressed in military uniform, the dark colours and heavy weave looking out of place amidst the fluttering multi-coloured cotton of people at the market. Michael had paused to reach into his shoulder bag for the second half of his stack of leaflets. He was smiling to himself; I don't know why. Feeling somewhat foolish and laughing at his own joke, perhaps. Pleased with himself for a job half-way done. Enjoying these moments of protest, these last instants of freedom, ahead of what was to come.

I wanted to shout out and warn him, my mouth already opening, already forming the word. *Michael*. Remembered too late I shouldn't, so it still emerged, but muffled. I remembered something else. I hadn't taken any photos on my phone, too wrapped up in watching and my inner thoughts.

Shit!

I scrambled to find the thing in my multi-pocketed rucksack. Couldn't find it. My sliver of electronics—a birthday present from Mum and Dad—was too slim and streamlined to easily come to hand. It didn't help that I was trying to find it by touch, alone, wanting—needing—to keep my eyes on Michael, on the way those men were closing in. I wanted so much for him to look my way, to be able to deliver a smile of solidarity, of encouragement, a thumb's up, a sympathetic grimace. Something. Anything. I couldn't find the damned phone. I was losing valuable seconds, footage in which Michael was standing tall, firm with resistance, holding out the leaflets and explaining what they said. First, in clearly enunciated English. Then, his attempt at Mandalian. I couldn't understand what the men were saying back, but their body-language spoke loud and clear. A hand reached out to grab the leaflets and hurled them to the floor. Another took Michael's shoulder bag, the brightly woven one I'd bought for him from the floating market in Bangkok. He wasn't letting them have it that easily; he was holding on, forcing them into a farcical game of tug of war, despite the fact they had truncheons and guns strapped around their waists and all he had was a braided belt.

A hand connected with his shoulder, pushing him roughly backward, and his foot slipped a bit as he took a backward step. My rummaging hand connected—finally—with my phone. Michael's hands were before his face now, half conciliatory, half protective. He was talking, gesticulating, but mostly it was lost amongst the heavy voices talking a foreign tongue, with just the occasional word that was recognizably English. *Stop. Come with.*

My hands trembled as I brought the phone up and the spectacle into view, seeing events now at one remove. I was supposed to take all sensible precautions. Stay well back. Immerse myself into the crowd that was swelling with curiosity and, I hoped, goodwill. But it was enough to try to persuade my fingers, swollen with fear, to do as I commanded. My hands moved as my finger clicked and I was mainly focused on the back of one of the policemen's heads. I carried on, as best I could, just as Michael continued on. Shouting slogans. Refusing to cooperate. Standing his ground.

But he was outnumbered and they were armed and the inevitable point came when his hands were being yanked behind him and handcuffed and the men were closing in around him and he was being marched away.

His head turned, side-to-side, taking in the crowds, seeking me out, perhaps. But he failed to look in the right direction, and all too soon he was bundled into the back of a dirt-caked van, the doors slammed shut.

Two of the men remained, seeking to shoo the crowds away as if we were a herd of feral cats. I knew I'd failed in getting any sort of reasonable shots, though I had at least been a witness. I had not, as far as I could tell, been spotted.

Then I noticed.

The leaflets which had been struck out of Michael's hand had landed in a solid clump. They had not been picked up and cleared away, taken as evidence or destroyed. A few fluttered feebly, trying to break free and take flight. But mostly they stayed in a pack, ruffling round the edges like cards being shuffled.

I didn't plan what happened next, not exactly. Simply acting on instinct, on the impulse and emotion of the moment, carried forward on a wave of love, compelled to complete what had been started.

I walked forward. I bent. Picked the leaflets up. I thought about walking out from the shadows onto the stage, and of having to act a part I felt unprepared for, of performing to an audience that was as best indifferent, quite possibly hostile, a crowd who, in all likelihood, did not want to be entertained.

Who, after all, was I, some privileged white girl, what could I possibly understand of what people suffered and the risks I might be exposing others to?

I needed to act. Now.

Now!

I clutched the wad of leaflets. They seemed so insubstantial, these red/orange/yellow pieces of A5 with their slogans written both in English and an unfamiliar script. They seemed far too weak a tool for the job in hand.

I followed Michael's list of instructions. No looking at anyone directly. No eye contact. I tried to focus my attention inwards, to discover a meditative rhythm, to find the certainty and strength.

Unsettled thoughts were buzzing up through the mantra, but they didn't stop me going ahead, dropping leaflets here and there, being sure not to thrust them directly into people's hands. I threw them upwards into the breeze, watching the flimsy paper petals flutter and fall.

My own heart fluttering. My sense of being in free-fall as I waited for the men in military uniforms to come towards me. Smiling for the cameras that failed to be there. The parameters of commitment—of love—still at that point unknown. Untested.

Day thirty

For the first time in thirty days I was allowed a proper shower. The cascade of half-hot water, the fragranced soap, the sachet of shampoo smuggled in from Mum's hotel room: They all felt alien in their luxury. The sallow-eyed girl staring back from the mirror did not look like me. She did not feel like me, either, as she dressed in Western clothes—proper underwear, a cotton dress chosen by her mother to look childishly demure, slip-on pumps. That girl followed her parents' careful instructions, going along with the deal that they had brokered and they were only acting in her best interest, after all, the way parents are supposed to do. *Just do as we say.*

She clasped her mother's hand tightly and she stood up in front of the flashing cameras of the international press and she declared that her protest had been a mistake.

She was very well treated in prison, she said.

She is extremely grateful to the powers that be for their clemency.

She understands how her previous actions were a result of misunderstanding. How her protest was wrong.

Nowhere does she mention Michael.

Nowhere does she plead for his release or state how his continued imprisonment is unjust.

Each statement hammers down her failure.

In the photo that is used in the papers afterwards, that girl is bookended by beaming generals in military garb. One of them has his arm around her shoulders like a favourite uncle. And she is smile, smile, smiling for the camera, too.

Sarah Evans lives in Welwyn Garden City, UK, with her husband and has had a career ranging from theoretical physics to economics. She has had over a 100 stories published in anthologies, magazines, etc., venues including: the Bridport Prize, *Bloomsbury*, and Unthank Books.

Hoffer Award Finalist

Lou the Mule
by Debbie Jones

I was born on the backside of a river town in New Jersey. You know how when you're riding on a train and you go through a town—any town—and you pass through the train yards in the big ones and dumps in the small ones, but either way, you come to a row of two-story houses that look like their backyards joined up before the tracks got laid? That's where I grew up. I had the second story bedroom on the back with the nylon curtains and a shade. Mostly it was two-thirds of the way down—the shade, the window was shut—all the windows on the backs of these houses were shut. Sometimes nailed shut. It's funny, I never thought about this until my brother went into the service and fell in love and we all took the train to Cincinnati for his wedding. That's when I knew where I grew up.

I was a nice kid. I wore knee socks and a blue uniform and I went to Catholic School. The uniform blouses had a certain smell. I used to put my nose in the puff and smell. I don't know what it was— maybe the factory they came from, maybe the cotton mill. Wherever it was, it was a place with a lot of women because, when I think of it, my uniform blouses smelled like a lot of women. That's another funny thing—Catholic School. It doesn't matter much where you're from, if you went to Catholic School back then, it comes down to the same thing. It was brick with chain link fencing around the asphalt that bordered it. The bathrooms were made of tile. They were clean and empty, like the nuns were saving them up for something. The classroom doors were wood and shut and marked with a black number. The corridors sounded hollow. Being in Catholic School was like being inside somebody's brain. You were never sure what was going on. You had to sit up straight and pay attention, and if you got called on you had to stand up straight beside your desk and have the answer. If you were a boy, the punishments for breaking rules was a rap with the ruler on the knuckles or, if it was real bad, the priest would come in and whip your rear end with the pointer stick right there in front of the whole class.

I was a girl. Boys who couldn't sit still got to clap the erasers on the asphalt in the schoolyard. The boys who behaved got to be altar boys. The girls got to sit still and wait. No girl was bad. They also got to sing in the choir. "Tantum Ergo" was my favorite song until I was 16. I also liked "O, Mary, We Crown Thee With Blossoms Today." We got holidays and holy days off from school, which was more than the public school got. The best one was All Saint's Day coming on November 1st. It meant we got to stay up late on Halloween.

My father was a weeknight drunk. It wasn't bad. On Saturday nights he worked an extra job as short order cook at Huey's Diner and Huey didn't like drinking on the job. By the time my father got off, the bars were all closed. On Sunday, drinking was out of the question. During the week he didn't bother anybody when he was in the house. He went out by the rabbit hutch my mother kept. It was out the back gate on the far side of the fence. All the neighbors kept stock. Most had chickens—one had ducks. The junkman lived ten houses down on the far side of the tracks. He kept a horse he used in his business in a one-stall barn. There was a horseshoe over the door but the horse had no name.

None of these animals had names for obvious reasons, but when Dad would go out there on a Tuesday or a Wednesday night, I'd stand by the inside of the fence and hear him talking to my mother's rabbits, calling them by name. I remember one he called Shortstop—it was black and white—and another he called Muzzle. There was one with smoky eyes. I think she was blind. Dad called her Rain. During the week, my father was out of the house; he was a conductor on the Erie-Lackawanna Railroad out of Hoboken. All this came to me later. When I was a kid, the house was just quiet.

"Shut your mouth, you kids—you want them knowin' our biz'ness?"

That's what my mother used to say to me or my sister or my brother. *Them* was the neighbors. *They* were the ones to look out for. She didn't want *them* knowing anything about us. She's probably rolling around in her grave right now for what I'm telling.

What's so bad—you got to hide it from the neighbors—*what's so bad?* Maybe if my mother bounced a check on purpose or shoplifted something she wouldn't want the neighbors knowing, but we weren't that kind of people. My mother dropped dead at 38 from worry in her head and literally pulling the lace shut against the neighbors. My father, who felt lost without her, drank for the next two years straight then dropped dead, himself. My brother saved the house from bankruptcy so my sister and I got all my mother's stuff. Sometimes when I'm cleaning one of her things—the blue creamer, her wedding cake ornament—I think *what was so bad?* My mother could be alive right now enjoying herself and her things instead of breaking her heart and his.

I was in the first grade. I had this novice nun for a teacher. She was good. All the kids wanted her for their teacher. Sister Anne wasn't spoiled like all the real nuns. When I look back, those nuns that taught us all sure were mad. It makes you wonder what went on in the convent at the end of the day. But Sister Anne was so good. That year, she was teaching us the catechism. None of the first graders had received Holy Communion yet.

"Who made you?"

"God made me, Sister,"

"Why did God make you?"

"God made me to know, love and serve Him, Sister."

Remember that—always Him with a capitol H and Jesus Christ, too. It was part of learning English. You always capitalized God and

Jesus Christ and all Their pronouns. Capitalizing Saint Mary's pronouns was optional. Saint Joseph got a small "he."

There was a lot of stuff about sin in the catechism. Remember those picture of three souls? One was pure white. One had spots on it. One was coal black. The one that was pure white was the good soul. The one with spots was having problems. The black one was damned. It used to scare me thinking there was a part of me I couldn't see that could get black spots on it that I couldn't get rid of. Only the priest could clean it off.

Every night before dinner, my mother asked me the new questions I was supposed to memorize the answers to out of the catechism in the dining room under the pull-down lamp. My father would come in, take off his conductor cap, hang it on the clothes tree, and go upstairs to change out of his uniform. He didn't make any noise up there, but while I recited, the pull-down lamp would silently sway.

"It was nighttime and the wind was blowing and all the people were moving along the dark, deserted roads to their hometowns for the census." Sister Anne was talking about the Nativity. The way she told it—it was quite an adventure.

"Whatsa' census, Sister, whatsa' census?"

"Put your hand down, Anthony Maragutondo, and listen."

Sister Anne would lift up her two hands with her thumbs and forefingers pinched together like she was conducting a band. At the same time her eyes would close to a scrinch and her voice would get mysterious.

"A census is when you count all-l-l the people in the land. So! Joseph took Mary out of Nazareth where they were living at the time and they went to Bethlehem where he was from originally. Where are you from originally, Patricia?"

"Weehawken, Sister."

"No, you're not. You're from God, originally, and someday you're going back to Him."

It was the details that got our attention. When one of the kids asked what the name of Mary's mule was, Sister Anne told us Lou. The mule's name was Lou.

When one of the kids asked if it was snowing, Sister Anne said, "Sure. It was winter. What do you expect?"

When one of the kids asked what color Mary's cloak was, Sister Anne said, "It was blue, blue as Noreen Kelly's eyes."

And so it went... *Mary was fourteen years old. The shepherds were ten. Their names were Michael and Anthony and, up until that night, they were pagans.*

The whole class went silent on that one. We all knew about the golden calf and what happened to pagans and idolaters.

There wasn't any tar on the streets—the inns were only two stories high so there wasn't much room in the first place. The barn was made out of stucco so it wasn't that bad.

That part bothered me when I was a kid; it still does. Joseph knocks on that last door and that innkeeper says he's got no room. Can you imagine? A woman out to here pregnant on a mule in the middle of the night in a strange town with no relatives and this guy's got no room? All I can say is back then things must have been rough all over, and they say times are tough now.

I got in a fight one morning on the playground with Roxanne Perotta about it. Roxie said the innkeeper was nice because he gave them the barn and I said the innkeeper stunk. Sister Anne broke it up.

"What are you so mad about, Mary O'Connor?"

"I'm mad at that stinkin' innkeeper, Sister."

"He didn't know It was the Mother of God," Sister Anne said explaining.

I don't think that's the point. I don't think I thought so then, either. Who cares if It was the Mother of God? That just makes what he did worse. And I know what you're thinking—pipe down—what's so bad about that? All I can say is that, compared to that innkeeper, my father never did a bad thing in his life.

My mother never said anything. My father would get drunk and disappoint her, but during it and after it was over she shut her mouth. I think she was pretending it didn't happen. Once he didn't come home for Thanksgiving dinner and, when he did, he didn't bring the turkey the Erie-Lackawanna Railroad always gave to their employees. He couldn't remember where he left it. We had sweet potatoes and cole slaw and the cranberry sauce and pumpkin pies with whipped cream and, to tell the truth, it wasn't bad except for my father sitting in his chair at the head of the table sobbing—he just kept sobbing—you'd hear him sobbing—all the way through the meal. I think—what if my mother yelled instead of shutting the lace—it would have been all right.

From the time I was three and a half straight through until I was ten or eleven years old, I couldn't sleep Christmas Eve. I believed in Santa Clause and the idea of somebody breaking in with a load of presents kept me awake. Break-ins happened in our neighborhood, but it wasn't a regular thing. The idea it was Santa Clause doing the break-in made my mind go crazy. The whole night I felt like a jack-in-the-box. By the time it got to be afternoon on Christmas day, I'd be conked out from exhaustion, my head on Dad's lap with the radio, then later the TV, playing low next to us.

The Christmas Eve I'm telling about is the one in first grade. We went to the 6:30 a.m. Mass that Christmas Eve because we had off from school and my mother was going. My mother believed in going to Mass every day in Advent. My mother honored Lent, also; so when I add it up, I figure as a kid I went to church more than anyplace except school and home. It was snowing and the tracks from the junkman's wagon were laying in the street. I pulled a snowball off a car hood and shot it at my brother. He ducked and the snowball hit my mother's black coat like a white splash. I remember standing there waiting for what my mother would do. There was steam coming out of my brother's mouth. Then my mother walked over to the same car and pulled off a snowball of her own and she chased me all the way down the block with my brother and little sister running behind us. I gave up at the church steps and let her get me. It was so good having her like that.

Sister Anne was there in the vestibule unwrapping The Holy Family out of brown wrapping paper from the year before. The stable was already set up on the altar of Saint Joseph but The Holy Family wasn't in it yet because They didn't get there until Christmas Eve. Sister Anne knew I thought Mass was boring. I told her. So she asked my mother if I could help. I remember my mother was out of breath and she was smiling.

"Mary would like to help? Wouldn't you, Mary?"

Was she kidding? This was better than clapping erasers in the schoolyard any old day. My brother was in kindergarten, but Sister didn't ask him. She asked me. This was the most important thing anybody ever asked me to do. And Sister Anne was so pretty. She was the prettiest nun I ever saw. I liked to watch her—everything she did—the way she moved her hands, the way she frowned her forehead. She was a pretty woman.

We got Mary out of the box. She was kneeling down and leaning over with Her hands opened up like She was delighted. My mother used that word. When she got a present she liked—*I'm just delighted.* Sister Anne gave me a damp cloth and told me to wash Her. I started with Her hands. Her fingers were long and pure and before you touched them they looked so warm, like they'd be good for touching. She had on a pink dress that had some orange in it with a gold rope around her waist. I cleaned all that. It wasn't really dirty, just some smudges here and there, and then I looked up into Her face. She was so pretty. Mary was so pretty. If Her fingers looked like good-mother hands, Her face looked like a saint's. It glowed soft—like a candle it glowed. And Her eyes were green like my mother's. What struck me even then was how young She was. Mary was just a kid like my cousin, Maureen. She didn't have lines on Her face like my mother. She had a kind of smile on Her lips that was less than a smile but more than a gentle mouth. All I could think was I wanted to kiss Her. She was cold like stone, but I wanted to kiss Her. So I leaned up and kissed Her on the mouth and, what was strange then and what is still strange now, Her mouth was warm and soft and I felt her kiss me back.

Sister Anne was looking at me. I felt funny like I'd done something wrong but I better not say anything in case I didn't.

"Let's get Lou out of his box," she said after what seemed to me a long time.

Lou was a mule. My mother said he should have been a donkey, but Lou was a mule according to Sister Anne. She said a donkey never would have been able to make that long a trip. Mary and Joseph needed a mule. A lot of years later, I saw Lou in a dumpster when they added the new wing and renovated the Church. I wanted him. It was crazy, but I wanted him. Mother of God, I wanted him. I thought I could put him in the side yard—hide his broken leg in a bush. Anyway, by the time I talked my husband into getting Lou out of the dumpster it was the next day and Lou was gone.

When we got him unwrapped—it was some struggle—he was bigger than Saint Joseph and his left rear leg was broken off just above the hoof. Sister Anne frowned. She told me she thought for sure she'd fixed it last year, but now she didn't know what she was going to do. She said she needed a miracle because his hoof was just about crushed. Part of it was powder. Lou the mule must have fallen on his weak ankle when the handymen were moving him out of storage.

We went down to the church basement. Sister Anne had a ring of keys on her belt and one was for the handyman's closet. I remember sounding out the word 'closet' in my head. We pulled out a bucket of water and a five-pound bag of plaster-of-paris and went back upstairs. Sister Anne said maybe she could stick Lou's leg—there were prongs hanging out of the part where the original hoof fell off—down in the plaster-of-paris, let it set, and pull it out. After that, she said, we could sculpt the plaster into a pretty good hoof. It sounded okay to me, so we dumped the powder into the water, sloshed it around, and put in Lou's leg. Then the Communion bells ting-a-linged. They filled up the whole church with their ring. I liked that sound. Sister Anne left me in the nearest pew and went up the aisle to receive Communion with the rest of the nuns. I wasn't old enough to get Communion yet. I was practicing for the big day, but I wasn't 7 yet.

It was a holy day. By this I don't mean a Holy Day of Obligation like Christmas or the Immaculate Conception. It was just a holy day. I could feel it inside. It wasn't only that I got kissed by Saint Mary; I got to help Sister Anne and it was Christmas Eve, too. I watched Sister Anne kneel down at the altar rail at the end of the line of nuns. Her black veil slid over to one side like long hair. The kids on the playground were always guessing at the color of nuns' hair. You couldn't always go by the eyebrows. Sister Anne was a novice, so her hair stuck out a little at the top of her forehead. It was reddish brown. I watched her hand reach back and up and her long fingertips catch the end of her veil and pull it straight. It was neat the way she did it. Everything she did was neat. There wasn't any organ for the early masses, so I watched Joey Cahill hold the gold plate under the nuns' chins in case the priest dropped the Host— fat chance. Joey was a 7th grader and a smart boy. The whole parish said Joey was going places if he kept at it, but I would have bet my green and white shooter he never got kissed by Saint Mary.

Sister Anne was coming back from the altar with her hands folded together straight up at Heaven. She looked so holy she shined. When she got to our pew, she slid in beside me and I tried hard to pray. I never could pray. I could kneel straight like an ironing board with my fingertips straight up to God. I could say the *Our Father* and *The Glory Be* and the *Credo*. But I couldn't pray—not the way the nuns said you could, not so God could hear. God never heard me praying for my father. Sometimes I think that's how come I lost the Faith.

Lou the mule was waiting with his foot in the bucket in the vestibule. The plaster-of-paris was set. It was almost as hard as the rest of him. Sister Anne tipped him against a pillar and pulled at the bucket with her hands. It wouldn't budge. She knocked on it with her knuckles all around and still it wouldn't budge. Sister Anne's pretty forehead frowned.

"It worked before," she said.

Then she got up and ran down the steps to the basement and all I could think was poor Lou. He'd look so silly in the stable with one foot in a bucket.

The people in the church started filing out through the vestibule and pretty soon my mother came along with my brother and my little sister.

"You done, Mary?" she asked looking for Sister Anne.

"Can't I stay? Can't I stay, please? We're fixin' Lou the mule, Mom." It was important to me.

I could see all the nuns coming down the center aisle. Just when they got to the vestibule, Sister Anne came running up the steps with hedge clippers in her hand.

"Good morning, Mother," Sister Anne said to Mother Superior.

"Looks like Lou the mule's on his last legs, Sister," said Mother Superior to Sister Anne.

All the nuns chuckled; it sounded like soft humming.

Sister Anne blushed. If I had to say why now, it was probably Mother Superior using the name Sister Anne had for Lou. At the time I thought Sister Anne was in trouble.

"Don't put him in the stable in that condition, Sister," said Mother Superior.

"No, Mother," agreed Sister Anne.

My mother left me after she straightened my skirt around and whispered, "Behave." We only lived three doors down from the Church, so I could walk home by myself.

Sister Anne tried everything. She tried cutting the bucket off Lou's foot with the hedge clippers. The 7:15 Earlybird came and went. She tried jimmying a carving knife down between the bucket and the plaster-of-paris. The 7:43 Commuter Special clacked on the rails out behind the church. She tried hitting the whole works with the blunt end of an axe. The 7:58 Express was Dad's first run of the day. I waited for it. I was looking up the side aisle by the confessionals. The air glowed there. It had a certain yellow cast from the amber in the stained glass and it reflected into the deep dark of the mahogany pews. Dad's train blew by on a long toot. I'd pretend I could hear it in the neighborhood all day even though it was gone.

"What time's it, Sister?"

"It's 7:58, Mary." She had her watch out—a little silver thing she kept underneath her white bib—all the nuns did. "You're a funny kid."

I told her how my father's trains were always on time. They were never late. I told her how sometimes in the Spring, I'd walk him to the yards and watch him cross the rails to his train and the early morning sun would hit the rails and shine and leave deep, long-running shadows. I told her how my father would make his way out across the tracks. I wasn't allowed out there. I'd watch his back until he climbed up the steps into his train.

Kids know when they're in the way. Sister Anne was getting upset with Lou the mule, so I watched the communicants at the next Mass. It was interesting how far people stuck out their tongues for Communion. And I listened for the trains; I learned to tell time by the trains. And I thought of poor Lou locked in a closet all year long just waiting to get out and here he was with a bucket on his foot.

Sister Anne was sweating. "Come on, Mary," she said.

We hid the Baby Jesus under an altar cloth in the vestry for midnight Mass. Then we went out on the altar of Saint Joseph and waited for the handyman and his assistant to carry Joseph and Mary up the side aisle and put Them in the stable. Sister Anne pushed Sweet Sue and Linda—they were the sheep—over to one side to make more room for Saint Joseph. He was standing up. Flossy the cow was already in her stall. Her eyes looked wet like she'd been crying. And there was a goat named Dutch. Sister Anne said the Baby Jesus was allergic to cow's milk. My brother was allergic to cow's milk. He almost died of it. Sister put Dutch on the side of Saint Mary.

"Get to work, Mary O'Connor."

"Doin' what, Sister?"

"Makin' a bed for Jesus."

I looked around. "Outa' straw, Sister?"

"Yes, Mary. We want it just like it was. Oh, and Mary?"

"Yes, Sister?"

"Make it comfortable for the Blessed Infant."

The Church went quiet. The handyman and his helper were gone. Trains didn't run as regular after 8:00 AM. The manger was in the center. I filled it with straw. Mary was beside me with her hands up looking like she was glad to see what I was doing. I tried hard. I tried to make the bed like a bird's nest so no straws stuck out. I patted it down and sat on it and got rid of the big pointy pieces and the whole time I was doing it, all I could think about was that stinkin' innkeeper. The straw crunched and sent up a yellow powder in the Church air. I got cut on a piece. It was bleeding in the middle of my hand. I licked it off and thought about how I could get even with the innkeeper if he was still alive. Maybe I could burn up his house or beat up his kid. But then I remembered—the manger had to be like it was. And maybe the stable was attached to the house. And if I burned it down, then it would all be different.

"What's gonna' happen to Lou, Sister?"

Sister Anne was pushing straw in around Saint Joseph. Her back was to me. All I could see was her black veil and Saint Joseph's face. He looked like he was watching me.

"It's bad enough They gotta' sleep in a barn."

"Oh, Mary." Sister Anne turned around. Her face was clouded up.

"What're They gonna' do without Their mule, Sister? How are They gonna' get back?"

"Mary and Joseph'll be all right. Lou the mule'll be all right, too. Try not to worry, Mary."

But I did worry. That's the kind of kid I was. When I got near my house I could see the junkman out front. He had his grinder going. My mother was standing there. She didn't have a coat on, so when she saw me she called out telling me to wait for her scissors. Then she ran back in the house.

I watched the junkman sharpen the blades. They shined like a mirror and the grinder threw up sparks in the cold air. I never knew the junkman's name. He looked old and he never said much. There was a doll high chair on the back of the wagon. Some of the spokes were missing, but a girl could use it. The junkman turned over the blade, and his foot started pumping the grinder again. I caught him looking at me and he sort of smiled. It passed between us that I wanted that high chair. We didn't say anything—just the sizzle of the grinder. I thought about saying a prayer for it, but then my mother's scissors were sharp and the junkman's horse was pulling the wagon off down our street. I watched it go.

My mother was baking gingerbread men with my little sister when I got back in the house and that's what we did most of that Christmas Eve. She was filling orders for the neighbors and some of the people at the church. We put on icing for smiles and eyes. The tree was already up. In between batches, I watched Felix the Cat on Channel 13 and then, in the afternoon, The March Of The Wooden Soldiers with my brother. My brother really likes that movie. The two of us watch it every Christmas Eve. It's always on Channel 11. He called me up last Christmas Eve when it came on. Funny the things you do with your brother.

At dinnertime Dad didn't come home. My mother turned on the front light. There was a wreath on our door. Then she sat in the chair in the dining room by the side window and watched down the street for him. There was a streetlight at the corner he always passed under on his way down the block. She pretended she was reading the novena, but my brother and I knew what she was doing. Our mother never rested. She said she didn't have the time. She was always on the move. My mother loved Christmas, but that night I watched it go out of her. It's funny how a parent's mood can change the whole house. The fake snow on the mantelpiece began to droop and a red Christmas ball fell off a branch and broke like a splash. I turned up the fire on the burner under the beans. They started burning and the smell of it got her up out of that chair. She put dinner on the table, then she went out in the hallway and made a few calls. She whispered when she made these calls. She whispered. It used to make me mad I couldn't hear what she was saying. What's she saying? My brother was chewing with his mouth open like a pig. I told him *stopit*. When he wouldn't, I hit his milk and knocked it over. My little sister got down off her chair and went and stood in the corner. That made me mad, too. So I took all our dinners and threw them in the garbage and my mother came in and took me by the hand up to bed.

I sat on my bed with my legs crisscrossed in the dark and watched my mother's shadow crossing back and forth in the slip of light coming under my door. I didn't care. I got her to move. I could hear her giving my brother and my sister a bath. Then she came in my room and pulled my dress up over my head and got me in my blue pajamas. I liked them. They were soft and old. Then she went out and closed the door. I didn't cry. I never cry.

If it hadn't been Christmas Eve already, I'd have stayed up all night, anyway. That's what I did on the nights he didn't come home. I pulled up the shade and settled in.

It was snowing. A salt and pepper snow, my Nana would say. Nana was a mother to my mother. It was hard picturing my mom as a kid. It was hard forgiving her when she acted like this. For a while I just watched the sky and the trees. The railroad tracks were powdered up and down. The moon was up with a star off its right. They were both blue. The star sparkled. My father said it was Venus. It was so bright out. The snow was blue, too. For a while I just watched the sky and the trees. It was interesting—all the thoughts that came in my head. The trees had dark armloads of spokes and spikes that brushed across the blue like rakes. The trees were waving at the sky, trying to get God's attention. The trees were people trudging back and forth in the snow trying to get home. I switched my watching to the backs of the houses on the far side of the tracks. Because of the fences that ran along our back yards, we didn't know the people who lived across the tracks and we couldn't see their first story from our first story. It was funny being strangers with somebody that close. Looking down from my window, I could see there was a Christmas tree in one of the dining rooms. I knew it was the dining room because all the houses were the same. It was lit with multi-colored lights. The rest of the downstairs was dark. My mother would say that was dangerous—leaving the Christmas tree lit. There was a kitchen window with blue lights strung around the outside that must have looked nice to passengers going by on the trains. I thought how good it would be if everybody's kitchen window was lit up like that. The front yards up and down our streets looked nice at Christmas, but doing up a backyard was rare and sweet. Somebody's father must have had an extra string of lights, or it could have been some kid put it up for her mom. I had good ideas—lots of them. My whole childhood I stored them up.

There were garbage cans by everybody's back stoop. A blue cat climbed across one. There was a blue snowman all alone by a clothesline. He had sticks for arms and a real scarf. I could see it blowing. I wished I could open my window. I even tried. I wanted to smell the outside. I wanted to take it in me—the blue—inside my chest. I began to think how the blue rays would shine in-between my teeth and come out my hair and my fingertips. I'd be blue and cold and fresh inside and nobody could get me. Nothing could get me. Nothing could get in but the blue. I'd be a tree icy and blue in the shine of Venus. I'd just stand there in the sky and nobody could get me.

All the shades on the upstairs' windows were drawn shut. I kept hoping somebody—some kid, maybe—would pull one up and I'd be able to see in, but nobody did. One by one I watched the lights behind them go out. I didn't see the Christmas tree in the dining room go out. It was just out when I looked again. The kitchen window stayed on. The moon was almost all the way up over our house now so even when I craned my neck around, I couldn't see it or Venus. Things just got bluer, like somebody dropping a blue sheet all over the backyards, or Mary's veil. The radiator in my room was off. I felt it. It would get cold in my room, now. It was so still out my window. It was like a picture I saw of winter in a frame in the 5 & dime—frozen forever because somebody thought it was nice enough to frame. I was thinking I was glad Mom named me after Saint Mary when I saw Lou.

Lou the mule was standing there in plain sight on the tracks behind my house. He was on the other side of the fence and down a little, but I could see him clear as day. I knew for sure it was Lou because he had a bucket on his foot. He lifted up his nuzzle and hee-hawed at the moon. I could just hear it through my window. Then he saw me in my window. Our eyes met. He looked me straight in the eye. It was like he was asking me for help. It was like he was sayin' *How come you left me in the vestibule?* I got up and pushed at my window hard, but it was stuck shut with paint and years. Lou the mule looked up at the moon and hee-hawed again. *I know this happened. You can say—come on, you were a kid—but I know this happened.*

I ran downstairs. I ran until I got to the bottom of the steps. It was dark. The blue was coming through my mother's lace in a patch on the carpet, but it was dark. I could see the shape of our Christmas tree, but I couldn't see if Santa Clause came yet. I moved slow. I didn't want to bang into anything. I didn't want my mother stopping me. She was always stopping me. I was afraid of the dark, but it excited me. It still does. I'm afraid of what's in it.

In the dining room, I could just make out the pull-down lamp. It was still. I could hear myself breathing—nothing else. I got in the kitchen. It was small in there—even then—even to me. Pots and pans were ready for tomorrow on the stove, catching at the night with aluminum shine.

"Mary?" It was Dad. He was sitting in a kitchen chair in a shadow by himself. I could smell the booze.

"Lou's out there all by himself on the tracks, Dad." I said it too fast.

"You should be asleep." My father never slurred his words. My mother said that was one good thing.

"I can't, Dad. Lou the mule's out there all by himself, Dad."

"Go to bed, Mary."

I couldn't see him, but I could hear anger. *Jesus—that scared me—that tone of his. If I heard it today coming at me, I'd still be scared.*

I felt bad—bad for Lou the mule, bad for myself, too. "Dad..."

"Go to bed."

There wasn't a choice.

I ran back upstairs. I didn't care about the dark or banging into something. My father was as bad as that stinkin' innkeeper. And there was nothing I could do. Girls obey their fathers. Boys don't. After a certain age, my brother did just what he wanted. But girls obey their fathers. I went to the window and looked up and down the tracks as far as I could see, but Lou wasn't there. He wasn't anywheres. I felt like I'd deserted him. I felt like I was just a girl and there was nothing I could do. I felt like nothing.

Then the back porch light came on like a miracle and turned the snow at the foot of the steps yellow. I heard the back door slam and watched Dad climb down the back steps and struggle through the snow to the fence. He had his boots on, but no jacket and only his conductor's cap. He pulled at our gate and let a wedge of blue cut into the shadow that ran along our fence. Then he lifted his head like he heard something. Then I heard it, too.

It was a train whistle.

The whistle post was just outside our gate, so it wasn't time yet for the train to whistle its way into town. There wasn't a crossing for a quarter mile in either direction. It could only mean one thing. The train was whistling at something on the tracks. When I looked back, Dad was gone from our gate. His boot tracks filled the snow, but Dad wasn't there.

I watched the whistle post. I watched the tracks. Everything was still as church. Then the rumble started coming. I wanted to go downstairs and out the back door and across the snow through the gate, but I knew I wouldn't because I was a girl. I felt bad for being mad at him. Dad wasn't like that stinkin' innkeeper—not one bit. He was brave enough to get out in the middle of the night on the railroad tracks and save Lou the mule.

There was a lady on the other side of the tracks. She was dark like a shadow. I was surprised to see her standing there. I thought maybe she was one of the mothers from one of the houses across the tracks—maybe the one with the blue lights—but she lifted up her hand and waved at me like she knew me and I didn't know any of the mothers over that side. I waved back. Then the trees started moving and the snow swirled up off the tracks and the wind caught at her cape and lifted it, and I saw Her face, and the engine went by on a blow.

It was a freight. It clattered along on a low-down rumble in the middle of that night and, when it got done going by, The Lady was gone.

Dad came in our gate, closed it, crossed the snow, and disappeared under my roof. I ran to the top of the stairs in time to hear him grunt with the effort of taking off his boots. Then he was on the stairs looking up at me.

"Mary?" He wasn't sure it was me.

"Yeah, Dad."

"Darndest thing," he said—he was breathing hard.

I waited for him to climb halfway up. When he lifted his face, there was sparkle like Venus in his eyes.

"Horse on the tracks," Dad said.

"It was a mule, Dad. Did you get him off?" I already knew the answer.

"Yeah, Mary, I did. Poor animal." He was climbing the rest of the way up. "Had a bucket on his foot."

I didn't say anything. I wanted to laugh. I wanted to listen.

"Crazy with it. Kept pullin' back—clanging it on the rails."

Dad kept shaking his head like he couldn't quite believe it happened. Then he stopped with two steps to go and he looked me in the eyes.

"You get it off him, Dad?" I felt almost happy—I remember in that exact minute, I felt almost happy.

"Yeah, I did." Dad looked surprised. "I kicked the darn thing, and it fell off—just like that—bucket fell off."

"Oh, Dad, that's so good."

"Ran off. Darn mule ran off." Dad looked worried. "I couldn't stop it."

"That's okay, Dad. There was A Lady waiting for him."

"Oh yeah? You saw a lady?" My Dad had a way of looking when he didn't quite believe what he was hearing.

"Honest, Dad." I was moving my head up and down.

"Well, good, then." He climbed the last two steps.

"She was by the tracks."

"Well, good." He crossed the landing.

"Oh, it is, Dad. It's Her mule."

"Well, good then... no night to be out on the road."

"No, Dad."

He turned back at their bedroom door. "It's late, Mary."

"Yes, Dad." My heart was so full it was pumping.

"Big day tomorrow."

"Yes, Dad."

The clock on the mantle piece chimed from out of the dark. I counted the gongs in my mind. It was Christmas and I couldn't wait to go to Mass and see Lou the mule in the stable. Then Dad came over and picked me up in his arms like he used to when I was little and carried me to my room and my bed and he smelled like booze and his cheek was cold and his arms were strong and I hugged him with all the love that was in me.

"Merry Christmas, Mary," he said when he put me down.

"Merry Christmas, Dad."

We each told that story for a lot of years coming. I told my version in the schoolyard and then later on to my kids. Dad told his to our relatives and I suppose the men he knew down at the bar.

After all these years, the thing I like best is sure—Lou the mule was Mary The Mother of God's Mule, but Dad didn't know that. As far as Dad was concerned, that mule could have been anybody's.

My father had character. He took care of us all those years, and he was a conductor on the Erie-Lackawanna Railroad—not some stinkin' innkeeper.

Debbie Jones is a produced playwright in NYC, a member of The Dramatists' Guild, and PEN American. Jones is delighted to be a part of Hopewell Publications' *Best New Writing* 2016.

Hoffer Award Finalist

Cassandra's Trump
by Stephen G. Bloom

Cassandra told Harry to make himself at home. The apartment building is directly behind the municipal fountain (which won't be working) in Gâvea, around the corner from a hole-in-the-wall *barzinho* with a large Pitú sign out front. You can't miss it, Cassandra said.

Climb the stairs to the third floor, that'll be the top floor. It's the first apartment on your left. No number. If I'm already gone, I'll leave a key on the ledge above the door. Two turns to the right, but be careful *to lift* the knob as you twist, or it's liable to fall off. Help yourself to anything in the fridge. There's cheese, crackers, some fruit, an opened bottle of wine. I'll put some fresh sheets on Claire's bed. She's gone for two weeks. Back to France. To see her boyfriend. Pillows are on the top shelf in the hall closet. Two are foam, the other feather. If that makes any difference. I'll be home late. Don't wait up. We'll talk over breakfast. Looking forward!

Harry had wanted to get to Rio by eight p.m. so he'd have a chance to finally meet Cassandra before she went out for the evening, but the bus from São Paulo had broken down on the toll road, BR 116, somewhere near a town called Volta Redonda. Brazil's intra-urban buses were notorious. That's why Harry had taken a *leito*, paying almost double for air conditioning, Brazilian Muzak, reclining seats, even a *roda-moça* (a bus stewardess who offers passengers refreshments onboard), but an hour southwest of Rio, Harry and everyone else onboard heard a disturbing clanking sound coming from deep within the bowels of the engine. The noise got louder and louder as the driver slowed from 80 to 40 to 15 kph, finally pulling onto the gravelly shoulder.

"*Que brincadeira!*" ("What a joke!"). A heavyset man with a moustache in 15B snorted to no one in particular, to which everyone nodded, as we sat in the hot, humid bus waiting for a rescue bus to pick us up as passing cars slowed, then whizzed by.

Harry had wanted to meet Cassandra ever since he had arrived in Brazil four months earlier. No one had come out and said it, and he couldn't very well have asked, but Stan, a middle-aged news editor at the newspaper where they all worked, did raise his eyebrows and removed his pipe when Harry mentioned Cassandra's name. "She's an attractive woman," Stan declared, as though he was testifying in a court of law. She'd have to be, Harry figured. What Plain Jane could pull off a name like Cassandra?

Harry and Cassandra were two peas in a pod. At least that's what Harry liked to think. Both had arrived in September to work for the *Latin America Daily Post*, a start-up English-language newspaper published in São Paulo. Harry had been hired to work as a news editor in the paper's main office, while Cassandra had finagled a job in the newspaper's four-person Rio bureau. It was a strange kind of friendship, Cassandra and Harry's, but actually, when he thought about it, no stranger than a lot of others. They talked every day, but had never met. Their conversations revolved around Cassandra's copy (Harry was her editor), their luck in finding apartments, news from back home, how well they were mastering Portuguese (not a piece of cake), and other general and sundry observations of two young, single people living and working abroad. Harry and Cassandra were the only Americans at the paper; actually, that's not technically true, it only seemed that way. They were the only Americans who had lived in the U.S. in the last five or ten years. The other editors and reporters were long-time expatriates, married to Brazilians, with thoroughly Brazilian kids, in-laws and mortgages. They were more Brazilian than American.

By the time the replacement bus had deposited twenty-seven grumbling passengers at the Central Rio bus depot, it was close to eight p.m. Harry stood in the taxi queue and got in a dented yellow Volkswagen Bug. Soon, the driver was speeding through the Rebouças Tunnel like he was on the last lap of the Brazilian Grand Prix.

"Easy," Harry thought. "I wanna stay alive to meet her."

Fifteen minutes on the other side of the tunnel, the driver promptly found Cassandra's place in a quiet, forested neighborhood in the Zona Sul, just as a sweet, almost perfumed, twilight descended on the city.

Harry lugged his backpack up the three floors, knocked on the door, and with no one answering, reached for the key atop the doorframe, as Cassandra had promised. Remembering her admonition, Harry ever so slightly jiggled the knob, and then pushed open the door, which prompted a lilting breeze to billow the sheer white curtains on either side of a French window opposite him.

The apartment was perfect, more than Harry had imagined. The floor was shiny parquet, the furnishings simple. Everything was in its place. Claire's room must have been the one to the right. He walked in there first, going straight towards several curled photographs tucked in the frame of a mirror behind a dresser: three smiling girls, all looking very French and very ruddy. Another photo showed a girl in a blue tank top and white shorts and a skinny boy with unruly black hair. They had their arms around each other and were mugging for the camera. On the dresser, Harry noticed a small French flag stuck in a terracotta flowerpot along with pencils, pens, combs, two hairbrushes and a multitude of swizzle sticks.

Cassandra had the smaller room, across the hall. Her bed was covered with a white muslin spread with little raised dots that formed a star pattern. She had books stacked on either side. John Reed, Hunter Thompson, Dorothy Parker, Herman Hesse, Lillian Hellman, Jack Kerouac, Allen Ginsberg, Henry Miller, Doris Lessing. On an oak nightstand, Harry noticed a framed color photograph of what must have been her parents, two brothers and Cassandra, herself. Harry picked up the picture. So this is what she looks like. Stan was right. The five in the photo were robust and tanned. It must have been taken at a restaurant; everyone was sitting around a table, smiling and wearing red-and-white lobster bibs.

Harry didn't feel right about snooping; just being in Cassandra's room, he felt like he was trespassing. But he was curious about this girl he'd never met, with whom he'd spent so much time talking and teletyping. As Harry turned to leave, he passed the closet door, which was open, and noticed an assortment of shoes, all lined up like toy soldiers—sandals, flip-flops, a pair of mid-heels, but also an assortment of platforms, high-heels and mules. This was a girl who knew how to have fun.

Harry headed to the kitchen, poured himself a tumbler of Concha y Toro, and made two cheese-and-cracker sandwiches. He sipped the wine and opened a rifled-through copy of the day's *Jornal do Brasil*. Harry tried to concentrate on a turgid political analysis of deteriorating Brazilian-Argentine relations, which he felt obliged to read considering his job.

He took a shower, made a passing acknowledgement of the loofa and long-handled wooden brush hanging from the shower-head, then dried himself with a folded bath towel left near the sink. In T-shirt and shorts, he went back to Cassandra's room to scan the piles of books again. He saw a paperback copy of *This Side of Paradise*, by F. Scott Fitzgerald; he carefully pulled it out so as not to disrupt the teetering pile.

Back in Claire's room, three pages into it, despite his best intentions, Harry put the book down, open-faced, mindful not to break the spine. He momentarily thought about Cassandra in her mules, dancing in a too-tight skirt and, for some reason, with a fringe shawl covering her bare shoulders, but the day had been long and Harry quickly drifted off to a sleep.

The next morning, Harry awoke early. He had forgotten to pull the curtains shut. He leaned on his elbows and looked out towards

Cassandra's room. Her door was closed, so she must have come home, tiptoeing past Claire's room, not making much noise—that, or Harry must have really conked out. He didn't quite know what to do, so he brushed his teeth, splashed water on his face, and put on running shorts and sneakers. He scribbled a note and left it on the kitchen table:

Gone running.

See you when you get up.

Looking forward.

H

Outside, the weather was already humid and it wasn't seven yet. Harry could feel the humidity. It was as though his pores had opened all the way and were straining to suck in more oxygen than the heavy air was willing to give. Harry started winding through the streets of Gâvea, then to a path that led through the Jardim Botânica. He soon found himself on a narrow trail that wound through a stand of gardenia bushes; suddenly their smell overwhelmed him. The aroma tickled his nose and he sneezed twice.

There's something exhilarating about running in a new, unfamiliar city, and that elation was heightened by the fact that the city, in this case, was Rio de Janeiro, and the sun had just risen. Whenever he passed other runners, he greeted them with a smile, nod, and *Oi!* (Hi!) or *Bom Dia!* (Good morning!). As Harry ran, building up beads of sweat, he looked upward, to the west, and saw the outstretched hands of Christ The Redeemer atop Corcovado. The huge statue was sending forth a benediction to everyone, Harry included.

He must have run for more than an hour. His legs began to go rubbery and he knew he ought to get back, but he wanted to give Cassandra time so she could get up and get dressed. Who knew what she had done the night before or when she had gotten home. In the distance, he saw the waterless fountain in the neighborhood plaza, and made a final sprint toward it. He ran past the fountain to

Cassandra's building, touching with his right hand its white stucco front as a sort of finish line, then walked in small circles to regain his breath. A vendor had set up a stall selling fresh-cut flowers, and Harry thought of buying a bouquet for Cassandra, but rejected the idea. We're colleagues after all, he thought.

Harry walked up the three flights and saw the door ajar. He could smell bacon frying, and as soon as he walked into the apartment, he sniffed fresh-cut oranges.

"Welcome," said a compact woman in bare feet, wearing a white terrycloth robe and matching turban around her head.

"Hi," said Harry, coming closer, reaching out to shake Cassandra's hand, and then on second thought, giving her a hug.

"I stayed out *way* too late last night," Cassandra said, laughing at herself in a sort of private-joke kind of way. "I tried not to make too much noise when I got back. Hope I didn't wake you. Here, take this orange juice. Just squeezed."

Harry sat down to take in all that there was. So this was Cassandra. In the flesh and in her bathrobe. She looked nothing like Harry had imagined, Stan's assessment included. The photograph in the lobster bib didn't do her justice. Cassandra was smaller than Harry thought she'd be. She looked European, maybe northern Italian or Czech, but also fully American. Her eyes were dark blue and she had a welcoming smile. She had small hands and wrists and she was very tan.

They talked over a spinach-and-mushroom omelet that Cassandra had made and split onto two plates with six strips of bacon. "Take some hot sauce if you like," she said as they sat sipping the orange juice. "I have some champagne, too, if you want to make a mimosa," Cassandra offered, but then said, "not for me. I drank *way* too much last night." Harry smiled and didn't ask for details.

All told that morning, they probably talked two hours—about how they had secured their journalists' visas (Cassandra had the moxie to convince the editors at *Rolling Stone* to make her the magazine's "special jazz correspondent" in Brazil; Harry had gone a more conventional route by talking the Field News Service into securing a visa for him); what they thought of Steve, Ed, and Stan, the *Daily Post* editors in São Paulo; how terrific Tom, a reporter in the Rio Bureau, was; and the quality of the newspaper ("It's O.K.; but it'll never be *The New York Times*—or the *Bridgeport Post!*" Cassandra said laughing). They exchanged impressions of Brazilians. How some of the women were hyper-feminine, like come-to-life, dark-skinned Vargas girls. "'Coquettes,' that's what they are," Harry said, a word he had assuredly never used before.

"But the men," Cassandra said, gaining steam. "They're a whole other story. I don't know how Brazilian women put up with them." They both laughed. "They're selfish, total egomaniacs, great looking, and they get away with murder. You ever watch how some of them walk? They strut, they really do!" at which Cassandra got up and swaggered around the breakfast table like a cross between a five-star general and Jean-Paul Belmondo. It cracked Harry up, and they both giggled at their cross-gender assessments, two Americans caught up in the elation of finding someone far away from home who got it completely.

Still laughing, Cassandra got up to clear the dishes. As she arose from the cane-back chair, she absentmindedly patted the towel wrapped atop her head, cocked her chin, moving it just so, then, putting the dishes on the counter, unfurled the towel. Out tumbled a mane of shoulder-length, thick, mahogany-brown hair. The scene reminded him of those old TV commercials for Breck shampoo.

But it wasn't just Cassandra's hair. It was what she did with her shoulders and head, how she moved them in counterclockwise directions, a sort of wriggling motion from her shoulders on up. The combination of opposing actions had the same effect as a dog shaking off after coming in from the rain. Harry felt a sudden mist spray his face.

They couldn't very well stay in the hot apartment the whole day, and when Cassandra suggested they go to the beach, Harry readily agreed. They took the bus to Ipanema, no more than a fifteen-minute ride, and joined what seemed like a pilgrimage of beach-goers hauling soccer balls, mats, boom-boxes, coolers and collapsible aluminum chairs. When they got to the sand, they agreed on a spot, and immediately started poking each other in the ribs whenever someone outrageous walked by. Cassandra wore a tank suit, which really was the only thing for an American woman to wear. You couldn't compete with the locals. Harry had never seen bikinis like these. They were called *tangas*, really nothing more than three tiny triangular pieces of cloth connected by a string. One girl after another on parade. But it wasn't just the women. The men, as Cassandra duly pointed out, were also wearing practically nothing, wedgies that went up their butts and form-fitting pouches girding their penises. Harry stole a look at Cassandra and caught her smiling, and when she realized that, they both broke out in laughter.

They continued staring at the procession in front of them, but now they had entered into another phase, and their conversation ebbed to a not-uncomfortable, bemused silence. Maybe the scene before them was just too mesmerizing; that certainly had something to do with it, but Harry thought that wasn't the only reason for their silence. Where do they go from here?

The last thing Harry wanted to do was talk about before Brazil. Why couldn't they stay exactly where they were? Why did everything always have to converge? Wasn't there some Flannery O'Conner story with that name? Why couldn't you just divorce yourself from your history and stay right where you were, at the moment now? Very Zen-like, Harry mused. That was one of the reasons Harry had come to Brazil in the first place. To plunge into a world of possibilities. Where anything could happen. Why'd he have to dredge up Katie back home and the possibility (however unlikely) that she'd make good on her promise to visit him in Brazil? The incident at the airport back home when he said good-bye, the false alarm when she thought she was pregnant, the time the black bear raided their backpacks in Olympic National Park scaring the bejesus out of both of them. He didn't want to forget. He just wanted to push forward.

Harry and Cassandra went back to bantering, how the water looked like glass, the geographic odds of a mountain so peculiarly shaped like Sugar Loaf so close to such a spectacular crescent of a beach, and then some on a guy with tattoos on *both* checks of his buttocks walking by. This was more like it.

But before Harry could do anything to stop it, Cassandra had somehow turned the conversation, dredging up her former job as an assistant producer (translation: go-fer) for an NBC affiliate back in the States, where she had met Evan Malone, the evening anchor, and how the two began going out, even though Cassandra knew full well that Evan was married and had two daughters, who, Cassandra noted with an arch of her eyebrows and a roll of her eyes "are older than me!" Everyone, Cassandra said, knew the marriage was over. Evan had moved into a townhouse in the city, his wife staying in the big colonial in the suburbs.

Harry wasn't sure he wanted to hear any of this, but the discourse seemed a matter of full disclosure that Cassandra wanted to put on the table—or in this case, on the sand between them.

"It might happen," Cassandra said, gazing at the ocean, not at Harry. "I talked to him last night, and he says he's going to come down in June. I doubt it, but he says he will."

What Harry thought at that moment was that Cassandra should have known better. Cassandra wasn't some Nebraska farm girl. She was smart, drop-dead gorgeous, able to read any man in seconds. You could see it. Then how'd she fall for this one? She certainly knew what she was getting herself into. But this was Evan Malone, after all. Could you blame her?

Cassandra talked about how wonderful a newsman Evan was, how respected he was, but also how humble he was. And how ethical. That was important. Very un-TV. And *everyone* knew him. Yes, he was older and that freaked her out. But he was in great shape. He'd given up smoking when he had split from his wife, and had taken up running three miles a day.

Did Harry need to know any of this?

As much for distraction as for thirst, Harry bought two lemonades from a vendor hauling two heavy aluminum canisters from his shoulders. They got up and waded in the warm ocean water, and then walked up and down the crowded beach. Close to five in the afternoon, they made their way to the bus stop and back to Cassandra's apartment. Harry took the first shower.

"Be careful with the curtain," Cassandra said through the door. "If it's not inside the tub, the water goes *everywhere*." Harry made sure no water spilled onto the floor. He thought to use the loofa to scrub his back, but rejected the idea considering the circumstances.

When Cassandra had finished her shower, she reappeared wearing the same terrycloth robe as in the morning. "I squeezed some lemons and made us *caipirinhas*, Harry. Let me put some shorts on and we'll go up to the roof."

They climbed up a vertical black metal ladder at the end of the hallway. Harry went first, carrying two tumblers. He pushed open a square piece of wood that served as a trap door. Cassandra followed, navigating the ladder carrying a pitcher of crushed ice, lemons, sugar and cachaça. On the roof were two director's chairs with faded canvas backs and a weathered, round wooden-plank table.

"Is this heaven or what?" Cassandra asked, beaming.

Harry would be less than forthright with himself if he didn't concede that Cassandra's admission at the beach had taken some of the wind out of his stay. Could he be jealous of Evan Malone, or was he just disappointed in Cassandra? He wasn't sure. But back on the bus to São Paulo Sunday afternoon, he decided he had no right to be feeling anything but sensational about—well—pretty much everything. He had gone to Rio de Janeiro for a weekend, for God's sake! How many Americans slogging it back home could say that?

And he was gainfully employed as a journalist. In Brazil, of all places. Although, as Cassandra had put it, the *Latin America Daily Post* was neither *The New York Times* nor the *Bridgeport Post*, it was a bona fide newspaper and the editors had seen Harry competent enough to be hired. And not as an intern, but as a staff editor who got paid (not much, but that wasn't the point). His fluency in Portuguese was gaining momentum. The taxi driver who took him back to the bus station had even asked whether he was from Rio Grande do Sul. That's how native Harry was sounding (or maybe the driver was just angling for a big tip). *And* he'd finally met Cassandra. That she had disclosed her affair with Evan Malone meant that she felt good enough about Harry to usher him inside her life.

They talked frequently over the phone the next few weeks. Rumors started flying that the newspaper was about to close its São Paulo headquarters and move lock, stock and barrel to Rio. Harry had warned himself not to think about living and working in Rio. He was lucky enough to have scored a newspaper gig in São Paulo. Don't ask for too much. Be glad for what you have. Yet, in the newsroom one Monday morning, the editor and publisher stood in front of thirty or so employees, and said that it was their obligation to duly inform everyone that the paper would relocate to Rio within sixty days.

Few could, or even wanted to, make the 430-kilometer move, so while everyone else groaned, this was terrible news for them, Harry could hardly believe his fortune. As soon as management finished the announcement, Harry called Cassandra, who answered "*Daily Post!*" on the first ring, and told her the news.

"That's wonderful, Harry! I can't wait!"

Harry stayed at Cassandra's apartment for three weeks while he looked for an apartment of his own in Rio. He took the cushions off the couch and arranged them on the living-room floor, which wasn't as bad as it sounds. Harry got to meet Claire, who was very French, which wasn't to say she was difficult to get along with, just that she took some getting accustomed to. The three of them usually ate dinner together, and over wine and cheese, they'd get to talking about everything from Sartre, the merits of a Brazilian hair conditioner called Neutrox, and the puckering sensation that cashew juice had on their mouths. Claire did not like much about the United States, although she had never visited there. Cassandra and Harry were hardly Chamber of Commerce types, and they probably agreed with Claire on ninety-nine percent of what she said. But it was a matter of principle. Harry was another voice in the apart-ment, a forged solidarity of two Americans holding their ground.

Cassandra continued to keep Harry posted on news of Evan Malone. After dinner, she'd leave the apartment and go down to an *orejão*, the pay phone outside the *barzinho* in the *praça*, to call him in the States collect. When she'd come back, she'd go about her business. Sometimes her faced seemed flushed. Harry never asked how things were going between Evan and her because, quite frankly, he didn't want to know. It wasn't any of his business. If Cassandra wanted to fill him in, she could.

Harry soon found an unfurnished apartment in a neighborhood near Corcovado called Laranjeiras, which means orange groves. It was a tiny place, but with a nice view of a wooded mountainside, and only twenty minutes by bus to Lapa, the district where the *Daily Post* had moved to in Rio. The apartment's previous tenant had left a mahogany dining-room set and a coffee table, and on Saturday Harry and Cassandra spent all day stripping off the finish. They celebrated that evening with takeout from an excellent Chinese restaurant around the corner.

The next Monday Harry had to buy a bed, and he and Cassandra went to a place down the block from the *Daily Post*, where they tried out an assortment of mattresses. The salesman naturally assumed that he and Cassandra were a couple as they tested out various mattresses, foam and springs, single to king-size, jabbering away in English while they rolled, lay, sat and bounced on the beds.

It was a toss-up. Cassandra thought that the foam would give out faster and recommended a spring mattress, but Harry rejected Cassandra's choice and picked a thick, foam *cama de viuva*, which translated to widow's bed, which meant that its size was between that of a single and a double mattress. Harry felt strange buying something called a widow's bed, but it was the largest size that would fit in the apartment's bedroom.

Cassandra had a great time with Harry's *cama de viuva*, mentioning it whenever she could. The first day after he slept on the mattress, Cassandra cracked across the newsroom, "Hey Harry, how was the widow last night? Too soft? Too hard?"

Steve and Ed looked up from their desks, first at Harry, then at Cassandra. They shook their heads, then went back to editing wire copy.

Within weeks, at a grand *feijoada* party that Andrew, a copy editor, had taken Harry to, Harry met a dark-skinned woman by the name of Anna Elena. By all rights, Cassandra probably would have gone to the party, but she had to finish a Sunday feature story about a Brazilian plastic surgeon reputed to have worked on Elizabeth Taylor and Michael Jackson. Andrew insisted that Harry join him, and it was a good thing that he did. Anna Elena was in her mid-twenties, with almond-shaped blue eyes, ebony hair pulled back tight in a ponytail and a perfectly oval face.

As it turned out, Harry's budding relationship with Anna Elena had many salutary effects, not the least of which was that since Anna Elena spoke not a word of English, Harry's Portuguese improved dramatically. In the limited grab bag of skills he possessed, language acquisition was one of them, and with Anna Elena at his side, Harry was able to make a quantum leap. Within weeks, he was using all kinds of Portuguese *gíria* (slang) that only a native could get away with.

One Tuesday after work, Harry called Anna Elena at her job (she was a clerk in a bank opposite the giant cathedral downtown), and the two made plans to meet at a sandwich place in Copacabana called Cervantes.

"Harry, I want to meet her," Cassandra pleaded when Harry told her he wouldn't be joining everyone else at Bar Brasil, the watering hole *The Daily Post* editors and reporters all went to after the newspaper got put to bed. "Everything *I've* told you, and you're not going to introduce me to her? No way! And you're sharing the widow's bed with her, Harry, the bed *I* helped you pick out! I get to meet the girl!"

They both caught the 434 to Copacabana.

Actually, the encounter went well, at least Harry thought it did. He, Anna Elena and Cassandra split a sandwich of pork and pineapple slices. All the talk about how jealous Brazilian women can get didn't seem to come into play. Maybe women have a way of knowing their competition, and Harry realized that both Anna Elena and Cassandra figured that each of them understood they had the fortune, or whatever you want to call it, of knowing Harry for their own reasons, and because of that, each was pleased in her own way to meet the other.

Back at the newspaper, Harry having a girlfriend seemed to give Cassandra license to open up more about Evan. The latest news was that Evan was finally planning a trip to Rio. "I have absolutely no idea how this is going to play out," Cassandra told Harry at Bar Brasil one evening. She wriggled her shoulders and head in the way Harry had become accustomed to by now. "I mean he's coming a *long* way." She paused to absorb all that meant.

"Have a good time," Harry said. "That's what Anna Elena and I are doing." He couldn't help checking a smile. "So why can't the same thing happen with you and Evan?"

"I don't know him very well," Cassandra said, lowering her voice, as though it made a difference among the loud Brazilians downing glass after glass of ice-cold *chopes* (draft beers) all around them. "I don't know him at all! And he's in his forties, probably his late forties. That sounds *so* old." Harry figured she and Evan had slept together a half a dozen times, then the job in Brazil had come up and Cassandra had left. Relationship interruptus.

"The worst that can happen is he leaves and you stay here. Besides, it's *my* turn now. *I* get to meet the guy."

Evan did come to Rio, and when Harry met him what struck Harry was what had struck Cassandra—his age. Evan was in great shape, except for a gut that Evan occasionally tried to suck in. And how he walked. He had a bad back, and whenever he rose from a chair, he seemed to wince. He had reddish hair, which he combed over instead of straight back. Harry thought that, too, made him look older. But more power to Evan if he could enchant a girl like Cassandra. Harry should have that luck when he's pushing fifty.

Harry surmised that it was *because* of the age difference that there was such an attraction between Cassandra and Evan, not withstanding Cassandra's assertions. What middle-aged man wouldn't fall for Cassandra? That was a no-brainer. And from her point of view, Evan was mature and well-respected (those were her words), *everyone* in the business knew him. He was a great newsman, and he was all grown up. There was no indecision, no lingering doubt about anything. You could see this when he walked. Once he got his back sorted out, he strode like he was on a mission, shoulders back, chin out. A man who knew what he wanted and had gotten it.

This might have worked in New York or Boston, but in Rio, it didn't sell at all. Beach-loving *cariocas* like to amble, chat, leisurely sip a *cafezinho* at a corner *luncheonette*, stroll, and generally enjoy themselves no matter what they're doing. Not taking themselves seriously is the only thing they take seriously. To be in a hurry, that was so *paulistano*, what people from button-down São Paulo do.

"Hey, slow down," Cassandra had to say to Evan not just a couple of times.

"What's your rush?" Harry chimed in. "You're south of the border, Evan. This is the land of siestas." (Actually, the Portuguese word was *sestas*, but Evan wouldn't have known that.)

Whatever Harry was prepared to think of Evan, Harry found him to be decent and likable. He was smart, too. He'd certainly taken on a tough act, coming into a distant, foreign land, trying to sweep a woman twenty years younger off her feet. If that wasn't enough, he had to do it with a tight circle of Cassandra's friends and co-workers scrutinizing his every move.

On Evan's third night in Rio, Cassandra invited Harry and Anna Elena over to her apartment for dinner. It was to be six of them since Claire's boyfriend had flown in from Lyon that week. "Harry, pick up some fresh limes at the *feira* in Laranjeiras and we'll start out on the rooftop for *caipirinhas*."

Cassandra had set out six director's chairs in a semi-circle on the roof. "The landlady doesn't like us up here, so please keep it down," Cassandra said to everyone, then giggled, realizing how impossible that would be.

Harry and Anna Elena played bartender, mashing the limes and sugar, as Cassandra produced two pint bottles of *caçacha* from the back pockets of her cutoff jeans. Evan and Claire had carried up the tumblers. It was a Tower of Babel party, since Claire and her boyfriend, Michel, spoke French, Cassandra and Evan spoke English, and Harry alternated in Portuguese with Anna Elena, and in English with Evan and Cassandra.

The Tropic of Capricorn sun was setting behind the Christ the Redeemer statue; it was one of those end-of-the-day pink, purple and blue spectacles that make you want to applaud. Harry couldn't have been happier.

He looked over at Anna Elena, who was absolutely remarkable, and for a moment compared her to Cassandra, who was leaning towards Evan's chair, touching his right knee just so to make a point. Ever since Harry and Anna Elena had met, she'd happily played city tour guide and linguistic interlocutor to Harry. She listened attentively whenever Harry and Cassandra spoke in English about American journalism, politics, how the folks back home ever could have elected Ronald Reagan president, even though she didn't understand a word of what they were saying. Anna Elena was enjoying herself, too, Harry could tell. She, too, had signed on for an adventure.

On the rooftop this evening, Harry thought about the singularity of the moment—six friends from three continents sharing a moment of collective intimacy. Anna Elena caught Harry's eye at that moment. She smiled, reached for Harry's hand, squeezed it, then kissed him on the lips.

"A toast," Harry said, tapping a twizzle stick against his tumbler. Three conversations gently interrupted, suspended in the moist evening air, floating skyward. "To Evan and Michel, friends we welcome to this magical place. To Claire and Cassandra, women who united to bring us this amazing sunset." Harry paused, as Claire dutifully translated for Michel, and then Harry did the same for Anna Elena. "And, finally, to Anna Elena," and here Harry spoke in Portuguese, *"uma campanheira de grande carinho e coração"* (a companion of great affection and heart). It all sounds way too corny, but if you were there, given the circumstances, it really was perfect.

"Bravo, Harry!" Cassandra said, followed by "Here, Here!" from Evan, *"Santé!"* from Michel and Claire, and *"Chin-Chin!"* from Anna Elena. Everyone raised and clinked tumblers.

Claire and Michel soon peeled off for a twilight walk on the beach in Leblon. Cassandra wanted to take Evan to *gafieira*, a kind of working-class dancehall where locals boogied to a twenty-piece (or more) band playing vintage music from the fifties and earlier, sort of a retro Brazilian version of Xavier Cugat or Harry James. For a moment, Harry thought of making a crack about this being the kind of music Evan grew up with, but (wisely) restrained himself.

The four of them—Cassandra, Evan, Harry and Anna Elena—took a taxi to a place called Club Elite (pronounced *Clue-bay E-leach*) near Praça Tiradentes, and walked up a very steep stairway to a large ballroom with a revolving mirrored ball hanging from the ceiling. There were two dozen men playing trumpets, trombones, saxophones, bases, guitars, clarinets, drums, to some of the hokiest but most exquisite music Harry, Cassandra and Evan had ever heard.

At one point, Harry caught Evan and Cassandra doing the tango (which Harry noted to himself wasn't even remotely Brazilian), hamming it up, cheek to cheek, and when the band took a break, en-route back to the table, Cassandra provocatively sashayed her hips, teetering on a pair of mules.

"Cassie," Evan said as they reached the table. "You want another *caiparinha?*"

Cassie?

And the way Evan butchered *caiparinha*, it sounded more like *copper arena*.

Cassandra immediately picked up on both of Evan's miscues, and realizing Harry did, too, she gave Harry a drop-dead stare that translated to, "Don't say a word."

Harry and Anna Elena danced side-by-side Cassandra and Evan, lots of laughing, lots of drinking. They exchanged partners for a couple of dances, Cassandra with Harry, Evan with Anna Elena. At 2 a.m., as the four of them tottered back down the steep steps to get a cab, standing unsteadily under a ripped awning at the curb, Evan put his index and middle finger together, stuck them in his mouth, and out came a shrill, deafening whistle.

The sidewalk vendors selling sugary *cafezinhos*, the transsexual prostitutes hanging out near the *praça* fountain, the unshaved men taking their last pulls of *pinga* from the corner *barzinhos*, even the fluttering pigeons atop the equestrian statue—all of them stopped at the exact same instant and looked at Evan.

Harry, Cassandra and Anna Elena didn't know what to say.

"It's what we do in the States," Evan replied, shrugging his shoulders. "At least, where I come from, it is."

Whether or not that was true, Evan's ear-splitting siren worked. A taxi materialized from nowhere instantly, screeching to a halt in front of them. Evan and Cassandra piled into the back, followed by Anna Elena, with Harry sitting shotgun up front. Harry gave the driver his address in Laranjeiras, that's where Anna Elena and he would get off, and then instructed the driver to continue to Gâvea to drop off Cassandra and Evan.

Harry, Cassandra, and Evan were chattering away in English about the evening, about the clarinet solo that Harry said reminded him of klezmer music, about the drunk girl in the strapless dress who had gotten into a fight with the girl wearing a hat and a dress without a back, when Harry suddenly felt that he had somehow abandoned poor Anna Elena in the backseat. He reached back with his left hand and started rubbing her knee. Or what he thought was her knee.

"That feels very reassuring," Evan said. "I like you, too, Harry."

In his celebratory state, Harry had picked the wrong knee, and when he realized that, pulling his hand back, he and everyone else, including the taxi driver, who somehow understood what had happened, broke out in gales of laughter.

Evan stayed for another week. On his last evening, he joined Cassandra and Harry after work at Bar Brasil for a last round of *chopes*. When Harry said goodbye to Evan outside the bar, he shook his hand, as American men of Evan's generation are wont to do, but that seemed hardly enough in this warm, proximal country, so Harry gave Evan what they call in Brazil an *abraço*, a shoulder-to-shoulder embrace. "Good luck!" Harry, for some reason, said to Evan, before walking around the corner to catch his bus home.

Evan's trip to Rio had done the trick. Cassandra pined for several weeks, making nightly trips to the *orejão* to call him back home. Then out of the blue, one day at work, Cassandra told Harry that she had decided to return to the States. She would quit her job at the *Daily Post* and try to get her news assistant job back at the TV station. For his part, Evan had taken a lucrative buyout and wasn't sure what he'd do next. "He thinks he might want to sail around the world," is what Cassandra told Harry.

On Cassandra's last evening in Brazil, Harry and Anna Elena were to take her to a Portuguese restaurant in the Glória section of Rio. Actually, it was supposed to have been just Harry and Cassandra. That way the two of them could speak English instead of Portuguese. But ever since the night of *gafieira*, Anna Elena had begun to raise an eyebrow at how much time Harry had been spending with Cassandra. Such a reaction, whether it was based on jealousy or something else, was totally out of character for Anna Elena, Harry thought.

"For God's sake!" Harry said, one of the few times he lost his temper with Anna Elena. "She's leaving! She's my best friend! A dinner, that's all it is. There's nothing between us. Don't invent a reason for there to be something."

As soon as the Portuguese leapt from his mouth, Harry knew he had flubbed what he meant to say. It was a convoluted sentence and a convoluted thought, and in Portuguese it probably made no sense at all. What he wanted to say was that Anna Elena was projecting a kind of relationship that didn't exist between Cassandra and him, and that if Anna Elena chose to manufacture one, it would undermine any fidelity and trust they shared. But how Harry's words came out, as best as he could figure out, was that no way could Harry ever see Anna Elena and him ever creating a relationship equaling what he already shared with Cassandra. It's hard to explain crossed linguistic gaffes, but that's at least what Harry thought Anna Elena thought. If that makes any sense.

"So, there's nothing between us?" she asked. "But you said I was your *campanheira*. When we were on Cassandra's rooftop. That means we are not just lovers, but a couple, if not married, two people as one, two people with a future."

Harry reassured her as best as he could, given the circumstances, but he still wanted to have Cassandra to himself, for dinner, her last night.

If their relationship was so innocent, Anna Elena insisted, then what was wrong with her joining Harry and Cassandra? Anna Elena, too, was losing a friend, she reminded Harry.

At work that day, Harry told Cassandra about the argument, who promptly said, "For God's sake, Harry, please have Anna Elena come along. Please."

It all led to a rather stilted dinner at the Portuguese restaurant, the three of them acting far too polite and restrained, considering the evening might be the last time all of them might ever be together. After the meal, in front of Cassandra's apartment, Harry and Anna Elena got out of the cab, each giving a hug to Cassandra, then got back in for the trip to Laranjeiras, during which they said nothing. Harry felt terrible.

Early the next morning, Harry took Cassandra to Galeão. Anna Elena had wanted to take off from work to join them, but Harry had persuaded her not to come. Cassandra had shipped home all of her possessions with the exception of her books, which she gave to Harry. He was thankful for her largesse, and was planning several weekends of doing nothing but holing up in his apartment and reading.

"Write me, Harry!" Cassandra said at the airport gate.

"I will."

"Take care of yourself."

"You, too." Then, "Make sure Evan treats you well."

"He better!" Cassandra said, flashing a smile.

They heard the final call to board, and just as Cassandra walked past the Varig ticket agent, just before she disappeared out the door to the plane, she started waving wildly, as though she'd forgotten something.

"Harry!" she shouted across the gate area.

"Don't wear out the widow's bed!"

In the wake of Cassandra's departure, Harry and Anna Elena continued to go out, but a wrinkle had turned into a crease. With Cassandra out of the picture, Anna Elena didn't have to share Harry with anyone. That's how Harry surmised the change. It led to an entirely different side to Anna Elena that Harry hadn't seen before. She wanted to know his whereabouts, almost hour by hour. If he wasn't at the newspaper, she'd want to know where he was and with whom. If he worked late, she'd call the newsroom, which led to the paste-up guys answering the phone and shouting from the composing room, *"Ha-Ree, Ha-Ree!"* One evening, she showed up unexpectedly at Bar Brasil while Harry was holding forth on journalistic idioms like -30- and (MORE). He was on such a roll that he didn't bother to translate for Anna Elena, even if he really could.

The next Saturday, Anna Elena called the newspaper, but there had been a power outage that afternoon, not untypical for Rio or the Lapa neighborhood, and everything the typesetters had set had gone *poof!* The other editors were going crazy, and Harry was in a panic. He pleaded to Anna Elena the English words, "blackout" and "deadline," saying he'd call her as soon as he could, then too quickly hung up.

Harry didn't hear from Anna Elena for a week, nor did he call her. He was spending time reading the books Cassandra had left him. Maybe the solitude was a way of coping with her departure. At dusk after work, while waiting for his bus to Laranjeiras, he thought he saw Anna Elena hurrying across Cinelândia downtown, but he resisted the urge to catch up to her.

In mid-August, Harry received a letter from Anna Elena at the newspaper. Her penmanship showed signs of strain. The stationery Anna Elena used was businesslike and thick, and the two horizontal folds she made in it were crisp. The envelope was postmarked from Recife, a city in the northeast. Anna Elena had quit her job and had moved back home, she wrote. She was staying with an aunt who worked in a lace factory.

They were too different, she wrote, like *"vinagre e óleo"* (vinegar and oil). They complemented each other, but could never be one. She realized this. She forgave Harry for any transgressions. She harbored no ill will whatsoever, she wrote, and wished him well.

For a moment or two, Harry thought of trying to contact Anna Elena, even flying to Recife and surprising her. Perhaps hopefully, she had written her return address in the upper left corner of the envelope. Harry kept the envelope propped up against the salt and pepper shakers on his dining-room table for a week, and then one evening he used it as a bookmark and eventually it disappeared.

This might be the end to this story, but there is a coda. Harry ultimately left Brazil, as Anna Elena suspected he would all along. Starting in the mid-1990s, when the practice of email grew worldwide, on New Year's Day every year, he would receive a note from Anna Elena, wishing him health and happiness. He always reciprocated immediately. Neither shared personal news in these dispatches. They commemorated an era past, warm and sincere, but also formal and transactional.

Harry and Cassandra ultimately lost touch with each other, too, Harry moving back to California, and Cassandra settling in New York. Harry worked as a reporter for a string of newspapers, and achieved a moderate degree of success. He never worked for the *Bridgeport Post*, but he never worked for *The New York Times*, either. He married a winsome girl from Florida he had met on a job interview and they had a son.

Through the years, Harry had tried to keep track of Cassandra and her career. He knew that she had worked for a host of magazines, mostly of the woman's variety, *Redbook, Mademoiselle, Better Homes and Gardens*. He assumed Evan was long gone and that Cassandra had married and had a family of her own. But he had nothing on which to base this. It just seemed how it ought to be.

One fall, Harry was in New York on assignment from the newspaper. He had finished his interviews and had filed his story.

He was staying at one of those convention-type hotels in midtown, just off Fifth Avenue with several hours to kill, and for some reason, he decided he just had to find Cassandra. It had been twenty years since they'd last seen each other. They were now just about the same age Evan had been when Harry first met him.

Harry put his reporting skills to work, first calling *Redbook*. He got an editor who told him that Cassandra had moved to *Savvy*, and when he called that magazine, someone told him that she recently took a job at *Self*. He called *Self*, talked to a series of operators, was put on hold, and after a couple of minutes, Cassandra picked up the phone.

"I finally got rid of that widow's bed," Harry started.

"Harry!" Cassandra said in an instant.

She sounded exactly as she had two decades earlier. Instantly Harry was transported to Rio and that first day they met when he had taken the bus from São Paulo.

Harry told her about his wife and son, going on fifteen, about his job, that he was happy.

"But how are *you*?" he asked.

Cassandra said that she and Evan were still together, despite all the time that had passed. Evan must be close to seventy, Harry figured. He doubted they had children (though Harry recalled Evan had two daughters). Harry was hungry for more, and just as he was about to ask, Cassandra interrupted his thoughts. "Harry, I have to go. We're closing the book today. Like right now. You know what that's like." She paused.

Harry didn't know what to say, but he didn't want this to be how the conversation ended.

"But let's meet for a drink when I'm done," Cassandra said. "It shouldn't be too late."

They decided to meet near Grand Central Station, at the bar in the Roosevelt Hotel lobby, at Madison and 45th. She said she ordinarily took the 6:38 home to Rye, but she'd stop by and take a later train.

It was only 5 p.m. Harry walked through Central Park, turning west to Broadway at 80th Street, where he stopped in at Zabar's, inhaled, thought of bringing some corn beef and a loaf of caraway-seed rye bread back home, but then discarded the idea. He picked up his pace walking back to midtown; it was beginning to get chilly. At the corner of 65th Street and Central Park West, Harry spotted one of those mini-cyclones of swirling leaves, which brought with it a medley of smells augmented by a nearby pretzel and hotdog stall. The walk and the aroma brought Harry back to when he'd first met Cassandra in her walk-up apartment, after he'd run through the botanical gardens, even though these smells were decidedly New York as autumn was about to turn to winter, and these days the closest Harry ever got to running was walking on a treadmill.

Harry got to the hotel bar early, and chose a table in the back so he could look out at whoever entered the bar. He ordered a beer on tap, and sipped it slowly as the place filled up. There was a raucous but pleasant chatter in the air, and he felt good. A blonde woman in her mid-thirties came in, looked around expectantly, about to meet someone. Cassandra? Could it be she? No, but it got Harry thinking.

Fifteen minutes late, Harry saw her. She waved merrily as she walked toward him. Harry rose from his seat and wrapped his arms around her still-small frame.

"Harry," Cassandra said warmly.

She was wearing a business suit and carried a bulging leather briefcase. She wore a knit hat that covered her hair, and as she sat down, she grabbed the cap in the front and started to pull it off. It was then that Harry saw it—the same gesture he had seen that first morning when she took off the towel from her wet hair; that wriggling motion, her shoulders, neck and head each shimmying in opposite directions.

As she pulled off the hat, Harry saw Cassandra's thick mahogany hair now had turned gray. It took him for a surprise. Either Cassandra noticed Harry's look or she was accustomed to the reaction.

"I know."

"You look *great*," Harry said, he hoped not missing a beat.

Harry caught the attention of the waitress, and Cassandra ordered a vodka gimlet, straight up, with a lemon twist.

"*How are you?*" Harry asked.

"Fine, really fine," she said, smiling, in the practiced way that Harry had remembered.

She and Evan had lived on their boat off an island in Maine, then sailed to the Caribbean and hired themselves out as cooks at a resort for another year. They ran out of money, and that's when she started with the woman's magazines. She enjoyed the work, but was concerned about the German conglomerate that had just bought the chain she was working for. "They're cost-cutters, and they don't know a thing about running a magazine, Harry," she said.

Harry couldn't resist. "How's Evan? What's he doing?"

Harry watched her carefully. Evan never returned to work in TV, she said. "He busies himself. He reads a lot. He's trying to write a novel, a western. He's got an agent interested in it; he won't let me read one word of it." She paused a second, then shrugged her shoulders. "He's got his pains, his back. Did he have a bad back when you met him?" Then, not waiting for an answer, "But he's doing fine. He really is."

As Cassandra continued talking, it dawned on Harry. She had let her hair go gray because she didn't want anyone to confuse her as Evan's daughter. That was the reason. It had to be, he mused as they talked back and forth, two middle-aged friends who long ago shared a fleeting moment that punctuated their lives.

So much might have been different. If Evan hadn't flown to Rio. If he had gotten back with his wife. If Harry had stayed in Rio. He might have had a family with Anna Elena. Or with someone else, living in Brazil. Or his old girlfriend, Katie, might have flown to Brazil. If he hadn't gone for that interview and met Audrey, the woman who'd become his wife, he might not have had a child. The core of their lives might have so fundamentally changed that it staggered Harry at this moment in the bar at the Roosevelt Hotel.

Cassandra tilted back her glass; by now, Harry had finished his beer. He didn't carry pictures of his family because he never wanted to be in this kind of position, in a bar with a woman from a long time ago, showing them off. There was a momentary pause between them, but he and Cassandra were too practiced to make it awkward.

"I hate to go, Harry," she finally said, pulling out a pair of red wool mittens, then grabbing her hat and briefcase. "It's getting cold early this year."

They both got up, walked to the lobby, and stood briefly under the large clock there.

"Next time you're in the city, call me. But give me some notice, Harry! You should come out to the apartment. Evan would love to see you. He still talks about you. We have a deck, and we'll barbeque something on the grill. It'll be terrific."

Stephen G. Bloom is the author of *Postville: A Clash of Cultures in Heartland America, Tears of Mermaids: The Secret Story of Pearls, The Oxford Project* (with Peter Feldstein), and *Inside the Writer's Mind*. He teaches narrative journalism at the University of Iowa.

Hoffer Award Finalist

Sinkhole
by Samantha Canales

It was a beauty—four feet across, and so deep that any chance of seeing Mr. Petryk's lawn mower was lost in its perfect blackness. The only proof that the ground had suddenly opened up and swallowed the machine was the gunning of its engine. The engine called out from the bottom of the hole for exactly an hour and twenty-two minutes—I know because I timed it with my watch—giving one final sputter before it ran out of gas. I had been the first to arrive after I heard Mr. Petryk scream. I stared into the hole and felt it pulling me down, toward its nothingness, and it felt good. Dad came running a few minutes later with some of the neighbors: Jon-Jon, Mr. Azer and his son, Andy—the one you used to watch skateboard down our street—and old man Nyguen. We all gathered around the hole, marveling at it as plans for rescuing the mower were discussed. Mr. Petryk stood on the concrete square of his patio, clasping his hands, refusing to set foot on the grass. It reminded me of when we used to play that game where the grass was really shark-infested water and if we stepped on it we would instantly lose a limb.

After several failed ideas, Andy rigged up a long rope with a towing hook and they pulled the machine up into the afternoon sunlight. Dad looked shaky. I knew what was coming next. I'd seen it after he'd moved a dying cat out of the road by Ducer's Market, when he fished my yellow balloon out of Jon Jon's tree, and every time he went to find Nana in some part of town she hadn't remembered driving to: the moment when he realized none of those things were you. Mr. Azer patted Dad on the back. That's when he went down on one knee, slumped over, pretending to tie his tennis shoe in the middle of Mr.Petryk's holey, shark-filled lawn.

A couple of guys in soiled coveralls pulled up in a city van that afternoon. They reported to Mr. Petryk, after several hours of poking around, that it was a sinkhole caused by some bad sewage pipes. That explained the foul smell that came up out of the hole, but I still didn't understand how bad sewage pipes could cause a perfectly good patch of grass to disappear. That night I stared at it from the upstairs window of your room. I turned off the light, so I could see it better. The darkness of your room made me feel better about being in there. There was no sixty-watt bulb shining down like a spotlight on your empty bed and the quilt Nana made from all of your old dresses. Everything I could see was outside.

Mr. Petryk's yard was in shades of grays and blacks, and the opening just lay there on his lawn like one of those trick holes we watched the Pink Panther use to escape Inspector Clouseau. I peeked at it through a crack in the fence the next morning before I hopped in the car to go to school. And later, during fourth period, I drew pictures of the hole while I listened to Mr. Marsh talk about how some lady, with your name, invented the school desk in the late 1800's. I wanted to blurt out, "Sure, she invented the school desk, which is what, wood and screws and possibly some nails, but can anybody tell me how a piece of earth just disappears?"

After dinner, I went up to your room again, and grabbed one of those horse trinkets you started collecting after the parents told you there was no way that we could keep a horse in the garage. It was the pewter one I bought for you at the truck stop last year on our way home from North Carolina. I shoved it in my jeans' pocket and squeezed through the spot in the fence that had the loose board. The gravity from the bottom of the hole pulled on my stomach. I laid down flat on my belly and hung my head over the edge. Next, I pulled out my black notebook, a pen, two cotton balls, and finally the little silver horse. I stuffed the cotton balls into each of my nostrils to protect myself from a smell that had gone from cow manure to dead cat. I placed your horse on the edge of the hole, nestled between two tufts of grass. The grass was heavy with dew, wetting my flannel and jeans; a drop from a nearby blade merged with the horse and slid down its muscular hind leg. With the notebook and pen in hand, I tried to answer some questions I had about the hole, but it was clear that I was not going to be able to answer them without certain tools, like a tape measure or flashlight. I talked into the hole. I told it things. Stopping to take a breath between sentences, I told it how I didn't put enough air holes in the container for that wolf spider I caught last week, about the time I didn't look away when I saw Uncle Hank rubbing the bare breast of a woman in the front seat of his pick-up. I even told the hole how you'd never returned home from school since that day— the same day you won second place in the school spelling bee, misspelling only the word "oriole." The hole's silence was somehow comforting. Before I left, I looked over at the horse, suspended in mid-gallop. I gently touched its flowing, metal tail with my finger— just enough to tip it over the edge. I never heard it hit the bottom.

Lake Jackson, Tallahassee, Florida, Lime Sink

Snapping turtles, soft-shells, yellow-bellied sliders and hundreds of frogs were doing their best to find refuge, even if it meant crossing one of Florida's busiest highways. I lost count at one hundred and twenty-seven. You might have been grossed out at the sight of so many amphibians in one place, but I can just picture you in the truck next to me, your eyes wide, looking up as blue heron and flocks of water birds filled the sky so completely, allowing only small patches of blue to flash in between wings and tails and woody legs. I still can't believe my good fortune. The university sent me out here to lead the project. Me. I mean, I'm just a newbie in the geological department—only been on the job for two short years. And this, well, this was big. If you had been with me, I would have asked you to reach over and give me one of your monkey knuckle pinches, just so I knew that it wasn't all a dream.

Jackson Lake was a short drive out from Tallahassee, appropriately called "Disappearing Waters" by the Apalachee tribe. I pulled into the gravel parking lot on the north shore playground where it quickly became clear that I'd missed most of the show. I walked past the trucks and vans in the parking lot, down to the sandy shore. The orange and white strand of buoys, sectioning off the public swimming area, was barely afloat in small, cloudy pools of water. I looked out at the rest of the lake and teetered back a bit as I took in several kilometers of muddy lake bed. The whole brown mess appeared to breathe as covered fish made last ditch efforts to move a tail or fin. Slender spike rushes shot up out of the ground, the water line still evident on their yellow-brown stalks. I expected to see a family of ducks come gliding around the corner at any moment, swimming on air.

The white sands crept in through the gaps between my laces as I walked back to the top to get a better view and spotted Jaguar Bennett, that big shot from the university's biology department, sitting on a park bench talking with a reporter who was dressed as if she were covering a mayoral speech in downtown Tallahassee instead of a vanishing lake. He held his hand up, gesturing that he'd be right with me.

"It was spectacular." Bennett peeled his eyes from the camera lens to look out intently at the lake bed. "Animals trying to scramble out, a whirlpool of gators, birds, and bass went down the hole."

The phenomenon had begun two days prior, but Bennett had sat on the information before informing the geology department this morning. He shook the reporter's hand before joining me at the top of the beach.

"Just look at all of that vegetation, all of it just living underneath the water, defying the laws of nature.

And look at the blue hyssop. Blooming! It was blooming underwater, Jack!"

"That's quite remarkable. I wish I could have seen it." The plants I had seen when I was down by the shoreline looked as though they had melted into the mud. "You really never know what you're going to find when one of these hole opens up, do you? Looks like I missed it, huh?"

"You think you missed something? I'll tell you what you missed: a giant bathtub draining. Nothing you haven't seen before. You also missed hordes of locals wanting to give innumerable personal accounts of what they saw, heard or—according to one nut job—sensed. Actually, you should thank me. I mean, let's be honest, you don't like dealing with people; all you want to do is get down that hole. Am I right or am I right?"

What I wanted was to be a part of this whole experience, but I said "True enough. The team will be here in the morning, and we'll figure out when it's safe for us to go down. I can't help but feel powerless looking at all of this. Those poor animals."

Bennett, already walking back to his vehicle, said to me over his shoulder, "Christ, Jack, we're scientists."

Driving a mile out to Midway just to rent a hotel room seemed pointless. I drove away from the North Shore, skimming the curve around the community cemetery on the East bank and turned down Harriet Road. The freshly asphalted road went past sprawling homes with lawns as big as parks, sitting right next to smaller homes nestled between oaks and sweet gums, clearly having been there long enough for entire front porches to decay. I followed the road to its end and felt my tires sink a bit as I eased my truck off of the asphalt onto the damp earth. When the sound of bugs filled the space around me and the mossy smell of wet stone was close, I parked among the reeds and tall grasses, what I guessed was about thirty yards from the lake bed. I knew I was near the hole. The night smelled of fish and mud. Not just any mud, it was sinkhole mud.

I fixed a tarp over the truck bed and unrolled my sleeping bag. It was cold and wet and not worth the trouble of getting out my propane stove to heat up a can of beanie weenies. I lay there thinking about the hole. Florida, as I've told you, is the Great Sinkhole State, rich with the geological promise of erosion, rife with opportunities to enter suddenly revealed doorways down into the earth, to explore the battles between water and stone happening right beneath my very feet. The Limestone Sink beneath Lake Jackson drained it about once every twenty-five years, leaving a treasure trove of unanswered questions every time. Lots of geologists had explored the hole, but they never made it more than twenty-five feet down, where apparently the caverns get complicated and dangerous. The sink clearly went down much farther than that. I couldn't wait to get down there. I knew I wouldn't find any answers above ground.

The bugs began humming louder. Something was moving through the brittle marsh grass, interrupting my thoughts. I *had* parked in alligator territory. My headlights lit up several intervening grooves in the grass when I drove in.

An older woman's voice called out, "Who's in there?"

"Ma'am, I'm just here to look at Lime Sink," I said after clicking on my flashlight.

A woman with fluffy gray hair stuck her head up under the tarp. "Well, I can tell ya that you ain't going to see a whole lot in the darkness, Junior. You might want to pack it up and come back when folks not sleeping 'round here."

I explained to her who I was and why I was here and she seemed to soften a bit. She unlatched my tailgate and plunked herself down on it so hard that her thick body caused my truck to move like a boat on the water. I noticed that she had hold of a large shotgun in her right hand.

"Aw, this is just for my own peace of mind. I been livin' out here a long time. A long time before all these rich folk came in and ran my real neighbors off. My husband's family set up house here in 1902. They built the first dock on this lake."

"Excuse me for asking, Ma'am, but why isn't your husband the one out here with the shotgun? There could be gators around here anywhere."

She let out a loud laugh that got swallowed up by the pulsing chaos of bug sounds. "It's people you got to worry about 'round here more n' the gators."

She rubbed her cheek as she looked out at the dark marsh. "Well, Junior, you better believe it would be my Stanley out here if he was still alive. He's been gone awhile now. He got killed rebuilding a boathouse for one of the new folks. The roof was so heavy from rain that it just collapsed right on him."

I didn't know what to say. I recognized the way her body drooped, and the way her hands reached out for something to clutch when she talked about her husband. These gestures betrayed her swamp-guard front and gave insight into her grief, the same way they did Mom. I'd always been able to see beyond Mom's lipstick-pasted smile and steam-pressed slacks.

When we decided to move from the pointy roofed house on Pepper Street, I was helping Dad clean out the garage, breathing in clouds of dust and fumes from motor oil stains, peering through webby windows at Mr. Petryk's overgrown lilac bushes. I wondered if I would miss their sweet floral parade filling up our small backyard each spring when I heard the screen door squeal open. Mrs. Nyguen was standing on the front porch talking to Mom. I moved closer to the front of the garage and rested my head on the cool metal frame of the door, hoping to hear what brought this private woman in her ancient gold slippers out of her house. The sound of the metal bike parts Dad was throwing into milk crates made it impossible to hear. I could see Mom's silhouette; her shoulders frowned, making her look as old as Mrs. Nyguen. When I saw her reach for the back of the chair that dad read his paper in, I knew that Mrs. Nyguen must be talking about you. What could this hermit of a woman possibly know? I was about to pull Dad out of his cleaning frenzy when I saw something I hadn't noticed before. It was a perfect, round orb. I saw the ball pass from one woman's hands to the others. Mom quickly took hold of it and held it to her chest. It rose and fell against her with each breath. I could feel the cement floor pressing against my thin sneakers. The old woman put her hand on the ball and mom stepped backwards. A portion of the ball revealed itself pink in the sunlight. I knew that ball. It was yours. Suddenly I could picture Mom out here in alligator country with one hand on a shotgun and the other clutching that bubble gum pink ball to her heart.

The woman used her sleeve to soak up moisture from a groove on the truck bed and mumbled, "Who ever heard of a boat needin' a house?" I wanted to touch my hand to her shoulder; instead, I moved the flashlight away from her face to give her some privacy and removed the tarp, revealing the entire night sky. We both looked up and marveled at it for a moment.

She looked over at me. "You study the stars?"

"No," I said, "I'm more interested in things down here on earth."

"I suppose it don't matter," she said while repositioning herself on my tailgate. "There's holes in space, holes in the earth, and holes in people, too."

I continued to stare up into the sky after the woman left and found myself thinking about the time we pitched a tent in the back yard. After we stretched our backs on the lawn and picked out which of the stars was Venus, we huddled together in the tent and took turns telling ghost stories. I told you the one about the ice cream man who lured children to his truck so that he could trap them and use them as the secret ingredient in his frozen treats. That story scared you so much that you slept in my bed for an entire week, your little toes pressed into my legs every night. We never had an ice cream man in our neighborhood, and I was glad for that.

Jakobshavn Glacier, Greenland
"Moulin Blanc"

A river of melted water rushed by, battering broken chunks of ice from one icy bank to the other—like some kind of glacial pin ball game. I walked behind Roger in my Arctic boots, looking down occasionally to see the alien-imprints the long, metal spikes from my crampons had made in the ice. I couldn't help but feel a bit like a member of KISS with these boots on. I knew they were instrumental to getting around out here in the middle of this ice plane, but the more I walked in the rockstar snow boots, the more ridiculous I felt. I remembered Dad that Halloween he dressed up like Gene Simmons. He tried to convince Mom that his face make up and shoulder spikes weren't going to scare you, but when you came down the stairs, he pretended to bite the head off of a rubber bat, and you stood frozen on the bottom step in your cowgirl costume, fringed leather gloves pasted to your sides. Dad spent a good five minutes convincing you that it was him. He even gave you the rubber bat, letting you stretch its fake wings as far as they could go. I imagined him standing out here in the middle of this white no man's land, playing air guitar and spewing fake blood everywhere, staining a patch of all this white ice red.

I'll admit, I've been in better spirits. Jakobshavn Glacier. I could have taken my vacation time someplace warm. Hell, I could have just stayed home and hung out with the lizards on my back patio. I looked at Roger piercing the ice ahead of me with confidence. The cold in my hands and feet were old news. All I could feel now was the wind slicing across my sunburned face. I knew Roger was no better off, but those were the arched shoulders of a man who appeared to have tamed a glacier.

"Come with my team," he'd said on the phone when I'd called him in Montreal. "This Glacier has never had a man's weight on its back. Completely untouched. We would literally be the first. From the air, Jack, this Moulin looks like a true cosmic rabbit hole."

Even in college, Roger had been a brilliant scientist, a scientist that also seemed to have an unlikely connection to all things metaphysical. When he and Sunny and I were members of Jon Coutilliard's crew off the coast of Southern Mexico, he'd excuse himself before each dive to go and do these strange deep breathing exercises he claimed would align the water in his cells with the water in the ocean. In other words, when we put on our diving gear and went down into the cenotes, those big, blue oceanic sinkholes, he needed to make sure he was one with the water. At night, curled up in our cabin, Sunny and I would laugh as she did hilarious imitations of Roger's breathing ritual. She was so beautiful that I think I would have applauded anything she did. Truth be told, I had always felt relaxed around Roger. There were even a few occasions when I tried his breathing exercises by myself, and I have to admit that one time I was relaxed enough on a dive that, instead of fleeing, an entire school of fish swam beneath me like a long, silvery shadow. Which is why I called him when the girl I'd been dating since Thanksgiving broke things off with me, and why I agreed to meet him here in Greenland. I wanted and needed that feeling again.

I knew we were getting close to the Moulin. The sound of the river falling into the giant hole was as loud as a jet engine and getting louder. Up ahead I saw the bright orange puff of three down jackets and knew it was the rest of Roger's crew. As we arrived at the mouth of the Moulin, I saw that they were piecing together their sonar equipment. Fifty-two glaring, yellow balls that they would throw down into the hole, which they hoped would travel through the glacier's plumbing system and come out into the ocean, giving them the information they needed to understand glacial melting.

The sonar toss on the first day was only rivaled as the glacier's premier entertainment by the onset of the furious chills I got right before falling into a nasty head cold. These two events, and the rare sighting of a lone snow goose flying low across the ice one morning, were the only happenings that would break up seven long days of white. I wanted to appreciate the beauty of the goose's sleek, white neck and peppered wings against the ice, but something troubled me about the way the goose kept skimming the ice. I finally figured out that if it got close enough to the ice it would leave a faint reflection. There were no green fields hiding grain, no water to lazily drift upon and, more importantly, there were no other geese. That smoky shadow was the closest thing it had to a companion. I watched it fly back and forth along the ice. Before I retreated back into my orange cocoon of a tent, I got on my knees and practically had to put my nose to the ice just to make out a grayish reflection that got darker near the top, which might have been my eyes. I blinked rapidly, but the gray spot remained unchanged.

I woke up from a fever-induced sleep on the fourth day to a sound I hadn't heard in years: Roger's breathing exercises. I knew they must be gearing up to go down into the hole. I pulled my aching muscles to the front of the tent and unzipped it just enough to be able to see out. Roger was standing outside of his tent, facing the direction of the Moulin—in his KISS boots. His eyes were closed, and his hands came together as if in prayer. He inhaled deeply, and when he exhaled there was a low, guttural vibrato that pushed past his lips. I laid my heavy head down. The cold air from the open zipper felt good on my forehead. I thought of Sunny, ocean-baked skin and blonde hair parted in the middle, her chest rising and falling as she did a perfect "Roger."

Sunny, the ecological journalist, the one person who I can now admit ever made me aware of the empty spaces in my life where I had not noticed them before her: the empty chair at my breakfast table, an empty sink that should have been full of unwashed dishes from dinner the night before, a mailbox empty of letters from someone, maybe even her, letting me know how saddened they were to hear a bird in Malaysia mimic the sound of encroaching chainsaws and also by how much they missed me.

Sunny said that both of our professions required us to distance ourselves emotionally from our work in order to do it any justice. At least once a week she would tell me the difference between us was that when she put down her camera, recorder, or pen, she reconnected, but I did not. I told her I didn't understand, that I felt connected to everything, and she said, "Exactly. Your love for me is no more than the love you have for that big hole out there."

It was true. I didn't understand why this was a bad thing. When Sunny left she said, "At least I'm leaving knowing there's a few caverns of mine I haven't let you explore yet."

And then she was gone. Just gone. I called Dad one night after a few tastes of vodka and told him what had happened. He agreed that women were mysteries, and then after a long, quiet moment he said in a low, defeated tone, "Mysteries are weapons of mass destruction." Even through the vodka, I knew he wasn't talking about Sunny any more.

Cocooned inside my sleeping bag, I tried to fend off sleep because a memory of you kept returning to my mind; it was a good one, the memory of you eating the blue Polar Pops. On the packaging was a cartoon polar bear, and in one paw he held up a fan of polar pops in every flavor, his exaggerated tongue licking them all at once: pina colada, strawberry, orange, watermelon, lime, and blueberry. Why you so devoutly coveted the blueberry is just one more question I will never be able to ask you, but I never touched that flavor, not once, not even when you melted my Elvis Christmas CD in the microwave. You'd greedily suck the blue from the plastic package and all that would be left was a sort of periwinkle crushed ice, which you crunched loudly, your mouth fully open, letting no sound be muffled. Following your protocol for eating the Polar Pop, I could usually find you sitting on the floor in Mom and Dad's room in front of the long mirror on the closet door, talking to yourself, sticking out your blue tongue in between words.

When you got bored of this, you would find me or Mom or Dad, inventing important questions that you had to ask us, like "What was the name of that guy that your band opened up for in the sixties?" or, "What kinds of vegtables will be in the garden this year?" Just so you could time how long it would take for someone to comment on your electric blue teeth.

Recently, I was at that symposium in Luxemburg on the Dead Sea, where I was to be given the Altman Peeder award in geology for a series of papers I had published on the dissolving salt pockets in the area. It was a stuffy event, full dress from head to toe, and I knew my jeans and Carhartt boots weren't going to cut it. I think Mom would have loved the blue suit and silver tie I used for these occasions, but the suit made me feel even more out of sorts about the social aspect of the evening. Two blocks from the university I realized my breath still reeked from the lamb kabob with garlic sauce I had eaten for lunch. I drove into the campus and parked near Zollverein Hall. The only thing in the vacuumed rental car was my battered briefcase and, in the far recess of a side pocket, I found a small, cobalt blue gumball. I popped it in my mouth and headed inside. The foyer of the hall boasted vaulted ceilings and a grand mahogany staircase, and I could hear clapping coming from behind two tree-high mahogany doors. I found the nearest restroom, hoping to give myself one nice, cold splash before entering the symposium. Right away two tiny pools of blue were revealed in each corner of my mouth. I folded my lips up into my gums and saw that the gumball had tinted all of my teeth blue. My tongue a deeper blue!

How could I not think of you as I sat at the table, drinking ice water from a wine glass, surrounded by some of the foremost scientists of the world, with my Polar Pop mouth? I felt giddy and asked lots of questions, laughing loudly and obscenely, and, as I received the honorable Altman Peeder Award, I gave a smile that would rival the Cheshire cat. Ah, Blueberry.

Guatemala City, Barrio San Antonio
Sink Hole, Zone 6

The Guatemalan government could have saved themselves a few dollars by constructing a cardboard cut out of me, placing it in front of the television cameras and reporters with a sign tacked on reading, "Jack Manuel, geologist and sinkhole specialist." Other than serving their credibility, there was no other purpose for me to be standing at the edge of this giant sinkhole—deeper than the Statue of Liberty was tall, with a stink that momentarily brought me back to Mr. Petryk's back yard. I felt totally useless.

For three days I'd been tied up like a junkyard dog, skirting the edge of the massive hole along with a dozen or so of the city's top engineers, all of us hooked up to safety lines. Clip boards and diagrams and hard hats—yes, hardhats; unless the sky fell, I couldn't see why we'd need them. It was clear to me that the enormous cavity had been created from the overflow of damaged sewer pipes, yet despite my fluent Spanish none of the engineers seemed interested in my conclusions. The city wanted to blame this one on the rain.

The sinkhole took out a good chunk of the road and several homes that were barely a step up from cardboard boxes. The bodies of two teenage boys were found before I'd arrived, floating in raw sewage and mud at the bottom of the hole. A third person, the deceased boys' father, had yet to turn up. I was sure the band of women that appeared each morning, huddling together on concrete chunks from a broken wall, were their family. I watched the women stare out at the hole, pausing every now and then from peeling fruit for the younger children to briefly close their eyes and make the sign of the cross. No one bothered them or forced them to vacate the area like they had the other residents. When the eldest woman wasn't placing her hand on their heads, she was spitting granadilla seeds in the direction of the hole or ceremoniously lifting another vibrant red fruit to the sky before tossing it in. A portion of the hole separated me from the old woman and her family, who were unexplainably beginning to feel like a basin of fresh water just out of my reach. One afternoon I was hardly able to think of anything other than the old woman's hand on my forehead.

Many of the residents found ways around the relaxed military barricade to collect mattresses and televisions. Not one person wailed or even cried. Everyone moved like ants, stopping only the few times a prehistoric rumble made its way to the surface. They made quick decisions as they sifted through the sum of their belongings in dark homes, where less than forty-eight hours before they had cooked corn tortillas on comals passed down from their grandmothers or rolled a spouse on their side during the night to quiet their snoring. I helped a young girl holding her baby brother gather some spoons and a bag of clothing and retrieved a caged bird for an old woman with gold earrings and no shoes.

On the fourth morning, I found it difficult to leave the comfort of my hotel room to return to the act of making myself look busy, while having to watch the silent grieving of the missing man's family. Several men that I hadn't seen at the site before were standing at the edge of the barricade where the cab dropped me off. Right away, a tall Asian man with deep laugh lines introduced himself as Jae-Sun Paeng, a civil engineer for the city.

"What a pleasure to meet you, Mr. Manuel. I've convinced the mayor that we can better benefit from your knowledge in the area of prevention. What do you think? You interested in accompanying me to a site about a mile from here?"

"Am I? Please put me to some use. There's not a worse torture I can think of than not working."

On the drive to the neighborhood of Colonia San Juan De Dios, I learned that Jae-Sun's father had been a self-taught engineer before he brought their family over from Korea.

"My father loved to say that the only time a king wants to take the time and money to make sure his palace is well built is after it has fallen down and the world can see him standing in the rubble without his pants on," he said as I followed him down a manhole.

"Your dad not only sounds like a very wise man, but like he's got a healthy funny bone, too. " By the time we were at the bottom of the ladder, the bright sunlight of Guatemala City had vanished.

"It's true. My father was a very humorous man, at one time, before we came here."

I flicked my light on, "Yeah, well, once upon a time my dad was a pretty funny guy, too."

We spent the rest of the day testing main collector pipes, finding sludge leaking from at least three. The gritty mud clearly indicated that several more main lines had broken. Pockets of stone underneath the earth were being further dissolved. More sinkholes were inevitable. Jae-Sun offered to drop me by the hotel and invited me to come by his house for dinner later that evening. It was a good day. I had a purpose.

Mom had advised me of two things years ago when my career first called me to travel, "Promise to keep your eyes open at all times"; she didn't need to explain that it was you I should be looking for, " And always bring me back something colorful."

I decided to venture out to an open market before I headed over to Jae-Sun's house for dinner. Men and women walked by me dressed in vibrant, handwoven garments that managed to steal the spotlight from the cramped, soot-stained buildings and honking horns. A woman held up a pair of carved jade earrings to her ears, "See how beautiful they would look on your lady?" I bought Mom the earrings and a wooden monkey with a pink body and lime-green tail from a boy at another booth. A taxi sailed by me, unable to hear my call over the clamor of people. I ran after it down a narrow street, but a man with a twisted jaw, using an oily crutch in place of a missing right leg, hobbled out in front of me. In Spanish he told me that his country had abandoned him.

He stuck his crutch out and came closer to me. "I lost everything during the war"; the names of his loved ones rode on wafts of booze coming from his mouth, "Maria Elena, Domingo, Jesusito, Hugo, mi amor, Rosa Maria..."

Another man—who was much smaller, yet boasting all of his limbs—came at me from the right, "You are going to help my friend out by giving him what is in your wallet."

I yanked out my wallet and showed them that all I had were ten quetzals, which was little more than one American dollar. The small one snatched the wallet from my hand, leaving me holding the money. I stood there dazed as they disappeared around the corner. I was shaken by the experience, but glad that I didn't carry credit cards in my wallet. I laughed out loud. They'd even left me with Mom's neon monkey and earrings.

I was freshly showered and shaved, sitting in the back seat of a cab on my way to Jae-Sun's for dinner when it dawned on me what *was* in the wallet. It felt as though my insides were falling down inside the big hole back in Zone 6. Out of seven empty plastic slips only one held a picture. It was the last picture taken of you. For picture day, Mom had bought you a bright orange jumper with matching ribbons, the same color as the safety vest worn by Craig, the crossing guard at our school. She loved being color-coordinated and thought it a good skill to pass on to you. Leaves in various shades of green filled the backdrop behind you. Those thin arms of yours crossed each other, leaving your hands to rest on your left thigh. Mom had pulled your dark hair up into two pigtails, highlighted by neon orange ribbons, tied in perfect bows. Dark eyes, and that wide smile—perfect except for the loss of one canine tooth. If I looked close enough, I could just barely make out a sliver of your tongue poking through the hole.

At home, Mom had dozens more of the same photo, strung up in a rhythmic pattern on the far wall of the family room. I wouldn't dare touch one of those, let alone take one for myself. Mom tended to this shrine of you, and we all understood nothing was to be disturbed. Besides, this picture had been with me, well, to the depths of the earth. How could I have let this happen?

The city had been invisible to me on the long drive to Jae-Sun's apartment in zone 10, but the hospitality of his wife, Olga-Maria, and her elderly mother seemed to pull me from the uncomfortable daze I arrived in. We ate dinner at a table underneath the spindly branches of a cieba tree in their back yard and bored his incredibly polite family with talk about the sinkhole. The women put the children to bed and left us to talk in the dimming light. I nibbled on chuchitos, dipping them in a tomato sauce as I brought up the two men near the market and the theft of my wallet. This seemed to light a fire under Jae-sun, "Yes, we know violence here, like the back of our heads."

"You mean like the back of your hands?"

"Hands, yes, hands. Just the other day my wife was on a bus after picking up my oldest boy from school when several members of a mara got on the bus and robbed everyone at gunpoint. All but one of the thieves got away. The people pulled him from the bus, beat him, stripped off all of his clothing and doused him with petrol. An old man had just thrown a lit match when the police showed up. They had to put out the flames at the same time they arrested him."

I hardly knew what to say, "Did your wife get injured?"

"She was fine. Barely shook up. The sad thing is that this is the sixth time it has happened to her. The people are getting tired of living in fear, many are beginning to take matters into their own hands... I wish I had been there to defend them."

Weak coffee turned to wine, as I took in every word Jae-Sun told me about the horrors of Guatemala City: gangs, violence, gun wielding vigilantes, dozens being killed daily, homeless children that were being "cleansed" from street corners. From my seat on the airplane, I had looked out over Guatemala, seeing lush patches of green, full mountains pulled out of the earth like taffy and the surface of blue lakes twinkling up at me. As we had begun our descent into Guatemala City, gray had taken the place of green, yet I'd naively thought that its perfectly gridded streets would hold a promise of some kind of order. I sipped on wine and thought of all the stories crowding the hearts of the people of this city. Stories they could never unknow.

I worked with Jae-Sun, doing research that he said the city would never use, during the rest of my days there and declined having dinner with him and his family again, claiming that I was working double time for a project back home.

I was desperate to be part of the city, a speck of dust, and was in no mood for the comfort and safety I would find sitting at Jae-Sun's table each night. Instead, I walked the streets, turning corners I probably should not have turned, going into zones I knew were not safe. I passed a bone-thin boy who was drawing invisible works of art on the sidewalk with a broken car antenna and imagined him already a ghost, leaving traces of his short life that no one would ever see. I wondered how many invisible stories you had left behind, traces of you that we had missed. I immediately longed to be back in the house on Pepper Street to look for those traces, things you might have buried in the yard, stick figures you might have pressed into the pane of a frost covered window in your room—frost made by your own breath. I obsessed on this as I walked and walked, until I came again to the street corner where I had seen the starving boy. I scanned the ground for a hint of a line or curve he had made, but found nothing. I realized that even if I found a trace of you in the world, it would still not be you, only a trace, which is really nothing at all, and that was what I already had. The weight of the nothing I had both hit me and emptied me in the same moment. I thought about you, the picture of you, in the bottom of some cold trash can somewhere out there. I felt livid and angry and robbed. When I thought about the two men who had taken my wallet, I was unable to summon any ill will. Instead, I recalled the man with the crutch repeating the names of his loved ones, "Maria Elena, Domingo, Jesusito, Hugo, mi amor, Rosa Maria…"

I watched the sun set and go down from my window, with very little sleep in between. I drank cup after cup of water straight from the tap and went to the market to stock up on fresh fruit at the end of each day, which I crammed in my mouth, anxious for the delicious flavors to break open on my tongue.

The day before I was set to fly back home, I watched as they hoisted the body of the father of the two deceased teenage boys up out of the sinkhole. His family was at their usual perch atop the crumbled concrete. The women buried their heads in their shawls and covered the children's eyes with their skirts. The old woman, whose hand had been pressed over her mouth when there was nothing to see but the long reeling of cables up out of the hole brought her hands together above her head when the body emerged. I felt relief for their family.

Kerr County, Texas Sinkhole Country

I was a sucker for country like this. The houses were mere specks compared to the gypsum-rich plains covered in centuries old sagebrush—which could look like an endless flock of sheep if you squint your eyes just right—with fragrant cedar and thick clusters of cactus to protect it from becoming much else. This was the karst region of Texas, which meant it was simply loaded with limestone deposits, and where there's limestone there are sinkholes. I arrived at the Chuvalos ranch, actually a commercial wildflower farm, around noon and was greeted by Tony. He was slightly stooped over when he walked, but it was easy to tell by his youthful face that he was still in high school. Tony's mother, Mura Chuvalos, had called the Texas Water Authority about a month earlier to report a possible sinkhole on her property. Since I was officially living in Texas, working as an expert geologist to help to protect the Lone Star State's water supply, I was the first one they sent out.

Decades ago, many money-hungry tycoons tried forcing oil from the ground by pumping in sea water from hundreds of miles away to dissolve the soft limestone pockets in the earth, creating what they hoped would be caverns that would fill to the brim with liquid gold. As you can imagine, this idea came crashing down around them, creating huge man-made sinks. Mother Nature played her part in the sinkhole business in the region, too, but hers were created the old-fashioned way, taking thousands of years for a final disappearing act that no one but indigo snakes and quail were around to see. For the most part, the state sees sinkholes as a menace, nothing more than potential polluters of the water supply. For me, they are the one beautiful thing that I get to be a part of in this life. I've always felt lucky to get a look behind the curtain at one of nature's greatest mysteries.

Tony informed me that he was the only one who knew where the sinkhole was on the property and that he would be my guide, on horseback. Their land had been mostly untouched and, other than walking, there was no other way in. I let him know that the last animal's back I'd been on was a pack mule in southern Mexico over a decade ago. The boy didn't make eye contact with me but said, "I'm letting you ride Sonora, she's older and she can make her way to the sinkhole blindfolded. She's my horse. You'll be fine."

I watched as Tony saddled two quarter horses: Buck, a young rusty colored male, then Sonora, whose coat was a shimmery gray-blue color, reminding me of the way the moon could look at times. You would have loved her. The moment I stepped near her stable she came right up to me, putting her nose to my shoulder. She reminded me so much of that horse you rode every week at your lessons. Sugarfoot, or was it Blackfoot? I can't even get a clear picture of what she looked like anymore. All I know is that the trainer said that the two of you fell in love after the first lesson.

I was nervous when we started out, but fell into a trance, watching as Sonora expertly stepped around crumbled rocks and the sunlit needles of prickly pears. Tony never looked my way or spoke a word. After traveling a couple miles I decided it would be a good time to ask him some questions about the sinkhole. He was not too far ahead, so I called out his name. He had his horse pause for a second until Sonora and I caught up. "You know, your mother didn't tell us much about the hole. About how big is it?" He looked straight ahead as we moved between two oak trees, "I don't know."

"I thought you were the only one who had been there."

"I am," he said as he stopped Buck and looked at me, "The truth is, Mr. Manuel, I didn't want Mom telling anyone. I didn't even tell her about it for a long time."

"How long have you known about this hole, Tony?"

"Ever since I was old enough to ride, about six, I think. Every time I got on Sonora's back she took me right to it."

I looked down at Sonora, who was sniffing something in the air.

"Is it that it's your private place? You don't want a bunch of officials on your land? You know we just want to look at it to make sure it's not contaminating your well water. That's all. Then we're gone. Out 'a here. Just like that."

I could tell he didn't want to talk anymore, so we kept on for another mile or so before Sonora stopped in a dirt clearing free from cacti, nothing but stone, earth, and one lone cedar tree with a curved trunk. That's when I saw the little black opening. The cedar tree's trunk curved up out of the opening, its branches almost hiding the hole completely. Sonora was done. She wouldn't go any further. I got off her and started unpacking my gear: a rope ladder, my headlamp, non-toxic glow sticks, a night vision recorder, a pack full of sonic measuring equipment, sample jars and various other tools. I asked Tony for help, but he just replied, "I've taken you this far, which is what I said I would do and that's already more than I wanted to."

I set up my gear around the entrance, which turned out to be no more than four feet wide and six feet across. The smell of minerals was heavy in the air, with a hint of what might have been bat guano. There really was something to this place that I just couldn't put my finger on. I was ready to go down. I looked back at Tony, who was sitting on a rock near the two horses, looking at the ground. Before lowering the line, which I had secured to the cedar tree and then to a large outcropping of rock about twenty feet away, I knew that there was something I needed to do first. I turned so that my back was to the boy and began breathing. I mean *really* breathing deep. In and out. In and out. I felt slightly lightheaded, but extremely relaxed when I was done. The last thing I saw were Sonora's gentle black eyes looking at me as I lowered myself into the darkness.

Before I went much further, I broke open a glow stick and tossed it. It landed on a ledge about sixteen feet down. Even then I could see that the sinkhole was much deeper. I reached into my pack and got the sonic measuring device and pointed it below me. A red beam shot down into the black and came back with a recorded depth of forty feet. The air around me felt warm and smelled like old leather. This sinkhole had definitely been made by Mother Nature. It felt ancient. I turned on the beam of my head lamp to get a better look. The sinkhole didn't drop straight down; there were small, half-formed caverns off to the sides and at least four different levels. The walls of the hole showed layers that dated this place to another time, and the black silt looked thick like fudge in some places and fine like powder in others. A white mineral compound mixed in with the layered silt and it sure wasn't limestone. I maneuvered myself to the surface of the four-foot ledge, immediately noticing large bundles the size of, well, people, some of them with large chunks of limestone tied to them. I ran my boots through the silt and instantly turned up shell beads and, yes, what were clearly bone fragments. The fragments stood out like stars against the dark silt. I walked to the lip of the ledge, shining my headlamp in every direction, revealing more of the same, in various stages and layers, throughout the entire sinkhole. This hole had been a burial ground. There was no question. I had been in sinks before that had been used for burials, but I had been one lone geo-logist among a swarm of anthropologists that descended on those underground cemeteries like ants on a breadcrumb. I'd spent a lot of time with the native people in the areas I worked in and had a good understanding that some tribes believed they came from the center of the earth, and when their loved ones died, they would send them back to the place where they had originated. In these underworld burial grounds, one thing was clear, without having to dig up bones and remnants of sacred objects, these people, down in these holes, were loved by someone, in life and in their deaths. This place I was in now, alone, was no different, and while some people might have felt edgy about being surrounded by thousands of years of the dead, I felt a peace I hadn't felt since I was a boy. I felt you.

I stepped off the ledge and let my line go. The farther down I went the lighter I felt, until I finally reached what could be consi-dered the bottom of the sink. I nestled into a three-foot patch of earth and turned off my headlamp. It was so dark that I could hardly believe I was separate from anything. I turned my head up to find the mouth of the hole. It looked like a tiny pinprick of light through a black curtain. There were questions, thoughts, little things I wanted to apologize for, like dropping the ceramic doll Nana gave you, and colossal things, like getting a stomach bug after the spelling bee and not being there to walk you home that day. There were stories, moments I'd forgotten to share with you, and so much more—filed away in sturdy containers inside of me, but now they were nothing. They no longer seemed important in the company of all of these ancient bones, minerals really, like us all. So many years had passed since the time of these people, yet the love still lived in their bones. The only truth I knew was that I loved you. Mom loved you. Dad loved you. That was enough. I sat with this for who knows how long before turning my headlamp back on and taking out my pocketknife. I pressed the tip of the small blade into the earthen wall, and began etching, noticing the way the minerals in the wall shimmered gold. My fingers trailed over the grooves, tracing each letter of your name, S-A-R-A-H.

Up and out of the hole, I was surrounded by sky and the breathing of horses. The sun was low enough to throw pinks and reds and purples across the landscape as we headed back to the ranch. A breeze at play hummed as it moved through the hollow space in a lightning-burned oak.

Samantha Canales lives in the heart of the second coming of the Dust Bowl, Fresno, California, where she founded a non-profit organization that introduces visual art and literary skills to incarcerated, immigrant, and at-risk youth. Previously shortlisted for the Glimmertrain Very Short Fiction contest, *Best New Writing 2016* is her first publication.

Hoffer Award Finalist

Memory Islands
by Cory Carlton

At the time, I thought it was quite clever to start with the line 'By the time you read this I will be gone.' I mean, I said *gone*, not *dead*. I thought it would be funny, lighten the mood; I wasn't trying to be mean, or morbid, or dramatic. I was only 18, though, and still a decade and a half away from having children of my own. I did not realize that for a loving parent there is a narrow range of ways to react to a letter like that found on your child's bed after a few days of unexpected absence. Oddly enough, that wasn't even the part that scared or hurt her the most. It was that I addressed them as Timmy and Jay, and not Mom and Jay. Honestly, I was trying to show her respect, top billing even. I just thought Mom and Jay had a funny ring to it, like they were something you'd serve to a seven-year-old for lunch without the crusts. Those are the only two things about that letter that I remember.

For most at the house on 13th Street, I was an idol. The Che Guevara, Kerouac, or Supertramp of my time. Leaving the mundane, broken home cliché behind and hitting the road with only my wits and whims to guide me. That night, the only pit stop on my journey south, we ate sandy, purple-spotted mushrooms, smoked sticky, dark green bud, drank cheap pale beer, and waited for the first-worlds to grind to a halt. Preston, Clint and I were out on the front stoop, one on each wing and me in the middle. Shouting at passersby.

"Y2K? A-Okay!" All in unison.

The house didn't even have a microwave, let alone a computer, and we were all far below the elite crowd of cellular phone owners. So what did we care, everything could crash; most of these kids wouldn't even notice the crisis. They'd keep working their shitty jobs, keep telling themselves they'd enroll in college next semester, then next semester, then next, keep drinking cheap beer, keep experimenting with whatever random thing floated around, keep trying to impress each other with one-upping tales of delinquency. Me, I was headed for adventure regardless. Let the corporate world crumble; surely that could only make things more exciting.

Sometime before the turn of the century, around 11:00 P.M., I guess, a light blue mini-van pulled to a stop directly in front of us. Now this was unusual, first of all because 551 Thirteenth was in the middle of the block on a three lane one-way street that was busy always and exceptionally so that night. Secondly, well, secondly I was very fucking high. The first thing I noticed about this van was that through the windows I could see there were no back seats, but, instead, in that big open space were at least six of those psychopathic yellow cartoon rodents from the Honeycomb commercials, spinning around like furry little tornados bumping into each other and rocking the van side to side. We fell silent and watched as the driver, a massive woman, pasty white, topped with an unkempt shrub of orange curls in what appeared to be a pastel flower print muumuu, struggled to first squeeze her arm down beside her then laboriously gyrated until the window was low enough to pop her head out.

We stared, frozen, mouths open, pupils like quarters. She looked at us and sighed. She must have known better, yet still she proceeded.

"Pardon me." Just a hint of an English accent. "Do you know where Whittier is?"

Unfortunately, due to the nature of storytelling, I must recount our responses one by one; however, all three of us reacted simultaneously as follows:

One—"Parrrrdin meeeEE!" I bellowed, English accent thick near to unintelligibility. "Da yew ave any Grey Pew-pon?"

Two—Preston, to my left, oldest and presumably most mature, took the high road and launched into directions. "Four blocks down take a right, go three blocks and then take another right, keep straight for four blocks, hang a right, stay on that road for three blocks, take your first right" and so on.

Three—Clint, on my other side, leaned over and, with what sounded like furious anger, threw up approximately five gallons of a rainbow-colored Slurpee substance all over Jake's ancient rusting Schwinn lying below.

This reaction lasted the longest, and must have been the most helpful, because once he stopped vomiting the woman promptly rolled up her window and drove off, nearly sideswiping two different cars darting into that far right lane Preston had recommended; presumably, she was now late for the appointment to offload her monstrous cargo at the sitters for the night.

Divorce. It was probably the best news I'd heard in my entire life, so why was I crying? Sitting on my mattress pad, barely off the ground, chin on my knees, hands clasped at my shins, eyes cast down at my blurry feet on the floor. Jay had his arm around my shoulders, an affectionate gesture so rare it could only be interpreted as manipulation. He was hollering out into the hallway toward my mother packing in the other room, *Look what you're doing to the boy*, and *He's just moved back home, we can try to be a family again*, and stern hissings in my ear *Tell your mother you don't want her to leave, tell her she's making a mistake*. Well, I could have said one of those things with honesty, anyway. But I said nothing. I just sat and cried. The move to Eugene had been a total bust, college and life goals no match for first-time independence in a drug-saturated city with no one to answer to but my own remorse. I hadn't even been back home a full month. Now, instead of the terrible but familiar routine that I had grown up with, here I was front seat to a whirlpool of great, unexpected, and inconvenient change. I needed a new plan.

Hours after the ball had dropped, and people had yelled and kissed, and drank until they collapsed or stumbled away, I headed back out to the stoop and found Sasha sitting there alone, smoking one of her never-ending Camel Wides, "How many people are staying here now?" I asked, honestly not able to tell. My move out had left four; there were at least ten times that many present at the party, most of whom had passed out there.

After a pause, counting out loud and on her fingers, she replied "Clint makes 13, oh, well 14, I guess, with Garret, but he doesn't pay us, and technically doesn't count, he's just always with Andrea. You can't go all the way down to L.A. Cory; you'll get mugged, raped, and murdered, maybe not even in that order."

"That's weird. I never understood the whole older guy thing with her and Garret. I mean, I don't agree, and we've never really seen eye-to-eye, but I can sorta see the appeal from her perspective. What does that say about him, though, or any other guys in that kinda situation; I mean, it's perverted, right?"

"I don't know; I like Garret, he's fun." Sasha never was one for easy agreement.

"Seriously, though, you're like my little brother, and I think what you're doing is cool, too, but... you can't go all the way down there. Stop somewhere safer, I don't know, Sacramento, San Francisco, or just stay here. Most of us would be super excited to have you move back, nobody holds a grudge, and Andrea's different now. They hardly even come out of her room anymore, anyway."

"You know I'm *older* than you are, right?" It was good to get some kind of attempt at responsible advice, even if it was the hopeless leading the lost.

"Great party Sash, Happy New Year."

How different would L.A. have been? Would I have lasted as long? Or even survived at all?

The crab season of '99 had started explosively, and I had gotten a job almost as soon as I had unpacked from my first failed attempt at freedom. For twenty-five days straight I had been leaving and returning in the dark. Twenty-five days riding my old, undersized Huffy back and forth through the sloppy, never-ending rain. Twenty-five days of uphill both ways; Astoria is built on a giant hill, you see, of which my parents' house and the seafood plant were on opposite sides. Twenty-five days of reaching into giant pots filled with very alive, pissed-off, click-clacking crabs. Twenty-five days of grabbing their shoulders and bashing their carapaces off on the blunt spike then separating what was left into edible bin or waste bin. Twenty-five days of *This will get me back on me feet.*

Then she made the decision. The decision I had in my own way prayed for since I'd reached the age of reason. The decision I had never thought she'd be able to make. The decision many women are never able to gather the strength for. The decision that, for me, could not have come at a worse time.

Maybe that's why I shed all those tears onto the floor beside my bed. Not for a maligned union finally divided, not for my longest, hoped for wish coming true almost too late to make a difference for me, not for that broken monster, not for his unbound victim, but rather for the dissolving foundation of my pitiful second attempt at claiming independence. So I, too, made a decision. Twelve hours lying awake dreaming of escape. Four days grinding it out waiting for my last paycheck. One afternoon to pawn my valuables and purchase the gear I thought I'd need, half an hour to write the letter, ten minutes to buy a bus ticket, and never a second to question myself.

I made it six weeks. Six weeks and I don't remember that city the way I remember any other that I've lived in. It's not a map, like the rest, this road leads to that; this place is here two blocks from that place; north south east west; ten minutes from here to there; did this, then that, which was before this other stuff. Instead, I remember Sacramento as tiny, individual memory islands, disconnected in space, and largely disordered.

The massive, hollow bus station where I slept for the first two nights until the guards realized I was a transient, not a waiting passenger. The homeless Philippine man that called himself "Darkwing Duck" that always had a smile and dressed in too many layers for that warm winter. The pristine Porta-Jon that I slept in one night, outside a new construction site. The bench where a smart-sounding man in a suit told me he could tell I was not from the city because I made too much eye contact; he gave me twenty dollars without me asking. The only outdoor benches in town without that damn deterring middle armrest, deepest into Capitol Park, which I spent many nights on; and that half of those nights the cops would prod me awake, and make me *move along*. The other bench in that same park where a middle-aged bald man sat down and inquired thoroughly about my situation before inviting me back to his house for a shower and some relaxation; making it halfway across the park on the way to his car, feeling funny, asking if he was gay and if he expected something related to that fact from me once we were at his place; the surprising, embarrassingly loud and dramatic reaction to my polite decline of that proposition. The big, circular fountain just inside the entrance of the open air mall where, many days, I would roll up my pant legs, remove my shoes and wade in trawling for the bottom-feeding dimes and pennies that would become my lunch money. K Street. The Light Rail. Loaves and fishes. The train yard. The hollowed-out, boarded up building right in the middle of downtown; the back alley entrance with the broken pad lock; and that it took weeks before the other squatter kids finally invited me to stay there with them.

When I left Eugene that first time I didn't own a car; no one wanted to make the six hour round trip from either end. I had, just barely, too much stuff for a bus. So I found myself behind the wheel of a moving-truck slinking up I-5, from Oregon's navel to her temple, headed home and wondering, why me? A few boxes, a tuner/cd-player/tape deck combo, and my bicycle. Half of it fit in the cab with me, yet I inched along as if dragging a sled full of iron weights.

Ignorance and uncontrollable flares of emotion, the unfortunately common bedfellows of youth, guided me to an undeserving target for my iceberg of rage. That slow ride home cemented, for me, a grudge that would last half a decade. Instead of considering the missteps of my own immaturity, I kept telling myself it was all Andrea's fault I was leaving. I just couldn't keep living with that stubborn, nagging cooz. Apparently I was unreasonable because I didn't see how storing their guns in a designated cubby hole by the bathroom while visiting made it okay to have the crackhead neighbors over for a beer. The phone was in my name; how was it not my right to run a fifty foot cord up to my room to keep it there if I wanted? What the hell business was it of hers if I had a different job every two weeks as long as I kept up my share? All I wanted to eat was pork chops, so why would I buy any other groceries? How many times did I have to say I didn't care about my portion of the safety deposit before she'd shut up about replacing that back window? I grew up taking abuse from a *true* nightmare, an American cliché, a stepdad. I sure as shit wasn't going to stick around and take lip from that incessant bitch.

I don't know when exactly, but I'm sure it was closer to the end than the beginning, if I had to guess I'd say it must have happened about four weeks in. I was asleep on one of the Capitol Park benches when I awoke to the soft pit-pat of raindrops on my face. I had experienced this a couple of times before and I knew that it wouldn't be a soaking, the way it would have been back home, still, though, I could not just lie there and take it, and there was certainly no hope of going back to sleep. I wriggled my legs out of backpack straps and sleeping bag in one move, packed up, shouldered my gear and went in search of shelter. I assumed it was a hopeless pursuit. At that time of morning, pre-dawn, and especially with a light rain, any squat with shelter was certain to be packed head-to-foot hours ago. Even so, walking in it would be better than just lying in it. I headed toward K Street and the mall; if I didn't see anything along the way at least I could keep under cover there while playing hide and seek with the night watchman. As I came to K and 11th, I glanced over at the Cathedral of the Blessed Sacrament, more out of habit than expectation, but to my surprise the front was barren. Perhaps I was the only transient in town to not have gotten the weather report in advance and the rest of my ilk were all snug as bugs in the various local hepatitis dens tonight.

The front entrance was underneath the center of three curving stone archways which were the foundation of the church's elaborate façade. I climbed the front steps and found a nice, dry spot in front of the tall mahogany doors. After a small nightcap bowl of pot, I bedded down and fell fast asleep. The second time it was not the tap of raindrops, but rather the clap of dress shoes and heels on hard stone which did the rousing. The doors behind me were open, people were slowly arriving, and there was a flabby old priest smiling down at me.

"Well good morning!" he said, watching me as I attempted to shake off the fog of a pot hangover. Then finally, "Would you like to join in our Sunday Mass?"

"Uh... sure," I said. *What the hell. It's somewhere to get out of this chilly morning breeze.*

"Go right ahead, take a seat anywhere," the priest said as he gestured an upturned palm into the belly of the church with a sweep of his arm.

Inside it was like a museum, massive, still, peaceful, and gorgeous. It was not at all like the newer little churches I had been forced to go to once or twice with my cousins, all sheetrock and oak, like a prefab home with crosses slung up. No, this was what I imagined the pope's house looked like. Not just church stuff hanging on the walls, but the epitome of church, a work of art. Front half of the ceiling a giant dome with saints carved all around it cresting in a massive cobalt blue skylight. Walls covered in ornate colorful patterns as if the entire shell were made of the world's largest and most intricate tapestry. Pulpit pure white marble, more desk than podium, in front of what I assumed must have been the VIP section, an area with padded pews and divine statues all bordered by a dark, decorative framework inlaid with Latin around the top.

Not wanting to seem too eager, or too disrespectful, I shuffled to the middle of a pew about halfway down the center aisle. I sat there with my pack between my legs and waited as the audience grew to capacity. I kept my head down most of the time, not wanting to engage with anyone. What would I say? *You come here often? Oh cool. Me? No. I don't believe in any of this stuff; just killin time, and keepin warm until the mall opens up; then I'll likely go steal some kid's wishes to buy lunch with. Real nice place ya got here, though, I thought they only made 'em like this in Italy.* I could already feel the eyes on me as people slid in and around me, I was not going to make this any worse by opening my mouth more than necessary. I just wanted to get through it, and then never make this mistake again.

Finally, everyone was in and had said their hellos to Jesus, and the service began. As I did not want to offend anyone, I attempted to act the part during the proceedings, humming the tunes, mumbling along as they thanked and pardoned and begged forgiveness and whatnot. Then after about the third or fourth time of standing and reciting and sitting, I noticed it was getting darker in the room. This seemed strange as the amount of sun filtering through the mammoth stained glass windows should have been slowly causing just the opposite effect. We all stood once more, and suddenly I became much less aware of everyone else as my vision began to fade.

It started as black around the edges, a bruised perimeter slowly oozing inward, then only a tunnel left where I could see the front wall, then a mere pinhole through which I could see the greying priest, and then, obsidian blackness. I could hear the people all around chanting along, I could feel the hard pew against the backs of my knees and in front of me with my fingertips, but visually there was nothing, I was completely blind. I sat down. Following along and staying unnoticed suddenly seeming much less important. *Is this a thing? Are they all aware? Am I being punished? Is this about the pot, or the pretending? I'm fucking blind!* I rubbed my eyes; I turned my head all around frantically searching for sight. I began to sweat as my body flushed with heat in outward waves. I removed my coat, my sweater, my t-shirt, down to my tank top. *Still too hot in here. Oh god, don't pass out!* I removed the night layers from my bottom half, pants, sweats, down to my shorts. Now in slightly less than my usual daytime apparel, I looked wildly at the people to either side of me, attempting to open my eyes as wide as they would go, as if that were the problem. I stared hopeless, my only sense of the other patrons their shifting rustles and murmurs as they pushed away from me. *Should I stop the service? Just yell out? Is this permanent? Oh my fucking god! I'm Blind!* This went on for what seemed like hours, however, after looking into Catholic services I assume it must have been about 45 minutes. They all sang, and prayed and listened. I sat there sweating, thrashing my head around trying to see something, anything, and trying not to vomit from the terror of not finding even the faintest light.

Eventually the service came to a close, the priest wrapped it up, and I heard and felt people start to leave. I sat there and gazed toward the front of the church on the verge of tears. Then slowly, much more slowly than it had onset, the blackness receded. I saw the altar, then the crucifix, the windows, the dome, everything. Just as it had faded in, the bruise faded away. I gathered up my pile of clothes, cautiously stood and shrugged my pack onto one shoulder. As I headed toward the doors, and also the priest standing there, stern, waiting for me, last of the congregation, my mind raced. *I should tell him. Are you insane? He will have you committed. What if this was a sign; he should know this happened, and probably what to do about it. Yeah it was a sign, a sign that you're a dope-smoking interloper. Don't tell the priest, you idiot! What if this happens again, I might need an exorcism or something. Don't tell him. Tell him. Don't tell him. Tell. Don't. Tell. Don't.*

When I got near the priest, he frowned, his wrinkled face folding, regarding me with expectant eyebrows. I knew he was waiting for an explanation of what the hell I was doing during his sermon.

"Thankyoufather." I didn't even look him in the eyes as I passed.

I walked out and around the corner. *That was fuckin weird.* I put a few clothes back on, packed the rest, then headed up K Street towards the mall. *Nice morning, should be a big crowd. Maybe I can fish out enough for a whole value meal today!*

All that weekend we had been looking for a place. We had to head back north that evening, and so far the only real prospects were townhouses and complexes, if we were going to stick together. Sasha, Andrea, Jake, and I, we hadn't all been best friends, but more like a chain of friends connected by each other. We did all want to move away, though, and to Eugene, and we thought it would be easier in a group. As we drove past the bronze fountain with all the big jumping salmon for the hundredth time that weekend, Jake proposed calling it a wash, and everyone agreed.

"Wait, what about this one?" Except Sasha.

"It's a little out of our price range, but it sounds amazing! Maybe if we like it we could find one more roommate and make it work? Listen to this. Three bedroom, with upstairs loft, fireplace, one and a half bath. Downstairs, separate fully furnished apartment with kitchen, one bedroom, one bath, fireplace. Available separate, or all together to right renters."

"Fine, but this is the last one," Andrea said. She had been calling the shots for most of the trip.

"What's the address Sash?"

"Five-Fifty-One Thirteenth Street."

It seemed like a decision made on impulse at the time. Looking back now, though, there must have been some hidden desire, an internal throwing in of the towel. I had written letters to my friends, had even called once, though it didn't last long, neither side could bear the long distance expense; but I had had no word to or from home. Until one day, right after Valentine's Day, I seemed to just have one of those big, black payphone receivers in my hand, and I heard him say, "Yes, I'll accept the charges." There was some staticky clicking, and then, "Cory?"

"Hey Jay."

"Where the hell are you? Your mother has been worried crazy."

I was a bursting dam. I attempted a reply, but it was just sounds muddled by whimpering. It was too much. I knew that her worry over me had kept them together. She had thought I might have killed myself. She had been a complete wreck for nearly 50 days now. I could see her pacing, hear her crying, and worst of all reluctantly accepting his sly comfort. All I remember clearly about that call are those first few lines, but I know she was there, too. We cried a lot, we apologized a lot, and we must have worked out the details of a Western Union transaction. I left the next day.

Slumped against the window of that Greyhound, a lot of thoughts went through my mind, but not one of them entertained stopping along the way to see my old friends. Of course, they would have accepted me, gotten me high, and outwardly delighted in the tales of my rebellious journey. Inside, though, they would know, I was the captain of the Titanic, the engineer of the Challenger, my act of emancipation a three mile island of disappointment. The contemptuous look on that bitch's face would have been a razor down my forearm.

Back home there were hugs, and quick claims of forgiveness. All I wanted was to go upstairs and sleep under my covers on my little single mattress pad after a nice, long shower. Instead, I was forced to endure a slow charade of nervous laughter and false guarded dialogue about how each of us had fared over the last six weeks. Once I was eventually allowed to go, I climbed the stairs, walked down the hall and opened my bedroom door. I stood for a moment and looked at the room I had left behind. My bed was not turned down, as if in a hotel room, not a sign of anxious waiting; in place of the nonexistent mint there was not an envelope. I did not shrug off my pack, and plop down next to my pillow. Inside the not-envelope was not a little card, dark green and yellow polka dots on a light blue background, on the inside of the not-card there was not a single line in my mother's loopy handwriting. It did not say,

"Welcome home, son. We Love You. Mom & Jay."

Cory Carlton is a native of Astoria, Oregon, currently working towards a Bachelor's degree in English literature at the University of Colorado. He is also a husband, father, and aspiring author of creative nonfiction. This is his first published work.

Hoffer Award Finalist

Under the Weather
by Mark Jones

Ben Browning dreams of her repeatedly, for now only in dreams is there possession: She is on her bed naked and supine, her knees drawn up and cocked apart, her hair fanned out on the pillow. He's almost on top of her when she thrashes her head at him, her eyes flare in angry alarm---No!---and then his unopened eyes are blinded by scarlet behind lids and he is a diver being hauled up from the dungeons of the ocean's depths to the widening circle of light. He feels as if he's being transported across a broad expanse of land to the lip of the continent in the time it takes to lay down in an alcoholic stupor thirteen hundred miles away, and awakes from oblivion to discover himself in this rented room's bed alcove, amazed at the swiftness and method of deliverance.

Lying wounded under the counterpane as though waiting for something to act as ballast to buoy him so he can rise to get the aspirin bottle on the sink, the room is soundless and there is no noise in the hallway or from traffic in the street below. It is as though he is at the center of a silence and the day seems pushed back, postponed. His ears strain to hear anything at all and he becomes aware of a thin and feeble filament of sound like electricity through exposed wire, so faint and tenuous he can't be sure whether it emanates from his own ear, or if it is an adjunct of that silence.

It is only in flashes like eye blinks that he recalls last night at the Red Lion Inn. Under the jet-engine decibel of music, he picked his way through the roistering moil and found a booth, which he didn't surrender for the rest of the night except to get another drink. He sat against the wall behind the table, segregating himself from the patrons that crashed against his booth in waves of rowdy drunkenness. He drank glassfuls of whiskey instead of his usual beer; and as he kept a sentry's eye on the roistering moil, it was as though he were looking through the wrong end of a telescope, until he got more and more inebriated and then that college town from where he had fled became a remote spot of light at the back of his head.

Light, soused and stupefied, pinpricks his eyes. He moves as if his joints are loathe, with a simian bipedal balkiness to the sink, washes down the aspirin tablets with cupped handfuls of water. Above the sink, in the mirror's reflected, dirty, gray light, he can't elude seeing his scar with its inflamed knuckles of bone alongside the fault line trenching across his forehead, gotten when he rammed his car into a wall on his way to coming here. What stares back at him is loose and haggard for its youth, both drawn and puffy. It is as though a joke is being played on him and he is confronting his spurious duplicate who would glibly claim his wallet, his name, his life.

Unwilling to contemplate his face any more, his stomach aching as much from alcohol as from lack of food, he sits at the desk's chair to pull on his boots, when he notices a teardrop of rain squiggling down the inside of the window. He glances out, but then his eyes snap back, confounded by what he sees.

The sky has merged with the ocean as though he is at the bottom of the bay, trapped under volumes of water, confined in wet suit and belled helmet, without direction of light or air. From his third-story window, the beginning of the bay can be seen, but fog obscures the rest of the water. The presence of ferries, tugs and fishing boats make themselves known by the deep, curt flatulence that cuts through the rain- and fog-saturated air. As if with great effort to reach his ears, the vessels sound without substance. Landside, the laborious churning of machinery on rails, the dying jangling clang of a train passing; and then, as the noise recedes, the whistle's long-pent shrill of reproach trails behind.

His eyes probe for where he thinks he last saw an arm of land curling out into the water as if slyly attempting to clasp the bay by its waist. The peninsula has disappeared as though it had never existed; he is bemused that his sight can be so easily deceived and he puzzles at how much trust he can put in the veracity of his senses. He can't penetrate the barrier of fog, but he's skeptical that something as solid and real as a spindle of land can be so easily concealed. As he squints harder to find any trace of the arm, the thumping that had been localized at his brain stem has grown tentacles and wraps around and squeezes his entire skull. Circum-ambient fog encloses the sky, cancels the day's horizon and affixes everything in suspension; and as he peers into the pearled gray that blends into itself, there is only the fluid, shifting fog bank of the present scrolling across his vision.

He shakes his head as he would to rid himself of a reverie, grabs his wool shirt-jacket and watch cap and double-checks the lock before walking to the middle of the hall to an opening no larger than a closet door. The stairs are narrow and steep, like climbing down a ladder frontward, and lit by one bare bulb above where the stairs angle hazardously and turn sharply left. Gut-sick and momentarily afflicted by vertigo, he braces a hand against each wall, painted an obscene yellow and tattooed by years of handprints. He feels his way down with boots that echo clumsy footfalls as if he's inside a barrel.

The lobby: The television blares to compensate for the deficiencies of the residents, but one young man takes exception and looks continuously annoyed as he tries to read his newspaper. He rattles the paper every so often as if its noise can compete with the pervasive public chatter and he can retrench behind his wall of print. On the couch next to the reader is an old man; his bald pate shines under the light, his head tipped back, and he snores as if each phlegm-snuffling stertor drags him deeper and deeper into sleep. The man in the chair beside him is smoking a pipe brandished in a palsied hand; ashes spark out of the bowl and fall to the carpet. He wears a crumpled fedora and greasy, knee-length trench coat; leaning forward and staring intently at the television set, he lets out a whoop like he is at a baseball game: on the set, two heads make small-talk between interviews. In the other hand, the old man waves a cane in the air; the stick pauses at the top of its parabola and then it falls, a hard thump. At intervals he raises his cane and lets it fall as if beating to music only he hears, his hispid face like scuffed boot leather crinkling into a mute laugh as deliberate as the thump on the carpet.

As Ben has done for the last three weeks, he clicks his key down on the counter and greets the clerk by name. Mr. Ridley partly turns, ignored work slips in his hands, and nods an averted, preoccupied acknowledgment. As Ben heads to the door, he spies a pair of crutches leaning against a pillar, but he continues toward the outside until he hears a voice behind him: "Whereya' goin'?" Nick asks.

"To the cafeteria around the corner. You hungry? Come on, we'll both go."

Nick shakes no. Ben tries to picture Nick chaining logs. Twenty years. Nick is a thin man for such work, his hair clipped so short it stands up on top, the sides the gray of iron that would endure through any weather. Ben jokes to Nick that it was beginning to look like a crips' convention in the lobby, and then tells Nick about how he had walked away from the hospital against the advice of his doctors. Ben supposed that might prompt Nick to tell him about his leg. Nick needs no prompting; he is unhesitant and candid. "I was chainin' logs and wasn't watchin' what I was doin." After Nick told Ben about his leg, he went on to describe how he got oiled last night.

Nick peers down as though questioning; his eyes become vacant, dark, querulous, his lips become taut and thin. Then, Nick's eyes leap up to his and he starts: "Sold sixty-three bulbs t'other day," the 'b' of bulbs like a small explosion. "Only had to sell twenty-four; because it was Saturday, I get the rest on commission. Damn light bulbs. Sit there and sell 'em over the phone like I toldya'. Goin' in t'night for four more hours. No gettin' oiled, least not till afterwards."

Ben smiles at the quaintness of Nick's word: oiled. "Sounds like you're doing all right."

"Yeah!" Nick's voice is sharp and crackling over the banal static of the television. Nick's eyes become grayer, opaque, vague staring down as if studying the chair, the carpet, what isn't there; then his head jerks up, his mouth cracks a sidelong pickerel grin like he's about to deliver a witticism: "You should eat at that Turf. Cheap. Only a dollar forty-nine for toast 'n egg and a pancake. And all the coffee you can drink." Nick tells Ben of the place's whereabouts as he scours the top of his head; hair bristles between fingers.

"Thanks, Nick; maybe I will. I'm tired of that cafeteria twice a day. Sure you don't want to come?" But Nick shakes his head.

Out of the cloud-corrugated sky the color of adulterated milk, the drizzle begins as a patter and steadily increases; Ben watches droplets stain the sidewalk dark, then the droplets intensify to steady streaks and the entire sidewalk is a sheet of water; the rain comes down so dense, hard and fast it is as though it has created and built on its own momentum and the torrent is unstoppable: It will rain forever. The intensity of the rain pounding down sideways slashes Ben's sight and objects appear in epiphenomenal flashes like images on a length of film. He doesn't hurry, nor does he duck in and out of buildings playing hide-and-seek; what's the use? He'll get wet either way. He walks at a leisurely pace, the throbbing in his head reduced to a walnut-sized pain at the back of his skull; he thinks neither of his past nor of what might come, but only of what is in front of him.

The rain sizzles as it hits the ground, beats against his eardrums until, in the rhythm of it, Ben hears it pant *now now now* on the sidewalk and produces the asphalt's counterfeit, jet-black smoothness. He walks past the stalls of the open-air market; fish goggle at him with eyes as large as marbles and thick-lipped mouths in jeering grins mug as if for the camera and are flopped across beds of ice. There are gray-skinned trunks of quahogs' lewd appendages. Ben passes the newspaper vendor as the vendor abandons his kiosk and skitters across the sidewalk for the dryness of the flower shop. The rain compels the pigeons to go to wherever they mysteriously retreat to when it rains. Couples under protective domes of umbrellas rush past while an executive, caught downtown umbrella-less, scurries from eave to eave to recessed doorway, those ten or twelve feet of quasi- public haven where vagrants, feet sidewalk-ward, sleep it off, though water has pooled beneath their feet and slipped into pants' cuffs. And he passes women who reveal, under raincoats, hot-colored hot pants and tube-tops or some other gaucherie of costume, and who dawdle in alleyways and stairwells and eye the men plastered with rain.

Since the cafeteria is on the way to Turf, Ben inches along under the restaurant's narrow soffit until he is near the glass double doors, his face pressed against the green-tinted windows. He shakes his collar of wetness, slaps his watch cap against his thigh while he observes the patrons, mostly older men, all with intense self-absorption in whatever occupies them. The only ones animated are three gesturing in the third booth back. Through the thick glass he can hear their rude boisterousness. A man and two women young enough to be his daughters; this older man keeps up his wise guy commentary and looks gratified when the twos' amusement amplifies to guffaws, too loud and gratuitous for whatever bon mot was offered. Then one woman adds her remark, laughing, and the other one's mouth screws tight as a sphincter. The wise guy leans over the table as she rises in a half-crouch; he captures and snaps her forearm upside-down, forcing her body to his, her mouth wrenches open in half-thought of scream or profanity, his open palm stopped at the side of her face. The other customers do not attempt to assist or even comment. They eat or drink coffee and read the newspaper, or stare outward at nothing or as though mesmerized in unbroken concentration or vacuity by the rain.

Ben dodges back into the rain before the abusive man sees him, briskly walks three blocks and turns before he believes his evasion is complete. He's beginning to feel the wetness as the wool sucks up rain into his shoulder blades and his watch cap is absorbing rain, too. But he saunters down the street forgetting about the violent man and his hangover; his mind is wonderfully free and he is thinking of nothing, until his peripheral vision snags an abrupt flutter, an attention-attracting movement.

His heart jumps. *How did you get...?* When he turns to the storefront, he sees a woman standing behind the glass, one foot hitched up on the windowsill; she is gesturing, Come here! Come here! mouthing something vitriolically, exhorting passers-by like she is a carnival barker, and then entreating them as though in great distress. As he approaches the window, pedestrians shoulder past him, and when the sidewalk is vacated, he realizes her eyes have been on him the whole time; hers is not a plea for help, nor is she a barker.

Ben stands transfixed by her exhibition, by her sudden and furious onslaught; she piles grievance upon agitation, her mouth torquing with the tart concision of her words until she is gesticulating wildly, pleading with him and damning his passivity, her fist pounding the window and the air. And when she sees he will not go to her, she twists herself into the shape of agony; her body slides down the window, her hand skidding down the glass and following her into a heap. And in what is seconds of watching her, he recovers enough to run blindly into the rain.

Somewhere across the corner and down the street is Turf. Ben plants a foot over the stream plowing through the gutter to pick out the Turf sign from the many hanging perpendicularly and blocking each other out. Gazing down the street, his sight is slashed by the persistent, driving rain like a flash of frames flipping upward in a blur; the street is a continuum running backward, replaying time in eye blinks. Then the film breaks in its showing and buildings on each side of the street are fog-blinded without windows or doors or spaces between them.

Once inside Turf, Ben's head is as riotous as the bar's denizens. The women are relatively quiet, but the men's voices are raised in a crescendo of cross-purposes and the camaraderie of sexual assignations, speculations and assumptions of parental ancestry. A long, untidy row of hunched backs fraternize above the wail of some jukebox cowboy's lament over the loss of his Sue, the singer and guitar twangy, the fiddle sliding and lachrymose. The stench of grease and smoke is combined with the powerful rawness of undiluted whiskey. Ben's stomach kicks once as he eyes the patrons, and then he takes a stool at the bar where no one is sitting on either side.

The waitress' lizard eye slithers sideways at Ben as she passes; she has a platter in her hands and she stares with penetrating and contemptuous disapprobation at the patron she is serving. She is between fifty and sixty, her face carved into hardness and lined like the pit of some bitter fruit. Ben lights a cigarette and smokes all of it as she passes him coming and going, and then he brusquely stands and exits. In the foyer, he feels his stomach about to erupt and he stumbles, lunging through the door before he gets sick. As the heavy oak closes behind him, another country-western song starts up, the crying fiddle announcing the next cowpoke's plaint.

Outside in the rain- and fog-impregnated air, he breathes deeply to get the vestiges of Turf out of his lungs. He walks off the steps before realizing he has nowhere to go and he's getting drenched. He retreats up the steps and lingers under the Turf sign, whose thin edge creates a lacuna of dryness. That's when the image of the woman in the window comes back to him until he walks out again into the rain.

He settles on going back to the cafeteria and starts up the long incline of the street. At the corner, a store blasts music from loudspeakers hidden in the overhang; pre-adolescents crowd under the triangle as they frenetically gyrate as though entire bodies are limbs meant to be shaken. Annoyed by the loud raucous of the music, he shuffles his feet, hands jammed in pockets, waiting there with them for the traffic light to turn green. His thighs are wet and the bottoms of his jeans' legs have a dark ring around them where they are sopped; rain has soaked through his watch cap to his hair, his collar and shoulders are wet, and he is still some blocks from the cafeteria. Even though the place is filthy, he can almost feel the warmth inside the cafeteria, the warming effect as coffee and food supplant the chill of rain and fog.

Chancing an opportunity to beat the traffic, he bounds into the street, stops stricken, mid-lane and looks off in the distance for someone beckoning him by name; car wheels screech feet away and fright shrieks through extremities. His head thumps once with a towering and almost unbearable bolt of pain, and when he looks around him again, through rain-stained glasses, he sees the driver carom off the back of his seat, slap an open hand against the steering wheel, his mouth forming unheard swear words in vehement rapidity behind the windshield. He curses, waves the driver on, and reaches the safety of the double-yellow lines.

Down the street the children dancing, pedestrians and people waiting for buses have vanished; an abrupt and complete silence has settled on the street. The rain abates and the slackening gives back to the previously fog-bound buildings, the precise delineations of their features. And as Ben desperately tries to locate the source of that voice, he simulates it in his mind: the two-note call, thin and high in its coquettishness as if attenuated by fog- and traffic-muffled air, biting in its familiarity, sounding grotesque.

Slack-jawed and arms akimbo like a man imitating a chicken who doesn't know he's imitating a chicken, Ben crosses and re-crosses the double-yellow lines; cars in both directions honk and swerve, but he gapes down the avenue at nothing in abashed and incredulous incomprehension. He takes off his watch cap for the rain to soothe his head, but he only gets wetter. He stuffs the watch cap into his pocket and finally surrenders himself to the weather.

Mark W. Jones was born in Detroit and hitchhiked out to Colorado in 1976. His short stories have appeared in *F.O.C. Review, Welter, Dan River Anthology, Re:al,* and in the *Overtime* chapbook series of Worker's Write.

Hoffer Award Finalist

Postcard from Amsterdam
by Cameron Martin

My soul was rotting in a brine of gin and Camel Lights. I needed to stop drinking and I needed to get out of London for a few days, so when Paul suggested we spend our weekend in Amsterdam, I have to admit I immediately saw it as a perfect alternative. I could smoke pot, not drink, and visit the Anne Frank Museum to get myself some culture.

"Whatever, I'll think about it," I said to Paul, and his shoulders collapsed, the poor sap. He was sitting at the table in our flat, chain-smoking Dunhills and flipping the pages of skin mags, his late afternoon routine. He'd been pining over his girlfriend, Kelly, who was back in Nashville taking classes for the summer and not missing him a lick. So said Trevor, one of our Vanderbilt roommates, who saw Kelly out several times a week at happy hours, drink-or-drowns and dorm parties.

"Amsterdam," Paul said. "I need to get laid."

I needed to get laid, too, but more than anything I needed to stop drinking, and that meant getting away from Moonie, Craig, T-Rex and Sally, the crew who each evening around 6 assembled on the picnic benches outside the Prince Monalulu bar, a stone's throw from our flat in the West End.

"You never leave the flat, man," I said to Paul. "That'd be good for you, take your mind off things."

"Don't call it a 'flat'; I fucking hate that. It's an apartment."

"We're in London, so it's a flat."

"What does that even mean? What's it supposed to say about our accommodations? A flat?"

I lowered *The Journal of the Plague Year*, part of my assigned reading, and raised my leg and ripped a fart. "It's short for flatulence."

He smiled for the first time since I saw him at the arrivals gate weeks earlier at Heathrow. Our interaction, then, went thusly:

"Important: The Camel Lights in this country taste decidedly different than the Camel Lights in America," I said in greeting him.

"I brought a carton," he said.

"I brought four," I replied, and he dropped his bags and grabbed me around the neck with a huggish forearm.

"We're gonna have an awesome time, man. London, home of Shakespeare," he said.

I wasn't going to correct him, not in that moment.

We lived humbly in the dorms of the London School of Economics on Fitzroy Street, beneath the shadow of the BT Tower. Some of us were taking both English and economics classes, but not me; I was taking a class on the comedies of Shakespeare and a survey class on 17th century English writers. The survey professor was from Vanderbilt, Professor Mack, an out-and-proud homosexual whose intermittently interesting classes I had taken back in Nashville; the Shakespeare instructor was Professor Howe, a bearded Englishman who rode a motorcycle and always looked as if he'd put on his clothes while still wet from a shower. That summer in London was atypically dry, and when I mentioned that a thunderstorm would be a nice reprieve from the oppressive humidity, Professor Howe scratched his hairy cheek and said, "Bloody balls," which made me like him henceforth.

During the break in our Wednesday Shakespeare class, Moonie and I hobbled outside with our hangovers to smoke cigarettes. Professor Howe pointed at me smoking and said, "Mind if I lick a fag?" I knew what he meant, but Moonie damn near keeled over with belly laughs and repeated the question several times, working it over as Professor Howe narrowed his eyes at this spoiled American twat, my friend.

"Sure. This is my last one, my last American Camel Light," and I handed it over.

"Oy, hold that," Professor Howe said. "I won't be having the last of anything."

"I'll take it," Moonie said, and the asshole grabbed at it and the cigarette broke in two.

Paul was hunched over at the table in our flat, sucking on a Dunhill and eye-fucking some naked Asian woman. He closed the magazine and threw it to the floor. "Done with her," he said.

"Moonie broke my last Camel," I said.

"Fucking hate that kid."

"Let's do it, Amsterdam. Let's go this weekend."

"No American Camels there," Paul said.

I sank to my unmade bed and leaned against the headboard. The torso of the BT Tower was framed by the windows. I yanked the letter from Liz out of the pages of *The Journal of the Plague Year* and replaced it as a bookmark with a five-pound note.

Dear Cam,

It was great to get your letter. My mom said you also called a few times. Sorry I wasn't home. It's good that you've decided to take it easy and not drink. You're interesting enough without drinking, whereas I'm pretty boring no matter what ☺

I wish you'd have come home this summer. It might have allowed us—

"All right, man, let's go," I said.

"I hate the Prince Monalulu. Bar stinks of old ass."

"Not there, genius. The home of the royale with cheese."

"You're lying."

I wasn't.

"Tell you what. I beat you in the dime game, you're going," Paul said.

"Fine. And if I win, you promise to stop beating off at night. Close quarters, man."

"Cute. I don't believe you."

"What, you need witnesses? Go grab Moonie, he'll vouch."

"Fuck that kid, and fuck you if you welch."

One night at the Prince Monalulu, a local drinking enthusiast in a Rolling Stones 1972 World Tour T-shirt showed us a simple game involving cigarettes, a dime, a shard of paper towel and a bar glass. You wet the rim of the glass and drape the piece of paper towel over it, the wetness holding the towel taut. Then you place a dime in the middle of the towel and take turns burning holes into the paper with the cherry on your cigarette. Gradually the paper comes to resemble Swiss cheese and the dime hangs precariously amid threadbare strands of paper. The game keeps going until someone's burn causes the dime to fall through the paper and land in the glass. That person is the loser and has to stab himself in the eye with the remnants of his burning cigarette.

"Either that or just buy the next round of drinks," the guy said and laughed.

The train from the Amsterdam airport into the city brought us into Central Station, and we de-boarded and a natty-bearded white guy with a Rasta hat and dreadlocks said, "Need some coke?" I put my hands up in surrender and he backed away. This was truly Sodom. I looked across the river to where the fabled Grasshopper coffee shop sat teeming with foot traffic in the midday sauna. I made a beeline and was halfway there when Paul grabbed my arm.

"What?"

"Let's go drop our stuff at the hotel."

This seemed rational.

"Fuck that," I said.

"I have to exchange some money," Paul said.

"You want some coke?" the rasta guy asked Paul.

Jesus, I thought. I should have just stayed in London and drank myself into oblivion with Moonie. I imagined waking up in a bathtub filled with ice, with my side sliced open and my kidney gone.

The lobby with its overwhelming scent of flowers smelled like a funeral home and I was reminded of my father's funeral and the unveiling of his headstone and its quote from Billy Idol: "If I had the chance, I'd ask the world to dance." That night, I resolved to find karaoke and to sing that song in honor of that irreverent dead bastard. We exchanged some money at the front desk and I bought a postcard fronted by the Anne Frank Museum and stuck it in my front pocket.

"You gonna write your mom a postcard from Amsterdam?" Paul said.

"As soon as I have something to tell her."

Our room, holy shit, you had to turn sideways to shuffle between the two beds, but we didn't plan on spending much time there, anyway, so we dropped the bags on our beds and I grabbed the complimentary pen from the nightstand and tucked it in behind the postcard.

"Motherfucker, let's do this. You want some coke?" I said to Paul.

"Funny. Does anyone even know we're here?"

"Yeah, Moonie."

"Christ."

Amsterdam is where amateurs get chewed up and spit out. That was Moonie's response when I told him of our weekend plans. He had said the same thing about New Orleans during Mardi Gras, Times Square on New Year's Eve and St. Patrick's Day in Boston. He frequently wore a T-shirt emblazoned with a quote from Hunter S. Thompson, "When the going gets weird, the weird turn pro," which nicely summarized his pedantic attitude towards drugs and alcohol. If it could be smoked, snorted, inhaled, vaporized, crushed, horked, drank or digested, Moonie had taken it—and in greater quantities than you or me, and in cooler places with cooler people: "Tripping on Bourbon Street"; "Shrooming in Key West on Halloween"; "Stoned sitting on the arm of the Christ the Redeemer statue in Rio." Paul always challenged him on the details—"How did you get on top of the statue?"; "How did you meet Keith Richards?" Moonie would just look at Paul and shake his head as if questioning the details was a silly waste of time.

The Grasshopper in late afternoon dusk: its indoor tables clogged with students disabled to varying degrees by the numerous strains available for purchase from the pot peddler in the glass-enclosed booth with the post office slot where the small Ziplocs were pushed through into the hands of kids looking for the genuine Amsterdam experience as they understood it.

Inhale, the lungs pierced by a fetid skunk freshness such as sifts through the air when two skunks fuck on a pile of Acapulco Gold. Thoughts like these arrived before I took my first hit, and Paul snapped his fingers at the bartender and said, "Hey, two Heinekens," and the bartender pointed with a full-sleeve tatted arm at a chalk board that read, "Kegs broke, soda only."

"I've always wanted to say this," I whispered to Paul. I raised my hand and the bartender raised his eyebrows. "Can we see a drug menu?"

The bartender lowered his gaze and swiped a hand towel and threw it to snag on a rack of glasses at the end of the bar. He shuffled down the bar and lifted the fold and strode into the assemblage of chairs and tables. A guy behind us muttered, "Ut oh. You. Fucked. Up."

The bartender put his donut hands on the table and leaned toward us with his black comb-over doing more of a hang-forward. He ran a donut through his hair and hung some strands over an ear.

"You're not funny, so stop trying, boy-o," he said to me. "The menu is right here," and he smacked the table where a menu had been inserted beneath a glazed veneer. "Sodas, so what do you want?"

"How 'bout a Fresca?" Paul said.

The bartender pushed off the table and it tottered and we leaned back against the booth back and waited for it to stop shaking. The same guy behind us muttered, "Strike two."

We drank our Diet Cokes and conferred with the guy behind us, who assured us the Hindu Kush was the best option on the menu. We nodded knowingly, unaware that pot came in so many different strains and flavors.

"Is that what you're smoking?" I asked him.

"Fuck no, wouldn't touch the shit. I only eat," he said, and he pulled a sandwich bag full of small tan cookies from his front shirt pocket and draped the bag across the table and shook it to spread out the contents. He offered us to dabble, and so we did, and we sat at the tan tabletop with its surface chiseled with initials and drank our sodas and listened to Paul explain his theory that Nicole Brown Simpson and Ron Goldman had actually been killed by O.J.'s son, Jason.

"On the night in question"—yes, he actually said that shit— "O.J. and Nicole were supposed to meet at Jason's restaurant after their daughter's dance recital. Jason was a sous chef, and this was supposed to be a big deal, an opportunity for him to showcase his skills. But at the last minute, Nicole cancelled and this made Jason furious. So he goes over to Nicole's place to confront her. He has a knife set in his car, because he's a chef and always has them with him. Moreover, he was trained in knife fighting by the Army.

"He runs into Nicole and Ron Goldman, this poor schlep who just happens to be there returning a pair of eyeglasses that Nicole's mom left at Ron's restaurant, and he kills them both using the knife training he learned in the Army. Then he freaks out, calls his dad, O.J., who comes to the scene to see what he's done. That explains O.J.'s footprints at the scene as well as the minor amount of blood in his truck.

"Afterwards, when the cops' suspicion focuses on O.J., what is he supposed to do? He knows who committed the murder, but is he gonna give up his son?"

"This is Nicole's son who killed her?" I asked.

"No, this is O.J.'s son from his first marriage. And he was supposedly obsessed with Nicole."

"She was hot," our pot brownie aficionado said.

"And so that explains the Bronco chase," Paul said. "O.J. couldn't give up his son, but he was going to be charged with the murder that his son committed. What do you do? You panic, you run. Also explains why the gloves didn't fit."

"If the gloves don't fit, you must acquit!" our new friend said.

Huh. This all made perfect sense to me. The defendant in the trial of the century, whom I had long assumed got off because of his mostly black jury, had taken one for the team. Team Simpson. Jesus, why had the prosecution not figured this out? And how had Paul? My flat roommate had solved the century's most infamous crime. We had to leave right now, go flag down a cop or something, make a call to a radio station! I bounced up from the table and said, "Holy shit, this is amaz-a-balls!" and our soda glasses tipped over and spilled and mine hit the floor and smashed before Paul and the pot cookie pusher corralled the other glasses with their arms.

"So where is his son now?" I asked. "Where is he?"

Paul chinned towards the bar, where the bartender was coming at me with a curled lip and a broom.

"Strike three."

Contrary to what I expected, the bartender did not swing the broom and bring me low. He pushed it into my chest and slapped a dustpan into my hand and said, "Learn to handle your drugs and clean this shit up," and the Grasshopper erupted with the laughter of boys and girls whose day had just gotten better—"Dude, you'll never believe what happened at The Grasshopper!"—in inverse proportion to how mine had gotten worse.

Crouched beside the table with a new angle on life, the slices and nicks in the floor of the shop and a beautiful blond girl with green eyes staring at me beneath a red bandana, her tablemates doubled over at my expense and her shaking her head with a look that told me she was grateful it was me and not her.

"Hurry up!" one of her tablemates said, a portly little girl with nose acne.

"Yeah, learn how to handle your drugs," Paul said, and I looked up at him and he leaned over and pushed me aside and took the dustpan from my hand and knelt beside me to finish cleaning up my mess.

I stepped outside into the dusk of an Amsterdam June, sat at a wrought iron table and patted my pockets for a cigarette. I came across the postcard and pen and began writing feverishly to my mother, transcribing Paul's thesis about O.J. Simpson. I underlined "It was his son, Jason!" and then I filled in the address for my mother in Connecticut, double checked the postage, and walked to the corner and dropped it in a mailbox.

I sat contentedly at the outdoor table and waited for Paul to exit The Grasshopper. My body felt warm from head to toe and my stomach felt giddy with the promise of adventure. The pot brownie, kicking in. A swirl of lights and laughter, the beauty in the red bandana joining my table and offering me a cigarette, and me asking her if she knew what "licking a fag" meant, and she laughing and saying, "No, you learn something new every day," and then I taught her the dime game, which she won both times. She kissed me on the cheek in parting and her hair smelled of strawberries. A starry night and my eyes in a swirl. I napped and Paul nudged me and said, "Dude, come on, let's go back to the hotel and clean up. We're gonna meet those guys later."

But instead we slept through the night and almost 'till noon. I swung my legs off my bed and hit the side of Paul's bed, and he moaned and fisted the pillow over his head and rolled towards the wall and moaned again. I felt remarkably refreshed, thanks, no doubt, to the absence of alcohol in my system.

After a hasty breakfast of grapefruit and seltzer waters from the lobby food court, we went to the Anne Frank House, followed by a hasty lunch of tripledecker turkey clubs and ice waters at an outdoor café. In the late afternoon we visited the Rijksmuseum and the Van Gogh Museum, where in the cafeteria we ate sausages and Paul drank gin and tonics.

Paul leaned back in his chair and patted his belly. "Pretty good day, man, got us some culture. You should send that postcard to your mom, tell her you saw the annex bookcase and kept your nose clean in Amster-sodom."

I imagined my mother opening the mailbox in a few days and reading my drug-induced ramblings about O.J. Simpson.

"What is it, man?" Paul asked.

My head. My stomach. My hands. My fingers.

"Seriously, man, you look ill," Paul said.

The waiter walked by and I flagged him down. "I'll have what he's having, but make it a double and bring two shots of Jack."

"What, why?" Paul whined.

I glared at him. "You better be right about O.J. Simpson, that's all."

"Why?"

"Jesus, because I sent your theory to my mom on a postcard."

He laughed. "From Amsterdam?"

"Yeah."

"Where is your fucking brain? Right or wrong, guilty or innocent, you fucked up."

"But is it true? Or did you just make it all up?"

"What difference does it make?"

"Dude!"

But he just smirked and shook his head.

Cameron Martin is a former journalist for *The New York Times*, ESPN, *The Atlantic,* and CBS. His fiction appeared in *Independent Ink Magazine* and *Doublethink Magazine* and *Spark: A Creative Anthology.*

Hoffer Award Finalist

Exit Strategy
by Olga Zilberbourg

Stepan's hope used to be his children—both of his sons showed such great promise when they were little! The first was the son of a poor father, born while Stepan was a simple engineer in Moscow, earning 120 rubles a month, and the second was born after Stepan had started a software company and made his fortune. Stepan had always, always tried to do his best by his family, but no good deed goes unpunished, and now was payback time. Look, just look at what they had done to him—his whole body aching, his hair white by the age of sixty!

Alone in his twelve-bedroom house in the Catskills, he cannot sleep through the night. Stepan wakes in pre-dawn darkness, crawls to the edge of his bed, lucks upon his slippers, shuffles across the hall to the music room outfitted with high-end vacuum tube amplifiers, and puts on a Kronos Quartet record. His music system allows Stepan to hear every scratch of the bow against the strings, to feel every vibrato in a soft spot at the back of his neck. The incoherent, dazzling jazz once could put him to the deepest sleep within minutes, but now he sits in his cold, leather chair, trembling.

In the dream that woke him, his oldest son, Gosha, in rags, was begging on a street corner, but turned away from Stepan's offer of alms. Gosha's face was lined with sadness, and no matter the stories Stepan told trying to cheer him up, his son stood despondent like a hundred-year old man.

At 10 am, Stepan is due in New York to finalize the sale of his software business. Everything has already been agreed upon; what remains to do today is a simple formality. The longevity of the business depends on new blood, fresh ideas. Stepan's too tired for it, and it's time for him to be tired—he has accomplished enough in his lifetime. The transfer of ownership will balloon Stepan's wealth; but what does money matter when Stepan's oldest son wants none of it, and his youngest can't be trusted with money? And what is Stepan to do next?

Stepan cannot fall back asleep. His stomach feels uneasy. He turns off the music and walks downstairs to pour himself a glass of milk. High cholesterol leads to high blood pressure leads to ten days in the ICU, and Stepan's not looking forward to that, but everything, including dieting, must come in moderation. Stepan is alone in his summerhouse, and milk is one sure way to calm his nerves.

He puts the glass into the microwave for one minute, then mixes in two teaspoons of honey, an egg, and a slab of margarine. The true Moscow Gogol-Mogol calls for butter, but Stepan compromises. He adds a dash of whiskey because doctors don't know everything. Stepan should move back to Manhattan—right now, he would give up the music room and the California King-sized bed to have a doorman to talk to—but he has just received the divorce papers from his third, American, wife, and she claims the flat in the city as hers.

Stepan's nightmare must have been provoked by his conversation with Gosha the night before. His son, Gosha, won't come close to the house in the Catskills, but at least he calls regularly to check up on Stepan. Maksimillian, Gosha's junior by six years, can be traced primarily by the drawings he makes on Stepan's bank account. The night before, Gosha called to give his father the latest on his brother.

"I just heard, Maks is in Moscow," Gosha said. "He's talking about opening a chain of Burmese restaurants in the Motherland." On the webcam, even on the crummy one Gosha insists on using, Stepan could see the threadbare collar of Gosha's shirt, his bulky and shapeless woolen sweater. Gosha—Georgij Stepanovich, or, as he insists on being called in English, George—has three graduate degrees, including a Ph.D. in philosophy from Columbia University, and makes a salary just above minimum wage teaching at a community college in Manhattan. "Maks will probably make a success of this crazy idea," Gosha said. "Although I don't see how. I mean, Russians hate spice. I don't want to scare you, *papa*, but he might be doing coke again."

"What hopes do you have of becoming a tenured professor, *George*, if you look like a bum from the nearest train station?" Stepan yelled at his computer screen, but Gosha didn't move an eyebrow. He was silent. Gosha has an annoying habit of calling Stepan and then forcing him to drive the conversation. If Stepan didn't say anything, Gosha could be quiet for hours.

"If you like wearing sweaters, let me buy you a set of new ones," Stepan begged. "You get your fashion sense from the bitter Brezhnev-era alcoholics, but you are a young man with access to unlimited resources. Don't be an idiot!"

Gosha took off his glasses and wiped the thick lenses with a sleeve. He continued to stare at Stepan from the monitor, but the feedback was missing. Gosha clearly saw nothing but the black eye of the webcam.

"Your brother's broken," Stepan declared, speaking to the computer. "And I don't know how to fix him. Nobody in Moscow is producing anything anymore. They're all users. People's hands have atrophied, and everyone with brains left a long time ago. The only thing the new generation knows how to do is to buy and sell. Burmese restaurants? These people will eat hot coals if you price them fashionably enough."

On the screen, Gosha's face looked grainy and sad. He put his glasses back on. "So, what are you going to do after your deal goes through, *papa*?"

"Did I tell you that the Russians are offering me a spot on Soyuz? For a discount price of $20 million, I could spend two days on the International Space Station."

Gosha laughed.

Stepan vividly remembers Gosha's dry, sardonic laughter, the highlight of last night's conversation. There should be no reason why later, in the dream, his son appeared so utterly humorless.

"Imagine me, at the age of sixty, chronic liver disease and all, being catapulted to the stars," Stepan spoke rapidly on the phone. "The Space program is out of money? Well, there are enough rich suckers in this world with their boyhood fantasies."

But the momentum was gone. In his glory days, Stepan could make a KGB colonel double over with laughter. His mind had worked quicker, then, and his liver had a lovely red color. Gosha was silent. "I'll see you tomorrow for lunch, Dad."

"My treat—and don't argue with me!"

The morning is nearing, and with it the 10 am meeting in Manhattan, but the *Gogol-Mogol* is slow to take its calming effect. Some of the milk has spilled on the floor, and Stepan goes for the mop. Blood rushes to his head as he leans down, and his stomach rumbles.

In Stepan's dream, Gosha was begging on a dirt street overgrown with acacias. The street was in Kalinin, the small city near Moscow where Stepan had been a boy. After leaving for Moscow at the age of seventeen, Stepan has been back only a handful of times. He still calls it Kalinin even though it was one of the first cities during Perestroika to restore its historical name, Tver. Gosha was born in Moscow, and he has never been to Kalinin; he has no business begging on the street of Stepan's boyhood.

Stepan wipes up the milk, then notices old stains and scratches on the slate floor. His regular cleaning crew comes in once a week to vacuum and wash the floors; Stepan's American wife hired them, and Stepan has never been satisfied with their work. If you look closely in the dark corners and under the furniture, there is always dust. This is not the first time Stepan fills the bucket with water and gets down on his knees to really scrub the place clean, like his mother taught him. You can't rely on anyone to perform even the simplest household tasks to perfection. "Cleanliness is the mother of success," his mother used to tell him. In Kalinin, keeping the dust outside their flat was a daily chore. His mother taught math in the local school, but she was never too proud to do the dirty housework. She swept the floors each afternoon, washed them twice a week, and always brought home daisies and dandelions to keep the air fresh.

When they were alive, Stepan's mother and father never—never!—had a reason to be anything but proud of their son. Life in the single room in a Moscow dormitory where Stepan and his wife tiptoed around baby Gosha stank of sour bread, but the difficulty had its rewards. Stepan's father subscribed to *Popular Mechanics*, and when an article about innovative "personal" computers featured the after-hours club Stepan had organized at his factory, the old man sent a telegram, "Keep up the good work!" Both of Stepan's sons are now older than he was, then, but neither is even considering marriage or children.

The kitchen floor is spotless, and Stepan moves his bucket into the large living room and entertainment area. After his American wife had moved out, Stepan got rid of the needless furniture and rugs. Now this space resembles a contemporary art gallery. Paintings on the walls look at each other across the expanse of a dark hardwood. The ceiling is very tall, admitting a lot of light through the skylight in the slanted roof, but now the sky is still dark, and the room seems woven of shadows. Even though it's hard to see, Stepan decides to wash this floor, as well.

Luckily, the possibility that Stepan's parents are following his career from wherever they are now is nil. Stepan has done well for himself, but what does this mean, when his children don't appreciate his achievement? Maksimillian has never had anything to do with Stepan's business except spend his money. Gosha's first degree was in Computing Technologies, and back when Stepan was still focusing on accounting software for the Russian market, Gosha had designed the first video game. He brought in his school friends to play and brainstorm ideas. It would only be right if Gosha called Stepan right now to say, "Dad, I want to help. Let me work with you, let me learn how to manage a successful, multinational company. I can do it, Dad. I want to do it with you."

Washing the floor is a better exercise than hours spent on the treadmill. His cleaning crew uses special solutions to preserve the polish, but the results are unsatisfactory. As far as Stepan is concerned, there's no cleaning solution more effective than a good mop and a bucket of water. This he learned from his parents, and this he tried to teach his children.

"If you want to live a noble life, give everything you have to the poor," the children's mother, Stepan's first wife, used to tell him. After Stepan made the first deal with the Americans, and the money started pouring in, she suddenly developed a fondness for the Russian Orthodox Church and told Stepan that the money was eating away at his soul. She befriended a *batiushka* who told her that the only way to salvation was regular, sizable donations to the church. At the time, Stepan laughed in her face. Gosha, a little genius who knew his multiplication table at age three and had written his first computer program at six, needed a world-class education, and they had their second son on the way. If his wife wanted to pray for his sins, that was her business; he needed all the money he earned. Stepan could never fully believe in the existence of God, not even when drinking with his friend, the former KGB colonel, growing more and more superstitious in his early retirement. No, Stepan thinks, if God existed, people wouldn't feel so alone.

He has finished up only a quarter of the room when the phone rings. It's the landline that never rings, and the echo sounds obscene in this empty house in the middle of the night. Stepan steps over his bucket and picks up the receiver in the hallway. He sits down on the floor to talk. He got rid of all the hallway furniture, too. Divorce was a good excuse for redecorating.

"Do you know what time it is?" he asks his youngest son. Both Gosha and Maks speak to him in English, like strangers.

"George—Goshka—tells me you're going through with the deal," Maks says. There's a lot of noise on the line, crackling and hissing that draws attention to the distance between them. "Don't do it, *papa*. What are you going to do if you retire?"

"It's done," Stepan says firmly. He feels nauseous, and his palms holding the phone are suddenly sweaty. "And don't count on the money! I'm spending it all on a vacation in space."

"You're overreacting. Just because your wife left you, it doesn't mean you should raise the white flag."

Stepan hears the ambulance siren on the other end of the line, distinguishes the noises of traffic of a large city. He should be in the city now, too. He always sleeps well in large cities, with the noise of other people to keep him company. He has never slept better than in that Moscow dormitory room he shared with his young wife and newborn Gosha. "Say, if you run into your mother in Moscow, give her my regards," he tells Maks. "If she still wants money for her church, she can call me."

"George is really concerned, Dad," Maks repeats. "Are you watching your diet, vitamins? Remember, doctors said no red meat, no dairy."

Stepan sighs. Talking to his sons is like shouting in the woods where only part of each echo carries. Neither of them hears what Stepan is trying to say. "What are you doing in Moscow, you idiot?" Stepan says. "Come home! You can open as many restaurants around here as you like. When are you getting married?"

"I can't chat right now, Dad. I'm late for a business meeting." Maks pauses, coughs into the phone. Stepan hears a car horn blaring, then another. Is the conversation over, and Maks simply forgot to hang up the phone? But no. "Dad?" Maks's voice is lower than usual, like he's about to say something very important.

Stepan's heart skips a beat, then beats faster. "Yes? Maks, what is it?"

"I'm thinking of staying in Moscow for a while, Dad. Things are really happening here!" He takes the slightest of pauses. "I'm going to need more money. . . Like, a lot more."

"Ah. Well, what else is new."

Stepan hangs up the phone and picks himself up from the floor. Milky bile rises to his throat, propelling him toward the bathroom. The moment he reaches the toilet, his stomach spasms, and he vomits up the *Gogol-Mogol*. When he's able to, he stands, holding himself up against the wall of the bathroom, and looks out of the small window above the toilet. Dawn is breaking, and he can see the silhouette of an oak tree a few feet away from the house. There's a slight ringing in his ears, reminiscent of the cacophonous Kronos Quartet. Perhaps there will be no trip to Manhattan today, no signing of paperwork. The second wave of vomiting brings up the remains of last night's dinner. Stepan notes with satisfaction that he did not throw up in the hallway, nor in the living room he has just washed. He inspects the bathroom floor and catches a few dark hairs hiding behind the sink. All the money in the world is not enough to have a clean house.

Olga Zilberbourg is a San Francisco-based writer with roots in St. Petersburg, Russia. Her English-language fiction has appeared in *Narrative Magazine, Hobart, J Journal, Santa Monica Review, eleven eleven, Prick of the Spindle,* and other print and online publications.

The Gover Prize for Short-Short Prose

We Were Those Girls
by T.L. Sherwood

In sixth grade, we would watch cartoons without any sound. Melanie would make up dialogue for the rabbit; the rest of us taking turns responding as the other characters. The next year, she acquired a boyfriend who took us out into the alley and got us stoned. Back in her mother's trailer that reeked from chain-smoked unfiltered Camel cigarettes, Mel would turn on Pink Floyd, then make out with the greasy-haired, mannish boy. We sat around, amused when the lyrics synched up with the cartoon action, but saddened that Melanie would not lend us her voice anymore. We all snuck glances back at the two of them on the couch. His hand rubbing over her perfectly formed bosom made our own nipples grow hard and wistful. Soon enough, we would have boyfriends, and they would seal off a part of us so that we became closed up to each other, too. Instead of puns and irony, we grew concerned with dances and perfume. We were those girls who learned how to go down without gagging instead of trying to make up silly dialogue that made us happy, or, if not happy, at least creating something that made us laugh. We'd lacquer our lips with purple lipstick scented like Bubbilicious, trip on our too-high heels looking for the grown up too soon groove. We found dependence on cheap sparkling wine, which we bartered for with sex at gas stations. We rode out into the country and suffered the inevitable rashes from doing it on the scratchy wool blankets flung out under the boughs of trees in the stands of pines. We were those young women who convinced ourselves that the mostly rape session with a college guy was the blush of first love. Our newborns were the ring bearers at our weddings. We had marriages, affairs, and shitty jobs. We divorced, carried on, and raised another generation. Now we are forty-something year old grandmothers who haven't gotten our voices back yet. We want to sing and strum. We'll whisper asides until we find our lines, mouth the lyrics until we find our song. We are as beautiful as a hummingbird's wing for we are the women who will not stop trying to recapture our tongues.

T. L. Sherwood lives by Eighteen Mile Creek in western New York. She serves as the fiction editor at *r.kv.r.y. Quarterly Literary Journal* and her work has appeared in multiple venues, including *Rosebud*, *Vine Leaves*, and *Vestal Review*.

Gover Prize Finalist

Night Journey
by Douglas Cole

—quiet hallway in green glow of fuzzy bulb and double row of identical doors warping like jellyfish as I move alone and now in terror of seeing anyone knowing at least in a distant way my condition and how vulnerable I am and that I could even get arrested and break parole and overwhelmingly have the desire just to get home going down twisting stairs that telescope from my feet and seem unreal as the green walls pulse and sway like inner organ flesh leaching wet emulsification that bubbles up bursting and breathing and I pray not see another person as I open into the lobby and the mirrors and see my face all ash and criminal monster mask so I slip phantom quick outside into the protective nightland of tilting streets swaying under a wobbly orange moon orbing over the towers as cars bend by with warplight where nightmare insects with articulated limbs and prowling feelers insert themselves onto this scary movie-reel my friend has given me and I take long strides in slow motion fast motion stop motion jumping jittering in and out of time down the steep hill and under troll arms of oaks and elms and onward down where I don't know with horns howling and cars sweeping as I stumble down through the empty market spaces and through a tumble of papers there at the edge appears a long coat with eyes that watch as I slide down a set of cement stairs with no railing on a sloping field all cockeyed with weeds dancing and creatures leering through wall cracks and hovels made out of overturned grocery carts and cardboard boxes with cookfires and shadows and twitching faces in overpass recesses and I see animal movement on the perimeter with my feet now gliding over railroad tracks how far I've walked I wonder and into pier lights and people on the stroll from whom I back away like some swamp thing exposed and creep crawl to an empty pier space and a ladder going down to a swaying boom dock where I crouch in cloacal dark on the water surging with green phosphorous suburnal imaginings as the mind goes down past sound and sight and rocking will to sleep it must and dreamless there repose with night upon my back my brain a fright of nightmare visions of bandits and cops and all kinds of phantoms I swear off as projections of the mind nothing more and the rolling black water issues up its drift dream debris of demon arms and murdered flesh and the sky's black mouth above coming down with cavernous hunger and devouring intent as I huddle inside the unveiling grainy insect hopping off things aflutter around my eyes and the race of the mind quieting as hour after hour I sing a little song to comfort myself: oh hey oh hey come on home come on home...singing this as a prayer as dawn light comes back sempiternal overall at last.

Douglas Cole has had work in *The Chicago Quarterly Review*, *Red Rock Review*, and *Midwest Quarterly*. He has published two poetry collections, *Interstate*, with Night Ballet Press, and *Western Dream*, with Finishing Line Press, as well as a novella called *Ghost* with Blue Cubicle Press. He is the winner of the Leslie Hunt Memorial Prize in Poetry; the Best of Poetry Award from *Clapboard House*; and First Prize in the "Picture Worth 500 Words" from *Tattoo Highway*. He is currently on the faculty at Seattle Central College.

Gover Prize Finalist

Finding Home
by Malinda Fillingim

I was headed in the wrong direction. My first grade eyes teared up with fear and sadness because my older sister had intentionally told me to ride the wrong bus home, hoping I'd stay lost forever.

At age six, I had already experienced homelessness, violence, divorced parents, a younger brother with cerebral palsy, poverty, and continued ridicule because of my rotten teeth. I was eager to go home and seek refuge in the closet where I often sat in the dark waiting for some light to shed on me.

The bus driver looked at me, the last student on the bus.

"Where do you live?" When I explained to him my address, he shook his head. "That's about twenty miles from here. You're far from home."

I cried, realizing my sister wanted me to be lost, to be far from her and our broken family. I was nobody to love. The bus driver showed me compassion and took me home to his mother, a woman dressed in cowboy boots, smoking Camels, and whose smile looked like a half moon.

She fed me food I had never tasted before, breads and fish cooked from scratch, warm and fresh, filling me until I hungered no more. We talked of my vulnerable state of mind. She hugged me like she meant it, like her arms were magical cures for a girl not familiar with affection. I cried knowing it was nighttime and nobody missed me at home and never would.

My mother begrudgingly told the woman who called her that she would come get me after she finished watching the news, she and Walter Cronkite the best of friends. Vietnam was where her new husband lived now and he was all she had room for in her revised heart, too small for her youngest daughter. War was all over the place.

The cowboy boot woman and I sat in her car watching shooting stars and feeling the marsh breeze, waiting for a woman who pushed me out of her so hard my head got misshaped, furthering my oddity. I watched her make doughnut circles with her smoke, evaporating where the Spanish moss hung low. I wanted forever to be there under that live oak tree, me rooted somewhere strong enough to grow.

I cried when I saw my mother drive up, blowing her horn angrily at a lost child who took up too much of her time.

"Do I have to go?" I asked my new friend.

"Yes, dear, you do."

"But I don't want to. I want to live with you. What if I get lost again?'

The woman pushed my hair out of my eyes.

"Soon," she said, "you'll be old enough to find your own way home."

I hoped there was a compass in my heart so I could always find a place to be loved as much as I was that night, the night when I first realized how it felt to be found.

Malinda Fillingim is a recent widow at 55, once again trying to find home.

Gover Prize Finalist

Girl Standing in Water Holding Bunches of American Lotus, Amana, Iowa, November 1938
by Kylie Grant

A girl wades into an autumn pond. It is morning. Quiet. Still. She treads carefully, keeping her eyes on the low horizon. Under the surface, her splayed toes sink into the thick mud. The pond is so dense with plant life that she feels like an intruder. She pushes forward. Rootless stalks coil around her ankles.

At the center of the shallows, she kneels in the cool water and, with her fingers, pulls at the flower stems, twisting them free. In later life she'll remember the water as algae-green, when, in truth, it is both brown and clear, like a tarnished mirror.

She used to collect the flowers for her mother, who would place one in every room, the smell thick like a forest after rain. But now she sells them to passing tourists, those lured by the romance of a fading town. She likes to watch the old women expertly fold the dollar bills small enough to hide in her bathing suit while the men look at the floor or play with their car keys.

After she's collected all that she can carry, she walks around the shallow edges of the lake. As she approaches the bank on the far side, she sees a man with a camera. He's arranging three girls for a picture. From behind she recognizes Lydia from school, her large white hat and summer-browned legs. Lydia turns around as if she knows she's suddenly being watched and recognizes her, calling her over. But the girl doesn't move. The calls grow more insistent, but still the girl resists them. Lydia soon tires and returns to posing, one arm held out at a perfect angle just like her mother taught her.

The girl watches as the man directs them into place. She waits for the moment to pass, for the photograph to be taken, and then moves back out into the water, feeling it working its way up her body until she can no longer walk and begins to swim.

The girls, too, have moved; they sit, now, on the bank watching the girl in the middle of the lake releasing her flowers one by one, leaving a trail behind her.

Kylie Grant is a novelist, short fiction writer and book hoarder based in London. Her stories have won prizes and have appeared in an eclectic array of publications, including *Stinging Fly* and the roller derby anthology, *Derby Shorts*. She is a self-confessed twitter fiend.

Gover Prize Finalist

Free Fall
by Barbara Hacha

One year has passed since Claire's husband plunged to earth, free-falling, unimpeded by the drag of a parachute, gravity pulling him toward his death at 120 miles per hour. In the end, there was no defying physics.

The U.S. Skydiving Incident Report listed the cause of death: *Failure to deploy either main or reserve parachute.* A brief investigation revealed that none of his fellow jumpers ever saw Eric "under canopy"—skydiver-speak for *his parachutes never opened.* His automatic activation device never activated, although the lab that tested it after the crash said it was functioning properly. *No definitive reason for this fatality was discovered,* the report concluded, with an admonition that, ultimately, all jumpers must deploy a parachute with enough altitude to ensure a safe landing.

Claire, having suddenly and officially become a 38-year-old widow, was left with her own free-fall of grief and anger. Mostly she was furious at Eric for taking such a risk, for proving her fears about his newfound passion. But that anger had no resolution.

"Haven't you ever wondered what it feels like to fly?" Eric had asked Claire when he first announced his desire to jump out of a plane.

"I know what it feels like to fly," she said, "*in* a plane!"

"I mean really fly—with nothing around you but air—like a bird."

"Eric, you don't have wings. You're not a bird."

"Claire, I'm almost 40. I need to do something I've never done before—something challenging—while I still can."

"If this is a midlife crisis, couldn't you just buy a sports car?" Instantly, she knew it was the wrong thing to say. Eric, the science teacher, grinned triumphantly, as he compared deaths per vehicle mile versus deaths per thousands of jumps. Claire quit listening; she knew she had lost.

Claire had photographs of one jump. Only once could she bear to watch, and only because Eric had begged her to come see his seventh jump. Lucky seven, he had said. Claire brought her best Nikon with its array of lenses, which pleased Eric immensely and let her hide behind the eyepiece and concentrate on the technical challenges of a photo shoot. Her husband, the jumper, became a subject, the skydiver.

After that first season, Claire had hoped that Eric's fascination with jumping out of planes would pass. But he was hooked. At the skydiving club, his friends shared his addiction and helped feed it.

Eric tried to describe to Claire how it felt when he jumped and why he was drawn to it, but Claire did not understand. They shared many things, but she could not share his love of skydiving. Where Eric thrilled at conquering fear, she saw only gut-wrenching danger.

And Claire was still haunted by that morning in June, when she voiced her apprehension about Eric executing yet another jump.

"Don't worry," Eric had said, kissing her. "It's a great day for flying. I'll be back on earth before you know it."

Barbara Hacha writes both fiction and nonfiction. Her historical novel, *Line by Line*, won an Eric Hoffer award in 2014 for Legacy Fiction; it also received a Bronze medal in Historical Fiction in 2012 from the Independent Publisher (IPPY) Awards and was a Finalist in the Best New Fiction category of *USA Book News*' "Best Books of 2011" Awards.

Gover Prize Finalist

A Man with a Millstone Around his Neck
by Christine Lind

Frank Bennett should arrive home around two o'clock in the morning. His truck rolls into the loading dock in about an hour. I gleaned all I could about his comings and goings from my brother-in-law who hauls for the same company. That's how I calculated the timing for our rendezvous.

Gazing out my bedroom window, a full moon illuminates the night, showcasing the snow on the lawn below. This must have been what inspired Clement Moore to write in his famous fable about a night before Christmas. It appears midday to me, too: magical, reflecting the feelings inside me.

I pull away from the window and lie down on the bed fully clothed. The clock warns of the time. Paul's promotion last year requiring him to travel has been perfect timing. He would never allow what I'm about to do. I haven't been much of a wife since haunting childhood memories erupted in my brain like Mount Vesuvius. For a time, I experienced a free fall into a deep abyss. But vengeance is a great equalizer and has catapulted me back out into the world.

It's time to go. I take Paul's handgun and place it in my purse. My black Suburban awaits in the driveway like a chariot. I squeeze the key in the ignition, turning it slowly, and back out the driveway of our two-story townhome. My trusty vehicle rolls silently through vacant streets to its destination, crunching on white-covered roads stealth-like while blinking yellow streetlights nod in approval.

Arriving at Frank Bennett's house, I park on the opposite side of the street and wait for the first sign of headlights. I settle in and feel the control. Two o'clock comes and goes. Clumps of snow fall off the bark of a nearby tree. And then, I see lights. Behind the lights, I see a truck. The truck pulls into the driveway as my personal flapdragon.

A man emerges slowly from his pick-up, his crew-cut now a bald head. As he maneuvers along a path to his front porch, I open my car door and step out onto the curb, exposing myself to a streetlight. Fixing my eyes on him, I slam the car door and walk across the street and up to his house. He wavers, cradling a large thermos bottle, glaring back at me, squinting in the moonlight.

"Frank Bennett?" I yell from a safe distance, my hand in my purse.

Startled, he yells back, "Who wants to know? What do you want?"

I forgive you, Frank Bennett. I silently pray. *I forgive you.* A millstone magically appears around his neck. Believing God's promises, the little girl smiles and he's cast into the sea.

Without saying a word, smiling, I turn to go. Who I am and what I want—accomplished. For in the moonlight and falling snow, I took back my power, in a magical fable of my own.

Christine Lind is a writer, wife and mother living in Omaha, NE. She contributes locally to Omaha.net with her column, "An Ideal Life." She created and teaches a women's Bible Study, "Saved Alive," and is currently working on her first novel.

Gover Prize Finalist

Deprivation
by Meg Pokrass

The mother had many terrible stories about Jilly's father. On Jilly's birthdays every year, they'd take apart the house. This made them feel excited, as though her father may suddenly show up at the front door. There were no photos of him anywhere, so Jilly patched together pieces of him in her mind.

Her father had gone after young women, would come in looking like he'd just won at Russian roulette, her mother said. Her mother would smell the woman on him, or else she'd find traces of eye makeup, or lipstick. The father's antique marble collection was Jilly's, but she never found them.

But he never fooled you, she'd say. *Even as a baby, you knew.*

On an airplane, thirty years later, Jilly wakes up thinking about sun deprivation, how her mother had lived too long without fresh air and sun. Since her mother's death, Jilly has been flying to see a man. While her mother was alive, Jilly had no interest in love. Now, in middle age, her body has been waking up.

She remembers her first flight—flying to college, years ago, looking at her hometown from the safety of the airplane. How old her young hands became in the waxy, yellow light. Why were her hands so old? Her mother was alive down there, back then, inside one of the tiny, glowing boxes.

Jilly finds herself crying when there is turbulence. This may have something to do with how she never learned to comfort herself. Or it may have to do with the man she is flying once again to see, who will never leave his wife. This time, Jilly will deposit lipstick on one of his shirts.

As the plane descends, she senses her mother as a bird, red in the face and free. Flying past. The bird looks at Jilly briefly, more interested in other birds now, no longer angry about what a person cannot be.

Meg Pokrass is the author of five flash fiction collections, including *Damn Sure Right*, and her work has been anthologized in *Flash Fiction International* from W.W. Norton & Co.

Gover Prize Finalist

A Working Philosophy
by Robin Rozanski

"You shouldn't worry about my dying," I say. This is supposed to be how bravery works. He stares at me. His eyes rove; his face looks like it hurts. What I try to explain to him is that there's a whole philosophy that maybe all we know is ourselves; the only thing that can be true is our own mind, our own body. When I say body, he puts his hand on my hand, just like he did the first time we waited in the hospital for the scans to come back.

He doesn't say anything, just stares at me some more and it's unsettling. His eyes are like ephemeral little globes, and maybe the whole universe is in his eyes, not my tumor-weakened brain. Or maybe I invented his eyes, too.

"Your doctors seem really good," he says. I have to look away. Maybe his concerns aren't real; maybe none of him is real. Outside the sun is starting to shine on the small patch of grass just beyond the window. Our least favorite squirrel is building up a nest, confident of an inevitable year ahead. We call him Mr. Acorn T. Fucknut and yell obscenities at him whenever he crawls up the screen door.

"You don't need to worry," I say. "I mean, if it's true, the philosophy, then if I don't wake up from the surgery you won't have to be sad because nothing will exist anymore."

"Don't say that. When this is over, we'll be fine," he whispers.

Yes. When it's over. If everything ends, he won't have to see my parents, whom he hardly knows, cry. He won't have to make single-size dinners, small, bland dinners like he made before we met. He won't have to go through my sock drawer, one sock at a time, matching the partners before throwing them away because I insist that Goodwill doesn't want used socks.

"What if *my* mind is making the world?" he asks.

I can't stand that idea. My throat hurts and I hold my breath. I squeeze his hand as hard as I can; suddenly I am angry with him, but it spikes instantly and melts back down into the breathless pain that is moving across my chest.

"No, that's not how it works," I say, "This philosophy. It has to be me."

But now I am scared. Now I feel his existence more than mine, and I cannot bear the thought of him strong and alone, creating a new world on his own.

Robin Rozanski's writing has appeared in *The Humanist*, *A Cappella Zoo*, *Thrice Fiction*, and elsewhere. She has an MA in Creative Writing from the University of Central Florida, currently lives in Minneapolis, and teaches at The Loft Literary Center. Follow her on Twitter @RobinRozanski.

Gover Prize Finalist

Vows Revisited
by Bob Thurber

At the altar, while reciting vows written a week prior and thoroughly memorized – a sort of long, rambling prose poem thick with sappy phrases expressing general exuberance, newfound joy, dumb luck, good fortune, all that, culminating with a mishmash of intimate pledges, really gushy stuff, all of it penned while I was stoned silly on some killer weed — about halfway through, my throat muscles tightened. I couldn't breathe or swallow, and my voice broke into this piercingly shrill falsetto that one might expect from a prepubescent choirboy. My legs started trembling, my knees felt ready to buckle, everything started to blur and I thought I was going down faster than you could say, "Take this ring."

My bride (whom I'll refer to only by the letter D.) detected my malfunction in a heartbeat. Under the pretense of adjusting her veil, she poked her elbow into my ribcage. The jab made me flinch, straighten, and gulp for breath.

Turns out, a little air was all I needed.

A few breaths later, still shaky but far less woozy, I was ready to continue from where I'd left off. Problem was my mind had frozen. Though I could have recited my vows from the beginning, mentally I'd lost my place. My thoughts raced. For over a minute the church was as quiet as a funeral. The priest wavered his eyebrows. D shuffled her feet.

All I had to do was reach into my pocket, bring out my typ copy, find my spot and continue. Instead, I stood there like an imbecilic fool, my heart thumping wildly in my ears, gazing at beautiful, bewildered bride. The same thought kept blaring: Sh deserves better than this. The priest whispered, "Is everything okay?" And I immediately understood this to be an inquiry directed not at me, but an urgent appeal for D to yank the leash on this witless heathen she'd brought into the holy church.

Fearing another jab, I coughed to signal my compliance, then skipped over most of what I had written, summing up in a croaky voice that I'd love D all the days of my life.

No one applauded, though no one cheered, chuckled or sneered either, such outbursts being a mortal sin in the Catholic doctrine at that time. Only the priest had reviewed my notes beforehand, casually and without comment, so no one else in attendance was the wiser. The thing is, I left out a large portion of what I had intended to say that morning, much of it gushy and sentimental, but all of it heartfelt. Considering how things ended up — our marriage imploded after eighteen months — that's just as well. This was in the late 70s, when camcorders were all the rage, and at least a dozen people were videotaping, making a permanent record of the event, so I'd really hate for D — or anyone, for that matter — to know just how foolishly in love with that woman I was back then.

Bob Thurber is the author of *Paperboy: A Dysfunctional Novel* and the recipient many awards and citations. His work has been anthologized over 40 times and frequently utilized in schools and colleges as teaching tools.

Chekhov's Cats
by Melora Wolff

In late afternoon, he sat at attention in the garden of his Yalta estate, coughing blood, a wool blanket draped around his shoulders. The pistol lay across his skinny knees. He waited for stray cats to appear. A dust of fine snow fell. At dusk, doomed, emaciated cats leapt onto the wooden fence around his property, their fur matted, their ears torn. The starving cats did not fear Chekhov in his weak and dying state. They did not know that a gun silent in the first act must be fired in the next—no, they had their nine lives to live. He watched the cats run along his fence on their scrawny feet and sniff the air for the promise of scraps. Chekhov focused his vision. He was an audience rapt to their hunger, their resilience, and their pride. Why, then, did he grow bored of them? He raised and aimed his pistol, and shot each cat—one, two, three. Their wasted bodies dropped on the far side of the fence, off-stage, out of sight. Chekhov sighed. He wiped the blood from his mouth with a monogrammed handkerchief, rose slowly, and walked with his pistol back to his study where he lit the samovar and resumed his work. Bent over his desk in that small room, he could not be bothered. But why had he done it? *The Seagull. The Three Sisters. Uncle Vanya.* He should have put a bullet in his own head! The last act must always be the hardest to bear! Konstantin, Tuzenbach, Voynitsky. He wept sometimes, tired of their fates. He stroked their matted fur. He stared out the window through webs of frost that formed in frazzled paths across the pane, but he saw no further movement, only the ghost-white limbs of trees. Acacia. Birch. Cherry. He knew that, soon, snow would bury each bloodied corpse. The house was dark now, quiet. A final draft swept across the desk and all his pages flew. Was there a faint rustle of satin in the wings? Was a woman nearby? He pulled the curtain, adjusted his monocle, and raised his pen.

Melora Wolff lives and works in upstate New York. Her other recently anthologized work appears in *Every Father's Daughter: 24 Women Writers Remember Their Fathers* (2015).

Gover Prize Finalist

Sing Me a Lullaby
by Caroline Mansour

I hear my mother whispering to my husband in the hallway and I don't want to know what they're saying. Nurses are moving efficiently about the room and my vague, pleading eyes follow them as they check my IV, adjust a pillow, lower the bed.

We have prepared for the inevitable, and there is very little to do but wait. The hospital room has been made comfortable, homey, even, and my husband and parents have kept an endless, cheerful vigil during the last two weeks. I am 32 and dying and this realization is so utterly horrifying that there are times I pretend that I am watching another person's life. The reality is too unbearable. My husband has tried to discuss "the situation" with me, quietly and gently, but I am so very frightened that I shake like a leaf whenever it is mentioned. Lately the pain has been so severe that conversing has been abandoned. The pain.

"Help me!" I moan between clenched teeth, wild eyes searching for the nurse. "Help! Help! No! No!" And my body begins to seize.

"Only morphine will help now, and it is essential that you not let the pain get ahead of her," I hazily hear a nurse telling my father before I drift. "It works quickly, but has a short life. At this point I think every 45 minutes is not unrealistic." My father bows his head.

I am awakened by pain so fierce that I am shrieking and twisting as nurses attempt to restrain me, and my mother, hands clasped to her whitened lips, cowers in a corner of the room. It is beyond my control and I cannot spare her this scene. I am in agony and it is like a demon twisting and convulsing in my head. I howl until I feel the syringe between my teeth. And I drift.

"Sing a lullaby," I say. At least I think I say it, and the way she leans towards me, all loving attention, eyes etched with sadness, makes me almost certain.

"Sing me a lullaby," I say again, struggling to focus on my mother's face, so dear to me, and I will her to raise her soft, cool hand and rest it on my forehead as she did when I was a child, smoothing the hair from my face as she sang to me in low, soothing tones.

"What is she asking?" a man's voice is saying from a corner of the room. It is somehow familiar, but I can't place it and so I let it go.

My mother isn't listening to him, but looking at me intently with such love that it fills my wretched body. I realize with vague interest that I no longer feel the excruciating throbbing in my head. The heavy, bloated sensation has been replaced by weightlessness, as though I am floating, and I turn my face to bathe in the golden light as it fills the room.

Caroline Mansour lives outside Chicago with her husband and two children. She is currently an MFA student with National University and working on a book of short stories.

About the Editors

Brittany Fonte holds an MFA in Creative Writing, Fiction. She has published three books, the most recent being *A.K.A. Charming*, and edited a poetry anthology. She is a 2014 Lambda Literary Finalist and is currently working on a middle grade novel about an adopted zombie.

Matt Ryan has published in many journals, including *Pindeldyboz*, *Ghoti* and *Opium*. He was nominated for the Pushcart Prize, holds the MFA in Writing from Spalding University, and teaches English at Concordia University St. Paul. His first book is *Read This Or You're Dead To Me*.

Christopher J. Helvey's stories have appeared in *Bayou*, *Kudzu*, *The Chaffin Journal*, *Best New Writing*, *New Southerner*, the *Dos Passos Review*, and others. His first novel is *Whose Name I Do Not Know*.

Danielle Evennou is a writer who lives in her own 90's sitcom. Her work has appeared in *Beltway Poetry Quarterly*, *Blue Collar Review*, and *Xenith*. She lives in Washington, D.C.

Tim Waldron is the author of the short-story collection *World Takes*. He received an MFA from Fairleigh Dickinson University.

Jamey Temple teaches at a small liberal arts college in Kentucky where she also acts as managing editor of its literary journal, *Pensworth*. Her prose and poetry have appeared in numerous publications.

Joe Peacock is a retired teacher. He holds a Master's in teaching and an MFA in writing. His words and photos have appeared in several publications. He and his wife live in the Louisville area.

Michele Ruby's fiction has appeared in *Shenandoah*, *The Los Angeles Review*, *Lilith*, *Alimentum*, *Nimrod*, *Phoebe*, *Inkwell*, *Denver Quarterly*, *The Louisville Review* and other journals. Her collection of stories was a finalist for the 2012 Flannery O'Connor Award.

Proofreader **Emily Vander Ark** is working on an MFA from Spalding University. She has been most recently published in *Garbanzo Literary Journal*, and works at a public library in Southwest Michigan.

About the Cover Artist

Thomas Gillaspy is a northern California photographer interested in urban minimalism. His photography has been featured in the literary journals *Compose*, *DMQ Review*, *Citron Review* and others.

CPSIA information can be obtained
at www.ICGtesting.com
Printed in the USA
FFOW02n2015051015
17385FF